Queen Anne Cowboy

Jay Kristensen Jr.

Praise for *Queen Anne Cowboy*

"Like '90s indie cinema, spectral prose and characters haunt Jay Kristensen Jr.'s second novel, *Queen Anne Cowboy*, with incredible detail. Through fragmented narrative and McMurtry-matter-of-factness, Outlaw musician and narrator Terrell Jamestone leads readers through a decade of the intimacies and loneliness of a family navigating crisis. Jay watercolors the Pacific Northwest's sweeping topography, revealing the similitudes of human and environmental drama."

—Tara Stillions Whitehead, author of *The Year of the Monster*

"Giving great attention to the emotional landscapes of domestic dysfunction, Jay Kristensen Jr. paints a poignant picture of redemption for his characters as they try to keep themselves together, while knowing the damage is done. Set against the stunning backdrops of the Pacific Northwest, *Queen Anne Cowboy* reminds us that mercy does not have to be as hard fought as it often is, and that love can be a beautiful antidote to pain, if we let it. I was cheering for these characters all the way through, and I felt deep compassion for them as though they were my own family."

—Taylor Garcia, author of *Functional Families*

For
May 7th, 2012

Without painted hunger
you never become a true person.
—Dōgen

2005

· Seattle ·

$\cdot$ One $\cdot$

Homeward

MY BROTHER'S EYES trace the tattoos like a fable across my abdomen. Ten years will pass before he knows how to read them: the sharp and teal century plant, the black live oak, the great-tailed grackle, the house of limestone and tin. When I roll over, the Balcones Faultline appears on the other side of my body, the ragged boundary where I first met the man I am today.

Something between a songwriter and a shitkicker.

Mostly a joke.

But my brother. He's no joke. Carrying himself like he's halfway dead. Only thirteen, protecting himself in withdrawn silence everywhere he goes. In the two months I've been home, he's worn the same clothes every day: white sneakers, black jeans, and a black hoodie. Under the hoodie's sleeves, the few times I've seen them rolled up, are cutmarks: thin notches on his inner forearms. Three on his left, two on his right. The scars are not something we talk about. Not yet. For now, they are for me to decipher at a distance, the same way he is trying to decipher my ink in the early morning light.

I yawn and smile.

How'd you sleep, friend? I ask.

I didn't, he says.

That's alright. We'll stroll down to the mercantile. I'll treat you to an espresso. How does that sound?

Espresso?

Ever had it?

Mom and Dad don't want me drinking coffee.

Would you try decaf?

Sure.

Then I'll get you decaf.

We stretch, looking up at the tattered ceiling of the van where we spent the night. Today—January 1st, 2005—we are in the village of Taholah, where the Quinault River meets the Pacific Ocean. We are in the backyard of a man who once rescued me from high tide. Down at Ocean Shores a few years back—before my fiancée, before my daughter—I'd been on a date with a woman I'd just met, a local who worked the resorts. I drove my pickup off the hardpacked beach into the soft mud, where I got stuck. Kissing my cheek and calling up a tow, the woman went back to work, probably vowing to share her affections only with townies from then on. People who could tell which parts of the shore were off-limits, anyway.

Edwin Guthrie was who came by. He looks the same now as he did then. Shoulder-length black hair, a round face. He dresses the same too, in black athletic shorts, Sonics jerseys, the classic socks-and-sandals combo. He still pretends to be impervious to forty degrees and rain. After hauling my truck in from the tide, we struck up a conversation about the sea and who you are when you spend most of your life at its side. He invited me to his home on the reservation, where we stayed up til sunrise. I drank beer after beer, and he drank diet soda after diet soda. He told me to keep in touch. I was welcome anytime.

When I took Edwin up on his offer, I brought my brother. Last night, everything was as free-flowing as our first get-together, though Edwin still only drinks diet sodas.

I don't think my brother said two words.

This morning, Ethan is lying under a mountain of blankets. He stays still as I slip yesterday's clothing over my plaid boxers: blue jeans, a white t-shirt, white socks, black boots, a prairie-yellow hat. I crouch low to the ceiling and slide open the door, hopping into Edwin's yard, inhaling the sea-sprayed air. Ethan steps out too. We look at our host's kitchen window, where we see him by the coffeemaker. He waves at us, and we wave back. Under a five-hundred-year-old western redcedar, Edwin lives alone in a light gray bungalow. Moss feeds on his damp roof like little guardians. Himalayan blackberry bushes push through the chain-link fence. Along with the van, Edwin's assets include a toolshed, a working garage, a stack of spare tires, an outdoor refrigerator, and an outdoor washer-dryer set. In the gravel driveway is my pickup truck, brown and beaten, with deep-tread tires and Montana license plates. After all the years and all the miles, that colossus can still run. Could be cleaner, though.

Our host opens the screen door, letting it slam as he lurches down the steps. He brings two thermoses of coffee, one for himself and one for me. We clink and inaugurate the day with deep warm sips.

Kind of you, I say.

Do what I can, Edwin says.

We were gonna get some smoked salmon omelets. You in?

You buying?

With whose money?

Sub Pop must've paid up by now. Or are you recording on spec?

We both laugh. I look out at Taholah. The waves, the river, the driftwood beach. The firs and hemlocks and cedars. The coastal mist, the stray dogs, the crows scavenging the alleys.

Know what this place reminds me of? I say.

What?

An old neighborhood in Austin called Clarksville. Used to be its own town, founded by freedmen in 1871.

No kidding.

Yes sir. When Austin expanded in the 1920s, the white government ruled that the Black residents needed to relocate to the eastern parts of the city. Well, a lot of residents complied. But a lot didn't. They stayed put in Clarksville. The city cut off all services in retaliation. Running water, garbage pickup, electricity. It was always a modest place. Most of the homes were trailers or shotgun shacks. Pride is what held it all together. Despite the city's worst efforts, the descendants of those first free founders held on for a generation or two. Everything is gone now, except an old church. But for a while, they made it work. Y'know?

Edwin shrugs.

You want my opinion, you're all hat and no cattle.

How's that?

Terrell, I know you didn't set a single boot in Texas until seven years ago.

So?

So how could Taholah remind you of what Clarksville used to be when you were never there?

More laughter. Unironic. In an hour, Edwin needs to report to his job at the seafood wholesaler, his second line of income in the off-season. After that he is participating in a ritual with the Shaker Church. Twelve hours of fasting and vision-seeking. The most important twelve hours a person can have.

Not that we can stay. We've got our own obligations, I tell him. The University of Washington is presenting my brother an award for his high score on the SATs, despite him only being in seventh grade. With the award comes an invitation to enroll this summer as an undergraduate. Ethan could end up skipping most of high school. If he wants to, he could be on track to make partner in a downtown law firm before he's twenty.

My brother looks away, cheeks reddening. I almost apologize.

Edwin nods.

Gifted kid, huh? I rode that rollercoaster. I was also supposed to be a lawyer. You'll create your own meaning from this world. Or you won't. But everyone will be a lot better off if you do, especially you. Remember that.

Edwin winks. I crack a grateful smile.

Ethan says nothing.

Well, we should mosey, I say. We'll come back for the truck. Take care, compadre. Thank you for everything.

We embrace one last time.

Ethan and I stroll into the cool dawn. We pass a smokehouse on a potholed street. Seagulls swoop and sing. The ocean noise is forever.

BY THE END of the decade, the glaciers that melt into the river from the Olympic Mountains every summer will cease to exist. With the disappearance of the icewater, the river will recede to its lowest levels since time immemorial, devastating the blueback salmon population, exposing mastodon jaws in the muck. Rising tides will erode the edge of the village closer and closer to the ocean. Ten years after my brother and I spend the night in Edwin Guthrie's van, the Quinault Nation will appeal to the federal government for assistance to relocate inland. Several news outlets will refer to them as the world's first refugees of global warming.

WE CROSS THE Copalis River on a low asphalt bridge. Deep along the curving water stands a grove of ghostlike trees. Accessible only by kayak or canoe, the crooked spears are victims of a three-century-old earthquake.

I tell Ethan the story. On a cold, drizzly night in the first weeks of the Eighteenth Century, the Juan de Fuca plate slipped violently beneath North America. In the resulting detonation, a tidal wave destroyed most of the coast. Raging saltwater crushed the roots of the forest, extinguishing the lives of giants. Through oral tradition, generations of Coast Salish storytellers have passed along the tale of the quake and its fatal tides. Thousands were killed. In Japan, thousands more died from what their historians would refer to as the Orphan Tsunami. The Orphan Tsunami's origins in the tectonic ignition five-thousand miles away would not be reconstructed until a few years ago.

What do you think about that? I ask Ethan.

Cool, he says.

He leans against the window. I glance at his wrists.

A BULL ELK stands alone in the Humptulips River, powerful as anything, raising his antlers under a curtain of drizzle. We glimpse him through a steel-trussed bridge. Around the King Herbivore, hemlocks and spruces drip towards the murky water, tessellated vines crawling up their trunks. Unkempt bushes erupt along the wet banks.

Do you know where the rain comes from? I ask.

Like the hydrologic cycle?

I'm talking about the rain above us right now. The essential Pacific Northwest rain. You ever learn that?

He shrugs.

In autumn and winter, I say, atmospheric rivers form in the sky. Currents of moisture stretching all the way to Asia. Isn't that wild?

I guess, he says.

Most of the time, I say, we only inhabit an impression of things. Rivers have a special way of opening up our environment. Our home.

I turn on the radio, searching for music.

OUTSIDE OF HOQUIAM, the first traces of community arrive, a sprawling complex of schools—elementary, middle, and high—nestled beneath a brooding hill. Concrete stands dominate the ends of a football field. Mist flows across, inundating the campus.

How would you like growing up in a place like this? I ask.

I don't know, Ethan says.

Seattle would look so different. Queen Anne would seem so small.

He nods.

In Aberdeen, an earth-tone neighborhood tells a story known from the Rust Belt to the Deep South. Weather-beaten houses, porches on the verge of collapse. Dead department stores, pawn shops, gun shops. Motels with neon signs, empty churches. Strangers sleeping under boarded-up storefronts, bodies nodding off under murals dedicated to the Golden Age of Logging. There are no murals to the maimed, the boys who fell victim to widowmakers, crushed by titanic shifts of wood and pine. In their place stand military recruitment billboards. Near the highway, a record store displays a permanent memorial to Aberdeen's most famous son. Flowers and photographs lie in tribute on the sidewalk as though he killed himself yesterday.

Kurt Cobain: The Saint Who Would Not Stop Dying.

I look at the shrine as though making a promise, then turn into a nearby neighborhood. Ethan sits up.

Terrell?

Yes, friend?

Where are you taking us?

Somewhere important. We won't be long.

In front of a rundown apartment building, young men eyeball us, the sons and grandsons of loggers. Little girls ride tricycles along a storm drain, yelling. Cars sit in yards, stripped of their tires. Behind everything, the Wishkah River courses a rough path.

I park the truck across the road from the cinnamon-colored house at 67 Simmons Street. Two stories tall, a mudroom in the front, a foreclosure notice pinned to the door. Broken down, rotting, lawn overgrown with dandelions.

See this house? I ask.

Yeah, Ethan says.

I bought it at auction for five-hundred dollars. I'm putting Mom and Dad's names on the deed, and when you turn eighteen, they'll add yours. Let me tell you something about adulthood, Ethan. Real estate is important. Even if this house is worthless, it'll be yours. How does that sound?

Ethan stares.

Are you serious?

Yes sir. This is where Dad grew up. Grandpa too. You know much about Grandpa Hugh?

Nope.

He was a drinker. A drinker with a mean streak. The papers called him the most hated man in Aberdeen. Do you know why?

Nope.

He was the most powerful foreman in a union town. What about Grandma Lilith? Do you know anything about her?

Nope.

She died in 1963. Drowned in Grays Harbor. Dad was five. Police called it a suicide, but most of her friends suspected it was a homicide. Hugh Jamestone died in 1993. You would've been two. The funeral was terrible.

Why are you telling me this?

Because Dad's always been in pain. Mom too. Do you know much about her side of the family?

Stop.

Stop what?

Stop pretending you care, Ethan says. You've been gone since I was in kindergarten. Then you came back with a fake Texas accent like you've been living on Crawford Ranch. All of this is dumb. Nobody wants this house. Nobody wants you either.

You don't need to get so carried away, I say. You don't need to cut yourself either.

What?

I'm serious. You could slash an artery. And what then? You end it all because you're in a bad mood one day? People got their reasons, but that's no kind of reason. You're smarter than that, aren't you?

Before I say more, Ethan pulls his hood over his head. He curls up in his seat. I open the glove compartment and pull out an unopened package of tissues. Ethan refuses them, wiping his face on the ends of his sleeves.

Hey, you're not in trouble, I say. Not with me.

He's crying.

I drive us away from the house at 67 Simmons Street. I won't be back for ten years.

Ethan, seven.

Leaving town, the highway rises over dark, silvery waters. In the distance, the harbor's remaining mills spew steam into the mist. Ethan presses himself hard against the door like he's prepared to throw himself out. I slow down and keep us in the right lane. By the time we cross into Thurston County, he's fast asleep. He wakes up as though he doesn't remember who I am.

RAINING IN OLYMPIA. We drive down a gravel road in the forest off Highway 101, arriving at the cottage where my fiancée and daughter are waiting. The homestead belongs to an older woman, Marjorie, widow to a physician whose pension has afforded her seclusion. Marjorie's home is a suspension of modernity: no television, no radio, no internet. Five minutes away, her nearest neighbor is The Sword Fern State College, an alternative public four-year school. A place that attracts many strange people, but so many good ones.

On our way up from Austin, my fiancée, Isadora, discovered Marjorie's spare room on a community bulletin board. Rather than continue to Seattle, she and our five-year-old daughter, Belinda, are staying in these woods while I record my debut album. For the time being, Isadora got an on-call job at a domestic violence shelter, using her social work degree as best she can. Our girl, Belinda, is between schools. We do not know yet if we're returning to Texas or staying in the Pacific Northwest.

We do not know what our family could be.

Billie sees us from the garden, squealing as we step out of the truck. Today my girl is dressed in a purple shirt and mud-colored overalls, bouncing and barefoot. She runs over, telling me she has spent her morning with earthworms and banana slugs, digging trenches near an old stump. She has something else to show me too.

Ethan stays back, hood still up.

Pulling me by the fingers, Billie leads me to Marjorie's woodshed. Painted on the side, a pronghorn antelope stands alone in desert grass, a pallet of white and orange against a yellow backdrop. The mural is in honor of Marjorie's late husband, whose first love was the high plains of Far West Texas.

Belinda points.

That's you, she says.

I laugh.

Why is that me?

Because that's what you do.

Know what you are? I say. A duckling. A muddy duckling who needs a shower.

With a second squeal, she races me to the house, opening the door, barreling past Marjorie and Isadora in the kitchen. I kiss my fiancée on the cheek, assuring her I will get our girl into a shower. Izzie rolls her eyes, thanking me. Marjorie tells me where to find towels. She is standing over a pot of soup: kale, carrots, onions, corn. Rolls are baking in the oven. Though she and Isadora are vegetarians, they are discussing recipes for pork adobo, Izzie responding with grace about her Filipina heritage. I wink and pursue our daughter to the bathroom, where she is trying to turn on the shower by herself. When I return, my fiancée is asking Ethan to peel a pile of Yukon gold potatoes.

His movements are slow and uncertain. But he tries.

I sit by the furnace, tuning my guitar. Izzie tries to congratulate Ethan for his award. She recently applied to the U-Dub's School of Social Work for her master's. She hopes to become a licensed therapist. Wouldn't it be a thrill if she and Ethan were attending the U-Dub at the same time?

Ethan's hands tremble. Izzie looks at me.

Suddenly, Billie streaks through the living room, dripping wet, shrieking with laughter. Mortified, Isadora wraps our baby up in an apron and carries her away. I double over in laughter.

Ethan sets down the peeler. Marjorie looks at her garden with a dreamy smile, remembering something.

EVENING MEDITATION. TONIGHT, we practice resting awareness. Marjorie leads the session. We sit on cushions on her living room floor, candles lit on shelves. Belinda and Ethan join in, closing their eyes and counting their breaths, opening themselves to inner stillness. Marjorie tells us to feel our shared emptiness, emptiness that does not care about achievement or acquisition.

Once we are done, Isadora takes Belinda up the ladder to the bed in the loft. Marjorie takes her rest in the room at the back. Ethan prepares the sofa where he has been sleeping for most of the week, settling in with a science fiction novel. He watches as I put my guitar in its case and prepare for a solo night out, meeting friends at a downtown diner.

I'm ready to talk, he says.

You sure? I say.

He hesitates.

Maybe tomorrow.

I nod.

Sleep well, friend.

He opens his book and reads. I step out with my guitar case. I won't come back until the early hours. Ethan will still be awake, lying in the moonlight, strained in every way. Strained but alive.

$\cdot$ Two $\cdot$

The Boy in The Room

WE PACE THE drizzly perimeter of Red Square, the brick plaza at the core of Sword Fern State's campus. Tucked amid the living timber of South Puget Sound, the college rises in concrete brutalism: a clocktower, a library, laboratories. Seminar rooms connected by outdoor gangways, lecture halls protruding out of verdant knolls. Pine needles cling to our shoes.

My brother is talking. Talking about the ventilation slot in the corner of his bedroom, a slot which shares a duct with the dining room. In the evenings, he sits on the carpet, listening to our mother and father's voices from downstairs. Before a crisis escalates, the triggers are hard to discern, floating like dregs in a bottle of red wine.

When he was younger, he used to intervene. Running, yelling, thundering. Screaming as though scaring off mountain lions. Trying to dominate. After exhausting himself with rage—and after our parents had exhausted themselves too—the conversation would always turn: our son has anger management problems. We've given him everything, and he still throws tantrums. He is inexplicable and ungrateful.

He is, in their words, how I used to be.

Now that Ethan has hit puberty, his outbursts have evolved. Now he burns alone, grinding through his homework, trying not to hear the cussing and accusations that ransack the house. This October was the worst of the fighting, and the worst month of his life. October, he confesses, was when the cutting began. This was when, layered on top of the rampages coming through the vents—layered also upon his honors homework—he was working through the SAT study guide alone.

As he tells me this, his posture is hard and clenched.

We are standing in front of the campus library, taking shelter. My brother tells me that everything got worse when I called Mom and Dad and told them I was coming back to Seattle.

It sounded like they were panicking, Ethan says.

They probably were, I tell him.

I take a deep breath.

So why do you cut? I ask.

He stares at the bricks.

What do you say when Mom and Dad ask this question?

They don't ask this question, Ethan says. I've caught them looking at the marks, though. Usually at dinner. They act like they don't see anything.

Trust me, they see. Not talking about it is just another way people panic. So is self-harm. Do you lose control?

A moment passes.

Yeah, he says.

Do you feel in control when it's over?

I don't know.

Do you do it so that people know you're in pain?

I do it late at night when no one else is awake. Sunday nights, mostly.

Before the week begins. You getting bullied in school?

I don't think so. It's more like everybody is an asshole to everybody else.

No child left behind, huh?

It's the kids in the honors program. Everybody wants each other to fail, so everyone treats each other like shit. Everyone thinks they're a genius.

Do you think your classmates are geniuses?

Nope, Ethan says.

There is so much I want to convey to my little brother. But he is shaken—I can see that—frightened by what he needed to say. For a few moments, we listen to the rain, watching the drops darken the slab façades.

You know, I say, I wrote poetry before I played guitar. Did that in high school. I was coping with all the same things you are now. Mom and Dad are trapped, Ethan. It's automatic for those two. You couldn't fix it if you tried. And school will always be school. You need to figure out where your control lies, and how to reach other people who need the same things you do.

He nods.

You ever thought about attending college at a place like this? I ask.

Here?

Sword Fern State is different. No grades, no departments, no majors. Every subject is taught in an interconnected way. Students evaluate teachers. Internships count as classes. It's not about ranking or competition. It's about cooperation and collaboration. Does that sound like something you'd want?

What do you mean they don't do grades?

They do evaluations. You write up your experiences. You hold yourself and your teachers accountable.

He shakes his head. I turn to the treeline.

I dropped out of college, I say. That's no secret. Dropped out of the University of Montana. I was supposed to get a degree in creative writing. Didn't last more than nine months. But if I were to try again, I would try somewhere like this.

Ethan says nothing.

We cross Red Square to the empty parking lot. The first on-campus residents are coming back from winter break, scruffy and pale, almost as lost as we are.

DOWNTOWN OLY, A coffee shop on 5th Avenue. A name I can't remember. Gothic and dim. Orange orbs illuminate purple walls. Ethan and I sit on a threadbare sofa, sipping chai. Old Time Relijun plays on a radio somewhere. We see all kinds in here. Madmen and madwomen. Crust punks. A middle-aged anarchist puts his arm around his starry-eyed girlfriend, talking about the Zapatistas. A homeless man named Elvis tells his comrades that the governor views them as the Scum of the Earth, repeating the phrase Scum of the Earth until the barista—shaved head, black lipstick—tells him to tone it down. As someone tunes a banjo, legislative aides plot how they'll survive the upcoming session.

I point across the street to the Capitol Theater. This is where, I tell Ethan, the International Pop Underground Convention took place in August 1991, the same week he was born. The convention brought together every artist from the local DIY and riot grrrl subcultures. Creativity in every direction. Autonomy and community. Things to consider.

Before my brother responds, a disheveled man approaches us, dressed in camouflage and combat boots. His name is Garrett. In 1991, Garrett tells us, he was serving in the Air Force, participating in the Highway of Death, bombing thousands of retreating soldiers between Basra and Kuwait City. Genocide is what it was, Garrett says. We killed them all. Now he sleeps in an alleyway.

Right now, he just wants an audience.

Years later, on a spring evening just after sunset, Garrett will get into a shouting match with a stranger in front of this same coffee shop. When the barista threatens to call the police,

Garrett will pull a semiautomatic pistol from his jacket and shoot himself in the head, dying in an instant, shattering the window behind him. By morning, a plywood board will take the place of the window, graffitied, replaced, and soon forgotten.

When Ethan and I leave, Garrett's eyes are as restless as the day he will die.

IN A TRAFFIC jam near the Tacoma Dome, I tell Ethan about the time I tried to jump off the Fremont Bridge. I was fourteen years old, fleeing the house during one of the worst fights, a marathon lasting til midnight, sprinting towards Nickerson Street. Mom tried to pursue, grabbing me by the arm. I yanked myself away and kept running. The neighbors called the police, who found me midway on the drawbridge. They shut down both lanes of traffic, chasing me back and forth before cuffing me. Took forty-five minutes of Dad doing his lawyer thing before I was released.

You would have been two, I say.

After the Fremont Bridge incident, Mom and Dad decided I would spend the summers with Uncle Roderick in Montana. Nothing was ever worse than that night, I say, and by God, nothing will ever be that bad for you.

I'll set them straight.

We're ninety minutes from the house.

WHERE DOES HEAT go in a rising home?

Twenty-seven steps lead from the sidewalk to the light blue Victorian farmhouse at 91 West Etrusca Street. Fifteen of concrete, twelve of wood.

Twenty-seven steps, building expectations.

The house sits high on North Queen Anne, on a final swell of asphalt before the downward slope to Seattle Methodist University and the Ship Canal. Broad and square, with a parabolic roof peak, symmetry defines the front view: four narrow windows, a cherry-red door, a porch with white curving posts. Tasteful, antique. First built in 1893, the property developed in phases. Underneath the main structure, a crude garage was built with the Model T in mind, now storing garbage and recycling bins. Mostly glass bottles. Sometime in the middle of the century, the house doubled in size. A remodel added a new dining room, bay windows, a generous kitchen, and a master bedroom upstairs, plus two home offices. At the backdoor, a second TV room also serves as a laundry room, host to dirty shoes and pawprints from Pepper, our black Labrador.

Midway up the stairs, a winding stone pathway leads past the rhododendrons and the cellar to the back patio, where a gnarled apricot tree lives alone. Coming up, we see Mom and Dad at the table, wine already poured, cheeks already red. Before Ethan and I come in, my mind conjures all the details we are not seeing: scuff marks on the kitchen's floor; crooked hinges on the door to the bathroom; dents in the plaster above the leather couch.

I hear snide remarks and caustic sarcasm. Jokes told to humiliate, told to provoke.

We step inside.

Mom and Dad greet us, open and sweet. Dad is wearing a navy-blue flannel, a tight belt, jeans. His glasses are thin and rectangular. His hair shimmers from rust to silver. He is affable and curious, a combination that serves him well in Seattle's law firm technocracy. Mom is in a yellow cardigan and blue jeans, eyes filled with vague worry. Her hair is in a messy bun, almost black, always windswept like mine. Both our parents wear wool socks. Hugs are exchanged. Mom pulls me to the stove, showing me dinner: pork chops and apple relish. She has also brewed a pot of coffee, knowing my late nights.

Dad asks Ethan about the Quinault Reservation. Mom wants to know if I'd be willing to reconsider staying here. My old bedroom is ready.

I remove my hat. We need to talk, I say.

Ethan vanishes.

Mom and Dad sit with me. What comes next is something between a son's promise and a hostage negotiation. Above us, Ethan is alone, listening. From his window, he looks out at the houses and apartments tucked into dusk-colored hills. He can see clear to Ballard, to a red neon sign for a petroleum wholesaler, the letters just beyond legibility.

But tonight, like most nights, he needs only to hear.

YOU DON'T HANG your shame on him. You do not burden him with your hostilities. You go into that master bedroom of yours and keep him out of it. He doesn't have much more than his own room, and when you two get to screaming and slamming, that's not enough.

You—do not—involve him.

He is not collateral. He is your son.

Or, if this keeps up, your granddaughter is collateral too. You won't see her. You won't come to me and Isadora's wedding.

You want me to be part of this family, you'll do right by Ethan. You'll stop trying to break his heart night after night.

You hear me?

Do you?

Night after night after goddamned night.

This is what I tell them. And this, in the end, is what they will accept. But the choice is not theirs.

WHEN THE NEGOTIATIONS end, Mom excuses herself for a bath. Dinner will go uneaten. The pot of coffee will turn tepid.

As Mom retreats, I almost bring up the house in Aberdeen, the plans for the deed. But I hold off. We'll discuss that document some other night, and when that time comes, only Dad will sign it. But right now, Dad is sitting with his hands folded on a placemat, the corners of his mouth twitching.

I'm sorry, is all he says.

I pat him on the shoulder. Upstairs, I go to say goodbye. Ethan hears me coming, I'm sure. Pepper, the Labrador, is lying outside his door, snout sunk between her front paws. She always comes to his door like this.

THE LAST TIME Ethan remembers hearing my voice in our household, I was coughing. That would've been the spring of '97, my senior year of high school. For almost a month, I lay in bed sick with double pneumonia, bacterial colonies constricting both my lungs, hacking after almost every breath. But as I lay in illness, I remind my brother, Mom and Dad took care of me. Mom took my temperature and prepared hot tea and soup; Dad came in when he could, supporting me on trips to the bathroom. Each of them took turns sitting at my bed, reading me poetry from chapbooks stashed around my room.

My recovery took place in their care, I say. Your recovery will too.

I promise my brother I will be at his awards ceremony. His face burns.

This is where heat goes in a rising home.

MY BROTHER STOPS cutting. Really, he should have seen a therapist. We got lucky. At first, he cannot say why he stops.

At first, he barely notices.

Part of it is that he can no longer hear. After my visit, Mom and Dad buy a television for his bedroom as a kind of apology, and also to drown out their fights, which do not slow down. The TV keeps their conflicts out of my brother's ears, downgrading them to peripheral chatter, something less than a laugh track. The TV keeps my brother up at night, pulling him into chronic sleeplessness for the rest of his teenage years. In some ways, his melancholy worsens. His loneliness.

But he does not cut. Reaching for the razor blade, he remembers our conversation. My voice. My worrying. He'll always put the blade back down.

DOWN 3ᴿᴰ AVENUE West, Seattle Methodist University is hosting an annual homeless camp maintained by student volunteers on its campus. The encampment is a Christmas tradition, a way to honor the Messiah. It will all be taken down soon.

Past SMU's chapel and dormitories, Mr. Lavender is waiting for me on his front porch. His house is another antique, one inherited with the passing of his mother. He waves with a generous smile, a not-quite hippie with shaggy hair, a shaggy beard, a wrinkled face, and dusty feet. Once my math teacher at Maynard Middle School, where Ethan is currently a student, we always stayed in touch. After I signed with Sub Pop, Mr. Lavender was one of the first people I contacted with the news.

In 2011, he will die in a fire that starts in his attic. After the ash is cleared, SMU will possess the ruined lot, rehabilitating it into a greenspace with a charcoal grill and a picnic table. Nothing will commemorate the man who lived here, the eccentric educator who taught probability to his students through gambling and lottery tickets, and once published a true crime novel. Like so many touchstones lost to New Seattle, Mr. Lavender will be left behind in a clean way.

But for now, he is untroubled. Neighborly. I park and come out of my truck with my duffel bag and guitar. Once I'm settled, he takes out a tobacco pipe and begins to smoke. He asks me about Olympia, how my fiancée and daughter are doing. He asks me about Texas.

Get me some whiskey, I say. I'll confess to everything.

Mr. Lavender guffaws. He goes inside in search of a good bottle. While I wait, I contemplate the underground springs in the neighborhood. One trickles beneath the house on West Etrusca Street, forever slicking the hillside, a place that will always need to be treated with caution.

· Three ·

Austin River Family

THREE SUMMERS ON Uncle Rod's ranch was all it took for me to get like this. Well, most of what it took. That's what I tell people who want to know.

Most people want to know.

Our crew was mostly from Northern Mexico. Sturdy and calloused, always brimming with jokes and stories. Only a couple spoke English. Together, from June to August, we hustled across the plains, branding and herding my uncle's beef in hot temperamental weather. Some nights, the men would drive into Great Falls, spending their cash in bars or sending remittances home. Other nights, they stayed on the ranch, gathering as I played guitar—one gifted to me by Uncle Rod and Aunt Dottie—covering the poets and pickers I knew and admired. I wasn't good then, but nobody minded. Night after night, those songs swept us into relief, a relief deeper than any of us could feel alone.

Mostly, Tanner Ranch was a place of labor. Predawn mornings and dark skies. The peace of the Upper Missouri. Occasional storms. When I wasn't on the plains, I was reading, writing, or practicing my guitar in my bedroom. The house only had one computer—the only computer for miles—which Aunt Dottie used to manage financial spreadsheets and communicate with the ranch's business partners. There were only two telephones, one in the kitchen and one in the cluttered home office, both compromised by dial-up internet. Electrification didn't come to this part of Montana until the late 1930s, and my aunt and uncle somehow still regarded electricity as a vice. But they did have a record player and a huge vinyl collection, an inventory I listened to many times over. They also kept an expansive library of Larry McMurtry books. McMurtry was an author they fell in love with while attending the University of Texas, which is where they met and decided to spend their lives together. Their four years in Austin was the only time they'd been residents anywhere else.

I read McMurtry every night, especially his essay collection, *In A Narrow Grave.* My favorite piece was "A Look at the Lost Frontier," describing a road trip from Houston to Matamoros, then to the Hill Country and the Panhandle, where the fierce wind comes down off the Rockies. In McMurtry's contemplations, the past accumulates into the present, a mounting of elements—hard country, hard history, the fading rural, the emerging urban. I began to see my own accumulations too: the pain of my parents, the open horizon.

Some nights, I would visit the spare room devoted to my mother's years as a concert pianist. Not quite a prodigy, but almost. Trophies and ribbons collected dust on the upright piano. I would try to square Nora Tanner's girlhood dreams with her unplanned college pregnancy, her quick marriage to Dad.

Every September, I dreaded coming home. Until, one year, I decided Queen Anne had never been my home.

MY LAST SUMMER working the ranch, Uncle Rod gifted me his thunderous brown pickup truck. He would mail me new tabs every year, so I could take Montana with me wherever I went. At first, I stayed close. In August 1997, I headed over to Missoula. My destination was a studio apartment near the Clark Fork River.

MISSOULA WAS SUPPOSED to be where I would thrive, but I didn't. Not with the rigid curricula, the witless lectures, the dreary canon. Winter was a problem too, all eight months of it. Though I made friends in that snowdrift—late nights in sawdust bars; midnight hikes up Mount Sentinel; dorm room intimacies—I couldn't stand it.

Returning to Seattle was off the table. And though they loved me, Uncle Rod and Aunt Dottie thought I deserved better than more ranch work.

On spring break, Uncle Rod suggested I try Austin.

In the '70s, he told me, the city had the cheapest cost of living in the United States, a premiere haven for weirdos and bohemian types, home to the Armadillo World Headquarters and the Outlaw scene. Willie Nelson, Townes Van Zandt, Steve Earle, Emmylou Harris, Joe Ely. Rebels to the prevailing Nashville Sound, speakers for the long-haired, the down-and-out. Neither Uncle Rod nor Aunt Dottie had been back since graduation, but they couldn't name a better place for a young man to chart his course.

I thought about it for a week.

The call to my parents—who were paying my tuition—was brief. I told them who I planned to be. They told me I could come back.

To my credit, I attended the remainder of my classes, sitting through every final exam, turning in every piece of homework. I dropped out with a perfect grade-point-average, the only student on the Dean's List to do so.

Uncle Rod and Aunt Dottie celebrated my nineteenth birthday with me. Then, early one morning, with some money, some clothes, and my instrument, I set out.

TWENTY-SIX HOURS, SEVENTEEN-HUNDRED miles.

June 1998.

TWO YEARS BEFORE my arrival, the Austin City Council rewrote the zoning laws, kicking off a real estate boom in downtown and East Austin. Pick any construction site and apply for a job. You'll get something.

That's what the pierced barista told me in Spider House, the elaborate coffee shop just off the Drag, not yet much more than a former party palace on a quiet street. I downed my espresso, thanking her for the tip. Sick of driving, I strapped my guitar case to my shoulders, endeavoring to walk. The heat index soon reached 108 degrees.

I WAS GRIPPING the chain-link fence outside a construction site on East 7th Street, sweat soaking through my denim shirt, when a crew of hardhats saved my ass from fainting. Taking me under the arms, they hauled me across the street into a tattoo parlor. Dumping me in the waiting area, someone told a young blonde woman I might need an ambulance. The tattoo artist asked why I had been brought to her.

Consider him your first customer, the foreman said.

The men ambled away, laughing. Flipping them the bird, the artist poured me some icewater and chilled my forehead and wrists with a damp washcloth, grimacing at my odor. I remember she was wearing a blue flannel, torn jeans, and scuffed up sneakers. That was when I first noticed the central air conditioning, as well as the music coming out of the silver cassette player on the floor, a jaunty combo of acoustic guitars and earnest voices singing about a Nicotine Queen.

Who are you? I asked.

McKenna, she said. Owner and artist. You?

Terrell. Outlaw and drifter. What are we listening to, McKenna?

Twang Twang Shock-A-Boom.

Huh?

Twang Twang Shock-A-Boom. They're local. You obviously aren't.

No ma'am. I am not.

McKenna did not care where I came from or why, but I told her anyway. When I finished, she was shaking her head. But I could see amusement in her eyes.

So you're a smart one, huh?

Smart as they come, I said.

Men always say that when they get into trouble.

We laughed.

You hiring? I asked.

McKenna looked me up and down.

You play guitar?

Yes ma'am.

You on drugs?

Not yet.

Okay, McKenna said. Minimum wage is what I can pay. I'll let you do anything you want. But you'll have to do something. Deal?

I nodded. She poured me another cup of water. That was how I got my first job in Austin, Texas.

FAR UP GUADALUPE—so far up it was almost North Lamar—I talked my way into a renting a room in a converted motor court for two-fifty a month. The building was made of old cinderblocks and overgrown with weeds. My neighbors either worked all day or stayed in all day. There was no in-between. With a bare mattress on the floor, a box-fan, and roaches to the ceiling, I couldn't recommend it as more than a place for shuteye and a shower.

But I'd still recommend it.

Seven days a week, I hung around McKenna's tattoo parlor from opening to closing. I was the only employee. She had me do everything from unclogging the toilet to running to the post office. The shop had been open two months when I came in. She'd named it Belclaire Ink & Design, in honor of the street in Dallas where she grew up. Her father was a C-Suite executive at an international jewelry company, though she would not say which one. She'd come of age in a neighborhood called Highland Park, a place of quiet mansions and elegant boulevards. I tried to tell her about Highland Drive, a street on Queen Anne Hill where manors overlook downtown Seattle, but she wanted nothing to do with it. She already had a story for us. She was the hardscrabble visionary staking her claim in the city, and I was the troubadour who wandered in one day and never left. There was some truth to this, but there was also money. The men at the construction site knew this, as did everyone else in East Austin.

Mostly, we all got along.

To boost business, McKenna drew up fliers for me to staple around 6th Street and the Red River District. Belclaire would pull clients from Austin's tourists and revelers, quick tattoos to remember wild nights and legendary shows. I introduced myself to as many venue owners as I could, who told me I could audition for their clubs once I had a setlist of at least ten songs, and eight originals. That setlist would be a work-in-progress for years. My presence in the store turned into a selling point: come get tattooed with live music from an up-and-coming singer-songwriter. Hell, he may be inspired to write lyrics based on you.

Only one client would ever inspire me like that.

ALONG WITH BELCLAIRE, McKenna also held the deed to a three-bedroom house at the corner of Rio Grande and West 29th ½ Street. Depending on the time of year, she had up to six roommates, mostly longhorns. Just before the new semester began, she told me she'd be bringing one into the shop, who'd get a tattoo at a considerable discount. The design was large and multi-layered, a thick crucifix requiring at least three sessions to complete. She came in one sweltering August afternoon, nervous but exhilarated.

I didn't even see her at first.

She was staring at me for twenty minutes before McKenna whistled to get my attention. I looked up from my notepad. In the tattooing chair sat a young woman with a sleek black ponytail, wearing a jean skirt, a burnt orange t-shirt, and lime-green flip-flops. I set down my notepad and came over. McKenna whispered something, causing her to blush.

I'm sorry, the client said. Are you from Seattle?

I smiled.

How do we know each other?

We went to the same high school, I think. Were you at Yesler?

Two for two. Yes I was.

I transferred to Franklin sophomore year. But I was pretty sure I remembered you. I think we had a typing class together. What's your name?

Terrell. Terrell Jamestone. You?

Isadora Madera.

Pleasure to meet you again, Isadora.

She clenched her teeth and turned away. McKenna's needle was darkening the underside of her right forearm into the contours of the Cross. Her spirituality, I could see, was grounded in the acceptance of pain.

Our girl is being brave, McKenna said, but we're far from done. Terrell, is there anything you can do for her?

I nodded. Kneeling at her side, I invited my future fiancée to take my hand. She seized my fingers, transferring her anguish into me, astonishing me with her strength. We looked at each other like this was the setup to a joke we were both in on. I asked what she was doing in Austin. About to enter her second year at UT, Isadora was majoring in social work and minoring in women's studies, attending college on a three-quarter-ride scholarship. On days she didn't have class, she volunteered for a reproductive rights advocacy group. Twice a week, she attended mass at the University Catholic Center. Her tattoo was a proclamation of reconciliation.

Isadora tightened her grip. She asked for my story. I told her all about the ranch, the songs I wrote. I stayed with her for two more hours, just talking. When it was over, she was wiping the sweat off her lips, looking at me with expectations rising in her gold-flecked eyes. She paid and scheduled the second session.

We left right then.

I took her to the Red River District, leading her into the Creosote Club, where I knew the crew that worked the doors. We danced under a hot downpour of rain, an electric blues duo jamming on stage, my hands on her hips, her waist on my waist.

MCKENNA CAME INTO her kitchen the next morning. I was cooking up a Denver omelet, naked except for my boxers. From the dining room table, Isadora said I'd insisted on keeping something on, despite her protests.

McKenna laughed.

She turned on the coffeemaker and wished us luck.

BEACON HILL WAS home, and Beacon Hill was with her always. In her bedroom on Rio Grande Street, Izzie showed me the photo album she put together before moving away, a visual essay of where she came from. Most of the photographs she took as a teenager, but a few important ones came from other sources. The first pages showed Pike Place Market in the '70s, gray and seedy. Her mother, Sunshine Madera, was a teenager then, working as a baker at a Filipino restaurant patronized by ship crews, men who sipped pork stew and devoured lumpia, missing the tropics with true and deep heartache.

One day, during her lunchbreak, sixteen-year-old Sunshine was impregnated by a Russian sailor. She never saw the sailor again.

She always seemed to blame Isadora for her father.

The photo album jumped to Izzie as a child, bright and energetic, running around Seward Park. With her biracial complexion, strangers assumed she was Hawaiian or Mexican, and she never corrected them. Always trying to please everyone, Isadora said. When she was ten or so, her mother opened her own bakery, Madera Panadería, on South Orcas Street. Her store, with its popular pan de monja, established a reputation as a staple of the community. Sunshine enjoyed her valorization as a small-businessowner, posing in press photos with her signature ensaymada, pan de coco, and colorful cheese breads.

Some neighborhood kids knew her differently.

Years after Empire Way turned into Martin Luther King Jr. Way, rumors spread about Sunshine Madera's temper, how she would run out of the kitchen screaming racist slurs, kicking out certain kids for coming in with backpacks or standing in groups. In a public relations coup, local papers ran a series of stories depicting her as a beloved hardass, her tantrums and harassment the cost of perfection. Sales shot up. But Isadora would always remember that one night in November 1991 when a judge handed down a sentence of time served to the storeowner who killed Latasha Harlins. Her mother was cheering. Sometimes, my mom feels like Rush Limbaugh in the body of a Filipina woman, Izzie told me, yelling in Spanish and Tagalog.

Sunshine, like so many of us, was mean and complicated. She had her graces too. She always encouraged her daughter to pursue whatever course in life she chose. Good grades were beside the point, as was a good salary. She just wanted a free and independent woman. In her bakery, Sunshine showed Isadora how to stand up to men, cultivating pride and ferocity. She could also be tender, consoling her daughter after bad breakups with boys who never deserved her in the first place.

Izzie closed her photo album and asked about my family. I didn't say much. We cuddled and fell asleep.

NIGHTMARES AWOKE ME almost every week. Screaming and slammed doors, the Fremont Bridge, the hard-plastic seat of an SPD squad car. Cuffs on wrists, Dad through the glass, neighbors gossiping. One night, after Izzie asked me why I never called home, I drank an entire bottle of whiskey by myself and woke up on the front porch. She told me to never drink like that again. But I would.

YET WE WERE in love.

Kissing and fucking in a dream of exemption.

We'd waste entire days in bed, talking about nothing, sheets soaked with sweat, a heart-shaped wreath of shotgun shells hanging above her pillows. When we were out in public, she would shove me against random trees, kissing me in front of cheering strangers. We swam nude at Hippie Hollow, picnicked nude, sunbathed and read paperbacks nude. We attended Chicken Shit Bingo at the Little Longhorn Saloon.

What a time. At Mount Bonnell after a thunderstorm, she jumped on my back and told me to carry her up the stairs—and I did. One afternoon, she asked me to paint her fingernails in front of her girlfriends, and when I did an excellent job, she painted mine. Then she took me into the bathroom, covering me in makeup, doing my hair. We went out to Waterloo Records, and nobody looked twice, even though it was only the late '90s, even though Austin was still Texas. Izzie laughed at what her mother would say. She told me I never looked so hot.

Romances spin their own tall tales. Ours was a second adolescence.

But we were serious, too. We had to be. She told me she had always been put off by the proud atheism of our hometown, convinced it was a cover for money worship, callousing its followers to the needy. This was the through-line between her religion and her reproductive rights advocacy: solidarity with the dispossessed. Rich women would always have a means to abortion. The legal fight was for everyone else. And fight Isadora did, staring down anti-choice protestors in front of the Texas State Capitol, unafraid. One day, a photograph of her leading a pro-choice rally while heavily pregnant would be the talk of Austin for almost a month. She was my hero.

Then and now.

She could be a creature of worry, though, wound up over term papers and tests, late nights spent ruminating over slights classmates had thrown her way. Sometimes, she succumbed to panic. She almost bailed on finishing her crucifix tattoo, revealing nightmares about getting HIV. I could talk her through that, but I couldn't help with everything. She didn't know how to drive—as of 2005, still doesn't, ever the city girl—so I tried to teach her in my pickup. Izzie accelerated by mistake, hyperventilating.

She worried about us too.

Many couples got by on novelty, Isadora said. Entertainment was all that kept them together, a swirl of endless amusements. She hoped we'd never be like that. And contempt, she said, was the one emotion that killed relationships for good. She hoped neither of us would ever feel it for each other.

Sometimes, she envied my lifestyle, until I told her I had no health insurance and no clear path for my career. I was in the Velvet Rut for sure. The only way out was trying. Mostly luck.

In some ways, Izzie was my muse, listening to me develop my voice, encouraging me to write more humor into my verses. She was with me for all the first shows, the bars and coffeehouses in the Hill Country, where I told jokes on stage, sharing my best stories with the crowd. An audience is nothing without rapport. We fell for the town of Dripping Springs, charmed by its stone storefronts, holding hands in gift shops, dashing into the best swimming hole in Travis County, holding each other under a waterfall, laughing at our own cliché. She cut class to come to my shows in San Marcos and San Antonio, my proud and excited roadie, whistling from the front row. When I got invited to perform in Houston, I could swear the sky was opening up, and that somehow, Isadora was the one who opened it for me.

In the evenings, we took ourselves to the movies. Arthouse, mostly. My favorite was a screening of *A Poem is a Naked Person,* the bootlegged documentary about Leon Russell and his hijinks in the Oklahoma lake country, never distributed because the subject disavowed it. Another one I loved was a documentary about Lightnin' Hopkins, our strutting Texas blues genius.

When we saw *Heartworn Highways*, the sight of Townes Van Zandt paralyzed Izzie. As he played guitar in the Clarksville trailer of a blacksmith named Seymour Washington, moving his host to tears, she turned to me and said:

You look exactly like him. You sound exactly like him. Have you just been ripping off Townes Van Zandt this whole time?

She meant it as a joke. In those days, that was the only time I felt hostility towards her.

SHE LEANED IN during *Gas Food Lodging*, whispering that I reminded her of all these movies somehow. Raw and high concept. You have a flickering way about you, she insisted. So unlikely, so worth it.

AND I TOLD her at the Wheatsville Food Co-op that she was a Babaylan. Her gift was transforming pain into joy. Holding a vial of bee pollen, she raised her eyebrows. Excuse me? How do you even know that word? She put the bee pollen down, waiting for me to say more, but I let my statement stand. We drifted up and down the organic aisles. Every now and then, she looked at me, my assertion sinking through her as though she were a jar of honey.

She tossed a tofu po' boy into our basket, and held my hand like she did in the tattoo parlor, her chest rising and falling.

IN ALL OUR carnality, we didn't always wear condoms. Holy fools. For months, we gambled off and on. Just to see.

OUR DAUGHTER WOULD be conceived on a warm winter night on the branch of an old oak tree, Spanish moss dripping above us.

We were on the Shoal Creek Trail, coming back after a late screening of *Paris, Texas.* Isadora pushed me hard against the trunk, closing her eyes. She had always reveled in her own lust, exhilarated by the force of attraction, losing herself to short breath and clenched toes. After a few electric seconds, she sat on a heavy sideways branch, kissing me deeper and deeper, whispering, Fuck me as hard as you can. She pulled down her skirt and panties, bare-assed and wet, unbuckling my belt. Please. Please. She clutched my shoulder blades so hard her nails almost cut open my shirt. She went through every one of her pleasured rituals—kissing her own shoulder, sucking her wrist so hard she left a hickey, writhing her abdomen—before we both came.

We felt miraculous, embarrassed.

Humid from the inside out.

As we collected ourselves, Izzie retrieved her flip-flops in disbelief. When I asked if she was okay, she nodded. We are both so lucky, she said. So lucky. She took my hand. A moonlight tower illuminated the prickly-pear and mesquite.

One day, we would agree that was the only way we could have conceived our daughter.

WE WERE SO young.

ISADORA WAS SITTING in a red-vinyl booth with queso and tortilla chips. I brought over two mugs of coffee, and sat at her side. Spider House was empty except for our friend in the kitchen. Izzie sighed, looking out the window to the parking lot. The light was faint.

How would you feel about visiting Alpine? I asked. Might make a fine place to settle down someday. Land's cheap. We could buy a house, get good acreage. The Big Bend needs social workers. You'd have a job. And I could drive down to Terlingua, jam with the porch sitters. Wouldn't that be a hoot?

Isadora turned to me.

I told my mom before I told you. I'm so sorry, Terrell.

What? I said.

We're having a baby.

Before I knew anything, she had already decided. Not only that, but she had already been to the health clinic, putting together an appointment schedule for her pregnancy. Being pro-choice, she reminded me, meant autonomy in both directions.

What did your mother say? I asked.

Sunshine Madera was incensed. She told Isadora to abort it immediately, break up with my wannabe-hillbilly ass, and be anybody but this. When the first test came up positive, maybe there was a single moment when termination crossed Isadora's mind. But she knew what she wanted.

They would not speak for nine months.

Izzie rested on my shoulder, wishing we had planned for this, hoping I would not resent her, but understanding that I might. She waited for me to talk. A great-tailed grackle descended on the asphalt outside, glaring with yellow eyes. I told Isadora I loved her. She wasn't scared, because back then, she knew I would never leave her.

BELINDA MIRANDA MADERA-Jamestone.

Our brilliant baby girl.

Our heart.

CURIOSITY WAS HER first and greatest principle, little eyes roving, tiny fingers touching. A strong-willed toddler, tearing through our babyproofed home in McKenna's basement, testing her velocity as soon as she could. Every phase of her growth enamored us. *Bat!* was her first word, and when she began talking in sentences, *Bats!* were most of what she talked about. She bounced in delight whenever we took her to see the Mexican short-tails under the South Congress Bridge. Her corner of the basement filled with stuffed bat toys, and when she could draw, she drew page after page of winged black blobs.

She loved echolocation, and true to form, loved to screech, which we convinced her to do only in the shower.

Reading was her other great passion. I taught her the summer of her fourth birthday, sitting on the front porch with picture books, waving at neighbors. Billie could recite the alphabet and write her name before she was five. I'm still proud of that.

Because Isadora needed her other life—her church and her activism—Belinda and I developed father-daughter rituals. She stood in wide-eyed wonder as McKenna tattooed me, hollering with joy as she received the same tattoos in temporary form. We would take walks to Shoal Creek, passing where she was conceived. I told her how Austin's north-south streets were named after Texas rivers, and all the streets ended at the Colorado River, meaning that all those rivers were connected.

My girl nodded.

I took her to the HOPE Outdoor Gallery, a graffiti park forged out of a failed condominium project, three concrete stories embedded into an earthen slope. Improvised art covered every surface: spray-painted saints, celebrity idols, prayers. A masterful serpent goddess could be painted one day, tagged by snickering middle schoolers overnight, then replaced by a new mural immediately. The park was a constant rainstorm of paint: bushes, trashcans, and abandoned couches drowning in color. Billie and I got to work spraying a boulder silver, then violet, then black in honor of the bats.

Belinda was fascinated by everyone around her, especially a crew of rappers gathering for a group photo, flashing their diamond teeth. We visited a dusty couple in the back of their van, where they sold crystals, beaded bracelets, and handmade enamel pins. Migrating from the Mojave Desert, they were careening through the South to wherever came next. They delighted in Belinda, giving her a free bat pin with my approval.

When the weather wasn't too hot, we'd hike the beer-can-cluttered trail to the top of the gallery. I would point at the Capitol and the UT Tower and the new skyscrapers, incomplete and winking in the sun.

This is where you come from, I would say.

She would just look at me.

Some of our favorite times took place in the backyard. One day, I caught her hosing a pile of dirt into a mess of mud. She plopped herself down, sculpting.

What're you making, Billiebat? I asked.

Mount Rainier pie, she giggled.

We had a poster of the mountain on our wall. Her mother and I had never spoken about taking her to the Pacific Northwest. She had never met any of her grandparents.

She was hardly deprived of attention, and raising her was sometimes a communal venture. Billie's favorite in-house babysitter was a woman from New Orleans named Giselle, who waitressed on the Drag and otherwise sat around in golden thrift shop dresses. Growing up in the Seventh Ward, she vowed never to return to the City That Care Forgot, but she also never shut up about it. Gisselle loved Billie, telling us that our daughter had opened her to the prospect of motherhood for herself. One night, Izzie and I came back to find a pajamaed Belinda dancing to the Wild Tchoupitoulas. Her favorite song was Meet de Boys on the Battlefront, and for a month, she refused to go to bed unless we clapped our hands and chanted the lyrics with her.

But motherhood was tough on Isadora, tougher than she wanted it to be. She took a year and a half off from college, convincing the administration to honor her scholarship upon her return, with sponsorship from her professors. Years 0-3 are the most important in a child's development, Izzie kept repeating. She wanted to structure our girl's every waking hour, and when she couldn't, she called me constantly to check-in. Even when she reenrolled, she studied part-time.

When she graduated at last, she took a job as a life skills educator for a wealthy family in West Lake Hills, working with their nonverbal, twenty-year-old son. Six foot three, his cognitive development had not advanced past a toddler's. The father of the family owned a local news station, and, Isadora suspected, hired her less for her qualifications and more because he associated someone who looked like her with domestic servitude. The pay was nine dollars an hour.

On a typical day, she divided her time between cooking, cleaning, wiping her client's ass, and accompanying him on medical appointments. Most of all, she endured his public outbursts. The mother of the house spoiled him, and most of the meltdowns were a form of learned behavior. Rather than replace his maladaptive strategies with positive strategies, Isadora was instructed to always yield. His worst eruptions occurred at Barton Creek, sometimes escalating into assault. We never visited Barton Creek as a family.

Within a month, Izzie would have done anything to quit. Grad school was a constant obsession. So was poverty. How long would we be raising our daughter in a basement? How do we tell Belinda her parents took a vow of indigence before she was born? Isadora cried into my chest. We'll be okay, I said. We'll be okay.

My own career was beginning to jump. The Creosote Club hired me as a bartender, and though most bartenders don't earn much, popular bartenders do. Eventually, I talked my way onto the stage, introducing acts, working the drunk crowds with my babble. Tonight, I'd like to thank Mr. River, a.k.a. Red. You know what they say around here, the redder the river, the better the blues. I convinced the owners to let me play a few songs, and my status jumped again when I helped a swamp-rock group from Baton Rouge whose guitarist was in jail. Quickly, I hired myself out to anyone who needed a replacement. They paid, and I got to meet some heroes: Bill Callahan, Rhett Miller, Jason Isbell, and Larry McMurtry's son, James McMurtry.

My first headlining show was in March 2004. It was the first night of South by Southwest, a for-locals by-locals showcase. I came on stage with my guitar, dedicated my songs to my daughter and her mother, and got into it. Taped onto a nearby amp was my setlist, with ten original songs: Pioneer Square Stole My Wallet, Whiskey French Toast, Born Without Eyelids. Etcetera. Leaving after an encore, a black-haired woman stepped in front of me. Introducing herself as Tina, she wore Converse shoes, a black tank top, and black jeans with busted knees. A former riot grrrl in the Oly scene, she now worked as an A&R. She wanted to know all about me and my vision.

If you were to record an album tomorrow, Tina asked, what would the title be?

I told her.

Tina took out her phone. She made a few calls. When she was done, she told me the score.

TEN YEARS AFTER Johnny Cash himself gave the keynote address at South By, I auditioned for a pair of Sub Pop executives on Spider House's patio. By this time, the café had expanded to a beer garden and the Ballroom. A neighborhood crowd whooped and cheered, convincing the suits better than I ever could by myself.

For my official debut, the label would wire a modest but crucial advance.

Isadora and Billie needed me. And I needed them.

McKenna would hold off renting out the basement for six months. Money was less crucial by then. Belclaire Ink & Design was succeeding, with a steady stream of clients and three artists working under her. The construction site across the street had long since turned into townhouses, which entrepreneurial types now called home. Many of the neighborhood's old businesses were gone, replaced by boutique and artisanal versions of things. As far as this version of East Austin was concerned, the neighborhood began with Belclaire and the daughter of a C-Suite jewelry executive.

JAY KRISTENSEN JR.

IN NOVEMBER, WE departed for the West Coast. We would stay with friends in Tucson, the Bay Area, and Oregon.

ON THE HIGHWAY to Alpine, rainclouds rolled over the vast countryside, the remotest vistas we'd ever seen, a Texas beneath Texas. A freight train led us into a cluster of peaks. We pulled into a gas station near Sul Ross State University. A desert hill loomed behind the school, the soil damp, the succulents doused. The rain was about to come back.

Isadora tugged my sleeve.

What? I said.

Will you marry me? she said.

Billie kept her eyes on us.

Darling, I said.

For seven years, we had never finished this conversation. I took Isadora's hand.

Yes.

She nodded. Then she unbuckled our daughter from her booster seat and took her into the store for a potty break. I stayed with the truck, filling the tank with diesel. I watched the vehicles on the highway, men hauling trailers of cattle and horses. We were spending only the night in Alpine, but I still thought about it as a place to call home someday.

ON THE LAST page of *In A Narrow Grave*, I underlined a sentence about unredeemed dreams.

· Four ·

Hill of Stairs

UNDER THE BLACK winter sky, where I am back where I came from, morning frost illuminates the brick and concrete gardens. Over one-hundred stairwells descend from Queen Anne Hill, the most in the city: some overgrown with ivy, some dropping beneath streetlamps on serene boulevards. Amid this vertical network, the hidden take sanctuary.

This, too, is what the frost illuminates: the unpropertied, the unsheltered.

The unwelcome.

Over the weekend, we attend the awards ceremony at the U-Dub. Standing on stage in a featureless ballroom, the provost gives a speech to the awardees and their families, telling us that the summer courses are only the beginning. Someday, this could be the first generation of middle school dropouts in history to lead the world's industries.

Laughter and applause.

Ethan is silent. His highest scores were in reading comprehension and writing, strengths his peers will leverage as corporate lawyers and consultants, extracting wealth for their already-wealthy clients. Those being honored for their math skills will go on to work in speculative finance, perfecting the commodification of society, or work for weapons manufacturers, innovating new ways to kill. A few will mature into lives devoted to community or artistry.

None of us know what the future holds for my brother.

As Ethan is called to the stage, my little Austin family cannot help but make a scene. I put my thumb and forefinger into my mouth, whistling. Isadora howls. Billie jumps up and down on her seat. The rest of the audience regards us with disapproval. We don't care.

As my brother shakes the provost's hand, he looks at us in desperation. He takes the certificate, gleaming with the magnitude of the future.

I ASK ETHAN if he wants to spend his summer at the University of Washington. The room is clearing out. We're alone.

Nope, Ethan says.

Why not?

They don't care about me. They're using me to make themselves look good.

Well, I say. Tell Mom and Dad.

He won't voice his opinion until May. When he does, he'll stand firm.

By then, I'll already be gone.

THE EVENING BEFORE the new quarter, I visit the house, sitting with Ethan on the porch, letting him share what he wants to. This is something I'll do between recording sessions for as long as I'm in town. The first time we hang out, he hesitates.

Then he asks about Eugene.

I tap my cigarette into a wine glass. I know who he's talking about. Bearded with jaundiced skin, always wearing the same denim overalls, black work boots, and brown wool cap. Old Man Eugene claims to be a former millworker from Aberdeen, fired by our grandfather. He's seen my brother with Dad, knows the Jamestone name, knows about the cinnamon-colored house on Simmons Street.

He's probably telling the truth, I say.

Neighborhoods of affluence can be as dangerous to a person like Eugene as the toughest inner-city blocks. I don't elaborate. One day, I won't need to.

MAYNARD MIDDLE SCHOOL conducts itself in a long brick building on the crest of the hill. This is where my brother spends every Monday through Friday. Beginning around 7:20 a.m., along the wide loading zone out front, school buses deposit hundreds of kids from distant neighborhoods: Mount

Baker, South Park, Rainier Beach. They rush the building, laughing and cussing. From the parking lot out front comes a different kind of preteen, chauffeured in luxury sedans by parents who expect them to hit a 4.0 GPA this quarter and every quarter, who wince as the bus kids engulf their sons and daughters, churning in kinetic crowds.

The lines used to be clearer.

Until last year, Maynard Middle School funneled its highest achievers into two parallel tracks: the honors program and the Urban Scholars program. The distinction between the two was nebulous until a lawsuit laid it bare. The honors students were almost completely white, with a few Asian-Americans, and Urban Scholars were almost completely Black, with a few Latinos. While the school district contended with demands to integrate, Maynard's parents were invited to express their views in a community meeting. Rejecting their customary self-restraint, some local residents took the mic in fury.

How dare the district undermine the honors program like this?

Bullying, they said, was their main concern. These Urban Scholars were aggressive. Street-hardened. Didn't the principal understand? These other children were in constant trouble, followed in supermarkets by assistant managers, told to clear out of candy aisles because they presented a fire hazard. When Urban Scholars hung out at the playfield, neighbors called the police, who arrived in multiple squad cars, searching their backpacks, demanding receipts to prove their snacks weren't shoplifted.

Where was the plan, local parents demanded, to protect the honors students?

The parents of the Urban Scholars were unavailable for comment. Most of them were at their jobs.

Maynard Middle School agreed to integrate, beginning in the 2004-05 school year, though most of one honors class is still white and Asian, and most of the other is Black and Latino. Neighborhood parents facilitated a relentless anti-bullying campaign, pushing for ever more severe punishments. The district congratulated itself on its progressiveness, and was relieved when, for financial reasons, a second lawsuit failed to materialize.

FOR MY BROTHER, he has concerns beyond politics.

Her name is Beatrix.

In the way of thirteen-year-olds, she is and is not his girlfriend. Like Ethan, Beatrix is an honors student. Pale and brunette, from West Seattle, hairbands hanging from her wrists. She always wears a pink-and-black hoodie, always wears jeans with sequined pockets. She loves parakeets. Her dream job is to work as a fashion designer, and to that end, she takes art classes three times a week in the community center. One afternoon, she asks Ethan to write his name on her sneakers in permanent marker. Sometimes, she sits on his lap at lunch, giggling. She rests her head on his shoulder on movie days, and has asked him, once or twice, if he has wet dreams.

Most of their closeness comes from openness.

When they hold hands, Beatrix's fingers and palms are cold, always cold. Poor circulation, she says. Mom smoked through all three trimesters of her pregnancy. She's never seen her biological father, and it spooks her to think she may have met him without knowing it. She lives with her grandmother, who screams at her. Beatrix always screams back, and over the holidays, her grandmother finally called the police on her. Living with Mom is not a possibility. Mom is in a studio apartment in Belltown, schizoaffective and alone.

On the morning Beatrix admits this, she will burst out in strange laughter, and slap Ethan hard across the mouth when he asks if he can someday meet her mother.

For now, they are still close.

Out of the January coldness, they wander up the stairs to their 1st and 2nd period block.

HOW MANY BASEBALLS would it take to fill up the Space Needle?

Mr. Bushwick writes the question on the whiteboard, bright and baby-faced, looking back at his unimpressed students. This is his first year as a teacher, charged with the honors program's math and science classes. Before winter break, most of his energy was spent arguing with students about his lesson plans, resulting in several in-class interventions by seething administrators. For the second half of the year, he is hoping for a reset.

The problem on the board, Mr. Bushwick tells his class, is the kind of question tech companies ask during job interviews.

Tech jobs are the future, he says. You need to begin preparing today. You don't want to end up on minimum wage, do you?

He lets out a nervous laugh.

Somebody else takes over, a man the class has never seen before, dressed in a black fleece vest, hiking shoes, and blue jeans. His light brown hair is spiked with gel. The special guest introduces himself as Mr. Dilner. Mr. Dilner works for Microsoft. An employee, he clarifies, not a contractor.

Tech companies want to hire people who show their work, he says. In programming and engineering, the approach to problem-solving can be more important than the solution itself.

The students will take twenty minutes at their table groups to write out their answers to the Space Needle problem, which they will present to the class.

Mr. Bushwick has high expectations for my brother's table. All four members attended the ceremony at the U-Dub. Beatrix is the only bus kid among them. She sits at Ethan's side in boredom. On the other end of the table sits Holly Johansson, a girl of Hmong descent, dressed in a sensible sweatervest, plaid skirt, and buckled shoes. Holly is the adopted daughter of two Scandinavian restaurateurs, whose Ballard oyster house is the epicenter of the new foodie scene. Years will pass—years spent far apart—but Holly and my brother will be the loves of each other's lives someday.

Next to Holly sits Wilhelm Kunst, a pimpled, Dutch-blond boy. Wilhelm is the son of a foundation director and a Google product manager. Every time you click an ad, he likes to say, my dad gets paid. He wears a Stanford t-shirt, where he will be spending the summer at a computer science camp. He already knows Python, has experience with Java and C++, and has even dabbled in UNITY.

After the groups give their presentations, Mr. Dilner announces he will be running an after-school coding club for the rest of the year, which they are all invited to join for extra credit. Today, he has brought laptops for each table. For the remaining ninety minutes he will be leading them in some preliminary Python exercises. In good faith, my brother will participate in the coding club, the same way he tried to participate in the chess club the previous year. His inquiring nature drives him, but he is also trying to stay above the future poverty line.

Then, Mr. Dilner will recruit Wilhelm to be his teaching assistant.

When my brother fails to grasp the distinction between an array and a list, his best friend tells him to go back to special ed. A miscalculation yields a smack to the face; a broken line of code, a condescending sigh. When Ethan writes a multiplication program and tries to teach the girl next to him, Wilhelm rolls his eyes. Damn, you're even being outthought by Ethan today. At this rate, you'll end up in a trailer park.

You're so stupid, you'll end up cleaning the windows of my office.

The same way Mom and Dad's fights punish Ethan for being their son, my brother's classmates punish each other for needing help. Ethan will retire from Python for the same reason he retired from chess club. Though he enjoys problem-solving, he would rather be alone.

OUTSIDE THE CLASSROOM one afternoon, Wilhelm sneers at Safeway employees striking for better schedules and higher pay. What do those idiots expect? the twelve-year-old asks. Poverty is a natural outcome for them, maybe the only fair one.

How do you feel about the strikers? I ask on the porch. Would you join them?

Ethan glares.

I'm never working at Safeway.

Alright, I say. Well, if you do, never cross that picket line. Solidarity forever. Vote with the union every time. Only we can take care of each other.

THIRD AND FOURTH periods belong to Mr. Finnegan, who teaches language arts and Washington State history. Piercing brown eyes look out from beneath his receding hairline, his round face electric with intelligence. The sleeves of his sweaters are always rolled to his elbows, his khaki pants crisp and ironed, his black shoes immaculate.

He has been teaching for twenty years.

His classroom is half the size of Mr. Bushwick's, and cluttered with textbooks. To optimize his space, Mr. Finnegan has a seating chart designed for the most effective distribution of personalities. Every morning, he takes attendance in front of his chalkboard, verifying that everyone has settled where they belong.

In this system, my brother sits with three former Urban Scholars: Bahk, Jermaine, and Ibrahim. For the rest of the school year, these three will also be his partners in a group research project about Japanese internment camps, as well as his educators on *Chappelle's Show*, crunk music, and the virtues of the Ying Yang Twins and Dem Franchise Boyz. Bahk is a Korean-born sneakerhead from Mount Baker, dressed in Jordans and a rotation of not-quite-official Sonics jerseys, his green-and-yellow basketball never too far from his hands. Jermaine is from the Central District, but at the end of the school year, his parents are moving him to Atlanta. Despite his starstruck excitement at the ATL, Jermaine fears the Ku Klux Klan, who, he says, keeps a list of every Black boy in every neighborhood, so they know when a new one moves in. Whenever he pushes this theory, Ibrahim plays the role of skeptic, asking how the KKK would be able to collect such information.

Because they all work for the government, Jermaine says.

Duh.

Ibrahim is the son of Nigerian immigrants. His ambition is to attend Rice University in Houston, where, he hears, lots of Nigerians are moving. He wants to be a dentist. Charismatic and sharp, he is one of the new honors program's obvious leaders. His best friend is a white boy named Zane, who once locked Mr. Bushwick out of his computer, and once told Mr. Finnegan it isn't fair that taxes are used to punish the rich for their success. With his perpetual smirk, Zane has asked Holly if her parents serve dog meat to make her feel like she's back in China. His friendship with Ibrahim fades when he decides that he can use the n-word too, as long as he ends it with an -a instead of an -er.

FIFTH PERIOD IS gym class. Most afternoons, weather permitting, the instructor, Ms. Zarofakis, takes the kids outside to the West Queen Anne Playfield. She is the subject of great rumor, Ms. Zarofakis. For many, her unladylike gray t-shirts, athletic shorts, and basketball shoes make a beyond-a-reasonable-doubt case for lesbianism, though nobody knows for sure.

Excusing himself from kickball, my brother sits with Holly in the dugout, watching her draw in a sketchpad, a new hobby taken up at Christmas. Proto-manga emerges from her pen, intricate and refined.

How come you like drawing now? Ethan asks.

Holly looks up.

I like the process, she says. The transformation.

Transformation?

I like seeing a blank page transform into art. Controlling how it happens. Think about it. All the things we do, the homework we get assigned, the classes we need to pass. We don't control any of it. We don't even get to choose where we go to high school. My parents want me to go to Ballard.

Not Yesler?

Too dangerous, Holly says.

She resumes her drawing, a castle on a hill with two lovers, a princess and a commoner. Eventually, Holly rips out a page and passes Ethan a spare pen. They get distracted when Ms. Zarofakis blows her whistle, halting the kickball game to prevent a fight from breaking out. She orders everyone up to the chain-link fence for a do-over. Team captains are now banned.

THE LAST CLASS of the day is Spanish with Mr. Paul, who pleads with his sixth period to sign up for his end-of-year field trip to Santo Domingo.

The bell rings and the students of Maynard Middle School liberate themselves. In the exodus, my brother separates himself in solitude. Some afternoons on his walk home, two crows divebomb him over and over, cawing and screaming. He cannot comprehend why he is targeted, and he begins to dread the crows as much as Old Man Eugene. He tries telling people about the corvids and how they torment him. Nobody believes him but me.

SOMETIMES, HE SEES my truck rumbling past, the dull paint and exhaust vulgar against Queen Anne's charms. Ethan loves when I drive by, even when I don't see him, even when I don't wave back.

YOUR TROUBLES ARE never too far from those of the people around you, I say. And theirs are never too far from yours.

My brother looks down the twenty-seven steps.

What about Mom and Dad? he asks.

Well, I say. I figure you could tell me more about them nowadays than I could you.

He sighs.

One afternoon, he tells me about the time Dad took him to lunch with his boss.

· Five ·

The Hiking Men

THE BOOTH IN the Centennial Steakhouse embraces them in velvet sapphire cushions and a table of madrone wood, contoured with golden trim. A small green lamp sits by the wall, lending the scene a businesslike atmosphere. Frosted glass rises above, emblazoned with the restaurant's founding year: 1951. This is the steakhouse where, in the late '80s, Dad took prospective clients from Japan to dinner and won their business. That was the moment our father began a hot streak, becoming Giske & Swain's preeminent young rainmaker, putting him on track to make partner.

In downtown law firms, Dad tells Ethan, attorneys come in three categories. Finders, minders, and grinders. Being a rainmaker means being a finder, an attorney who courts and captures spectacular new clients. Minders are subtler in their work, and in some ways, more valuable. They tend to relationships, strengthen connections, serve as key nodes in business and legal networks. Grinders are workers who handle the nitty gritty, spending late nights running down files and drafting memos. You want to be a rainmaker at some point in your career, especially in the beginning, but longevity is key.

And the key to longevity, he says, are your relationships.

In this restaurant of high-end negotiations, most of the diners are in suits, despite the Pacific Northwest's casual traditions. Ethan is in a button-down shirt and khakis, the least comfortable clothing, he tells me, he's ever worn. Waiting for the boss, Dad passes Ethan a menu.

You've never eaten real steak before, he says.

The menu lists angus, kobe, and wagyu. Fifty-dollar cuts, seventy-dollar cuts, hundred-dollar cuts. Appetizers include Dungeness crab cakes, encrusted scallops, calamari with cognac cream sauce. The soup of the day is lobster bisque. Every menu item is written in cursive. Before Ethan can read further, Dad nudges him.

In he comes: the Giske in Giske & Swain, tall and silver-haired, striding through the restaurant like a politician, shaking hands with seated diners. Dad steps out of the booth, grinning. He sweeps his arm towards Ethan, introducing his second-born, whom Robert Giske acknowledges with respect. The two men sit across from one another. A bow-tied waiter comes by, asking the gentlemen if they'd like to place drink orders. Mr. Giske puts in for bourbon. Dad and Ethan take water.

Mr. Giske looks around.

You know, he says, when I first began practicing law, everybody in here was smoking cigars. You wouldn't believe the waitresses. That was a different era. It's your era now. You're still young, Hunter.

Mr. Giske turns to Ethan.

And someday, it'll be your turn. Your father is so proud of you. Your achievements.

Ethan says nothing. Then Mr. Giske looks at our father in a strange way.

What? Dad says.

You're one of the first people I'm telling. I'm getting appointed to the Supreme Court. Governor Gregoire called this morning.

Are you serious?

I am. This has been in the works for months. I was with Christine the night she won. We had a conversation then and there. The announcement will come Monday during a press conference. I'll be in Olympia by the afternoon.

Congratulations, Robert, Dad says. Ethan, did you hear?

Congratulations, sir, Ethan says.

The waiter comes back. Mr. Giske inspects his bourbon.

Each term is six years, he says. Retirement is mandatory the year I turn seventy-five. I'm sixty-three now. I only need to get through one election. After that, I'm on to my golden years. It's the honor of my life. But first, I will need to divest myself from the firm. Get bought out. Conflict of interest and so forth. Cash flow is excellent. In fact, in the coming reorganization, there will be many new opportunities. For most people.

Mr. Giske takes a sip.

What are you saying, Robert? Dad asks.

I'm saying I got you a meeting, Mr. Giske says.

Where? Dad asks.

Howard, Warwick, and Moore. You've always been something of an obsession for Warwick. He's always insisted your talents are wasted with us.

Are they? Dad asks.

You know I've always had you in my corner. But things are changing. I don't know what's in store for you, Hunter, but you may find yourself sealed in your office, tending to assignments you haven't had since you were an intern.

Why am I getting punished?

Do you remember a few years back when we developed all those employee benefits plans for those contractors and small businesses? Do you remember how you fought, again and again, for more time off for the employees? More PTO? More maternity leave, more vacation days, more sick days? Do you remember when Hank finally lost his temper and called you a communist?

Hank Swain never liked me.

Of course not. I'm the one who hired you.

What can I do?

Take the meeting. I scheduled it for twelve-thirty. You can tell everyone you're taking an extra thirty minutes for lunch. Perhaps you'll be out celebrating my good news.

Howard, Warwick, and Moore? Dad says. Really?

Could be the best thing that ever happens to you, Mr. Giske says.

They defend war criminals.

You refer to Lockhart-Brisbane. No. They're an outstanding company operating on the frontier of innovation. Just wait until you see what they do for your bank account. You won't be so fast to judge. Ethan could go to any law school in the country.

Leave my son out of this, Dad says.

Mr. Giske shakes his head in a pantomime of embarrassment.

No, of course, he says. My apologies. How's your other boy? Terrell? The hellraiser?

Terrell was never a hellraiser, Dad says.

The waiter comes back for their lunch orders. Mr. Giske declares that he will be paying for everything. He insists Ethan and Dad enjoy the finest beef on the menu: the one-hundred fifty-dollar filet mignon, carved from cattle raised in Hokkaido.

Dad orders bourbon for himself. He orders several rounds. By the time lunch is finished, and he and the future Justice Giske are bidding each other farewell, he almost stumbles into an oncoming taxi.

IN A FEW years, when Ethan is in high school, he and Dad will be watching *The Sopranos* while Mom attends a writer's workshop in Capitol Hill. Dad will tell Ethan the mafia works the same way as corporate law firms. Crews of angry men jostling for rank, whose value is contingent only on who they work for and whichever capo is closest to the top boss. Just like the mafia, he will say.

AFTER LUNCH, DAD takes Ethan to a men's barber shop in the underground level of his law firm's building. Sitting in sleek leather chairs, they are attended to by two young women, one of whom pretends to be fascinated as Dad tells her all about the Centennial Steakhouse. He laughs, saying he can't believe how lucky he is.

But y'know, Dad says, when I was little, what I really wanted was to be in the Forest Service. I used to do the junior ranger program up in the Olympics, if you can believe it. I was the only kid from Aberdeen. All the other kids came from Seattle.

Dad looks at Ethan.

We should go hiking, he says. Next weekend, maybe. We'll see what's open. Hopefully the highways aren't all closed.

Dad's stylist and Ethan's stylist finish at the same time. My brother avoids looking in the mirror. Dad pays with his credit card, tipping handsomely. Rather than take the elevator up to see the office, Dad suggests they get back home. He needs to take a nap. But next weekend, he vows, they will hit the Cascades. Ethan asks if I'm invited too.

Sure, Dad says.

ONE SATURDAY LATER, they are waiting for me inside a North Bend coffee shop. Waiting and waiting. Rain keeps the Snoqualmie Valley dim and elusive. Daylight is faint. Passing the time, Ethan is drawing in a sketchpad with an ink pen, rendering boulders and conifers with realistic detail. Our father reads the weekend edition of the *Seattle Post-Intelligencer*, and when he gets bored with that, *The Seattle Times*, grimacing at an op-ed on the homeless problem. Eventually, he takes out his phone. He calls me up, checking on my arrival time, assuming I've been trapped in a studio session. When the call ends, he looks over at his second-born.

Where is he? Ethan asks.

He's in Olympia, Dad says.

Olympia?

Billie's sick with the flu. Isadora took her to the doctor. She'll be okay. I just wish Terrell had told us sooner.

Dad folds his newspaper back into its proper sections. Ethan packs up his pad and pen. They step into the midday twilight.

The rain is pounding now, but they will try hiking anyway. Dad swears under his breath as he takes the driver's seat in his Jetta and turns the key in the ignition. Ethan rests against the window, glancing into the gloom. In a few minutes, they come to the parking lot beneath Mount Si. An old man with a white beard descends from the trail, shuffling towards an RV. He glowers at Dad and Ethan as though they're the reason the temperature is dropping. On the windshield, the pelting raindrops transform into snowflakes. Even with the windshield wipers running, the glass turns opaque in seconds.

Crap, Dad says.

They turn around.

IMMEDIATELY, DAD AND Ethan are stranded with a thousand other vehicles on Snoqualmie Pass, a chute of red brake lights under snowy black ridges.

Dad tunes to KUOW for updates. Everything is at a standstill. There are rumors of a landslide. Snow is falling more and more heavily. Dad and Ethan are too far from an exit to turn around, and besides, Dad doesn't have chains, which were supposed to be in the trunk. Nothing in the forecast suggested there would be snow at this elevation, Dad says again and again.

Eventually, he tires of the radio. He taps Ethan on the shoulder.

How are you holding up?

I'm a little bored, Ethan says.

I bet. This was supposed to be fun. Last weekend wasn't so fun either, was it?

I just don't like haircuts.

Do you still want to be an attorney? Dad asks.

Nope, Ethan says.

Dad nods.

Traffic suddenly crawls again, then stops. To boost morale, Dad begins listing all the places he wants to hike as a family. The Olympics, the San Juans, the Columbia River Gorge. Wherever you end up in this life, he says, I want you to hold on to the Pacific Northwest. Not everything is about money. Not everything is about success.

For six more hours, they remain stranded.

IN OLY, ISADORA and I are at our own impasse.

We've been here for months.

She sits on a moss-covered rock in Marjorie's garden, looking at me from under the rain. Belinda is inside, covered in sweat, her fever broken like an unfinished thought. Without any privacy in the cottage, and with Isadora refusing to get into my pickup truck, we talk out here. She's frantic. Everything is too much. Her shifts at the domestic violence shelter are too much. The up-in-the-airness of our lives is too much. She doesn't know what to do about Billie's schooling. She's in kindergarten again, but for how long?

I can't do this, Izzie says. I can't. I can't.

We'll be back to Austin soon, I say.

We're not raising our daughter in that fucking basement.

Are we gonna raise her in the woods?

Isadora shivers. She's considering moving in with her mother. She and Billie. She could look for jobs while waiting to hear from the U-Dub. The decision is coming any week. In the meantime, the hiring market in Seattle is far more lucrative than down here. And though Marjorie is lovely, Marjorie is not a parent. Belinda is boisterous, unpredictable. She needs structure. She needs her own bedroom.

Living at home again is the single worst thing you could do, I say.

My mom is an imperfect woman, Isadora says. But she knows what it means to raise someone. Motherhood is a collaboration. Don't you understand that, Terrell?

I'm here, ain't I? Don't you see me?

You've been drinking, Izzie says. I can smell it on you.

Shut the hell up.

Do you drink because you need to?

I take off my hat. I put it on my fiancée's head to keep her from soaking, then remove my denim jacket and place it around her shoulders. She does not move. I step into the house to see our girl, who is waiting to take a bath as Marjorie draws it. I kiss her on the forehead, but leave before we can play in the tub. Isadora is standing in the dark.

I'm not staying, I say.

Why would you do this to me? she asks.

She returns my hat and jacket, standing by as I crunch the gravel back to the truck. I take myself to downtown Oly, where I drink at a bar until two. I spend the night in the cab of my pickup, waking up to screaming tweakers. Driving back to Seattle, I almost close my eyes.

· Six ·

Two Bricks

CHIEF JOSEPH GBAGBO has come a long way to hear out our mother's concerns. Profiled in a recent story by the *Seattle Post-Intelligencer*, the guidance counselor's unique background has made him a local legend. He is the bloodline ruler of a village in Ghana, who first arrived in the United States on a full-ride scholarship to Seattle University, after which he attained citizenship by enrolling in the Marine Corps and serving in the Gulf War. Since his honorable discharge, he has worked at Henry L. Yesler High School. Regal in his dashiki and kufi, he is rotund now, well past his days of combat-ready physicality, but no less commanding. Wherever he strides, he creates a wake of students competing for his attention. Students in the Advanced Placement program assail him with requests for letters of recommendation; students in the regular program tease and joke with him; teachers nod in respect. When Chief Gbagbo strides through the hallways, the marks of deprivation seem to fall away. The graffitied walls, the broken furnaces, the lightbulbs that are never replaced. His laughter booms. His capacity to hold several conversations at once is legendary.

Mom has brought Ethan here to try to secure his seat in Yesler's best-in-the-city(-for-a-public-school) A.P. program, the same one I attended in the '90s. I came in with the first wave. We were bussed across Seattle as part of a real estate scheme, the theory being that turning Yesler into a magnet school would raise area property values. Mostly, the scheme seems to be working out for those concerned, but only if you own a house, and only if you can afford the property taxes or plan to sell.

Anyhoo.

Chief Gbagbo remembers me. He remembers how I absorbed everything I could about the Central District's blues and jazz and funk scenes, and how I wrote poetry for the school newspaper. He recalls the reactions I got when I first showed up in a ten-gallon hat, fresh with stories about roping steer and assisting in cattle births.

But unfortunately, Chief Gbagbo says, I fail to see how I can help Ethan.

How is that possible? Mom asks.

Before he responds, three East African girls in black burqas burst into the office, giggling. Chief Gbagbo stands up, pointing to the waiting area.

Get out of here, you old goats! he yells. Masticate your cud elsewhere! Gracious!

The girls laugh and shut the door. The counselor sits back down, shaking his head with paternal amusement. He regains his seriousness.

The district controls high school assignments, Chief Gbagbo says. Not the schools. If you are coming from Queen Anne, you are most likely to be sent to Ballard or Roosevelt. Both are good. Submit your preferences, and prepare for every outcome.

Yes, but, Mom says. We're talking about a seventh grader who scored higher on the verbal SATs than ninety-three percent of college-bound seniors.

Chief Gbagbo grins.

He's a clever boy, eh? Be sure to tell that to the bureaucrats.

The students in the highly capable program at Washington Middle School get into Yesler automatically, Mom says. It doesn't seem fair.

Yes ma'am, you are correct, Chief Gbagbo says. Things aren't fair around here. Some of our ninth graders come into this school at a second-grade reading level. We have gang leaders waiting off-campus to recruit our kids for war. In the mornings, we have to time our buses so that our students aren't mingling with rival sets. We have pimps trying to lure away girls as young as fourteen to work for them. None of it is fair. But we do the best we can. Now, if you don't mind, I would like to hear from our clever boy. What are your thoughts, Ethan? Do you have a strong opinion about any of this? Do you have any questions? Any at all?

My brother shifts in his seat.

Are you a licensed therapist? Ethan asks.

The counselor laughs.

A therapist? No. I wish I were a therapist. We need a whole committee of therapists here at Yesler. I need a doctor to fix my weak knees too, but you don't hear me complaining. Well, maybe I just complained. Nevertheless. Do you have any other concerns at this time? Either of you?

Is all that true? Mom asks. About the gangs and pimps?

Yes, Chief Gbagbo says. But not to fret. Your son will be fine if he enrolls here. Trouble does not seek out students like him. He'll see a lot, but he'll never get involved. Colleges always love somebody adjacent to tragedy, but not in the tragedy. I've seen it a thousand times.

I don't know what to do with that, Mom says.

Neither do I, the counselor says. Now, if we are done, I need to tend to my goats. Can't you hear them outside my door? Bleating?

On cue, the girls boil into the office again, laughing and talking over one another. Mom shakes Chief Gbagbo's hand as he scolds the girls for not waiting their turn, compelling them to issue an apology.

Mom and Ethan depart.

Near the front entrance, an officer with the Seattle Police Department stands guard, a freckled, light-skinned man wearing a duster over his uniform. He is six foot five, genial, assigned after a rash of muggings and robberies near campus. Strict curfew hours are in effect, prohibiting students from loitering after 4:00 p.m. or before 7:00 a.m.

Mom and Ethan pause in front of a mural of Malcolm X and Martin Luther King Jr., their arms linked, their unity powerful. Across from them stands Chief Si'ahl, grave and sepia-toned. Remember the Suquamish and the Duwamish, he says. Next to him, Yuri Kochiyama, her hair under a thick headscarf, speaks into a bullhorn. One hand, tender, stretches towards Malcolm.

Out of nowhere, a middle-aged man with rich dark skin throws open one of the doors. Dressed in a purple and white jacket and a purple and white cap—and missing most of his teeth—he is a Central District rambler named Rick who, with the principal's blessing, is permitted to drift through Yesler during school hours. Beloved by everybody. Rick points at the police officer.

Who built Yesler with two bricks? he yells.

You did, Rick! the cop says.

Rick cackles. Mom feigns a smile. She opens the door for Ethan. Dozens of concrete stairs descend to the parking lot below.

You two have a nice day, the cop says.

AS A REWARD for his patience, Mom takes Ethan out for lunch at Pacific Place. The levels of the underground parking garage are identified with major cities around the Rim. Hong Kong, Sydney, Vancouver, San Francisco. They park on Taipei, ride a gleaming elevator to the lobby, and join the throngs of midday shoppers. Restaurants, clothing boutiques, jewelry stores, and coffee shops spiral under a glass atrium to the cloudy sky. Ascending an escalator to the second floor, they arrive at a high-end dim sum restaurant. Waiting for the waitress to come by with the cart, Mom lets out a long sigh.

How are you feeling about Yesler?

Alright, Ethan says.

Terrell always felt safe there, in case you were worrying.

I wasn't.

Good, good. Because their academic rigor is second to none in the district. I wanted to ask you about something else, too. Your father says you're thinking about going to Sword Fern State. The alternative college.

I guess.

Why's that?

Terrell said students collaborate on the curriculum. He said you get to evaluate your professors, and that they don't do grades.

Interesting, Mom says.

This is all she will say about Sword Fern State until 2009.

Before their conversation continues, the color drains out of Mom's expression. A few feet away, a blond man is smiling at her. With his lean physique, he is either in his late thirties or early forties, wearing a cornflower-blue sweater, jeans, and hiking shoes. A leather satchel hangs from his shoulder. Though Ethan cannot say for sure what is taking place, he can perceive that the man and his gaze are unwanted.

Well, this is splendid. I thought that was your Subaru in the garage. What are you doing downtown, Nora?

My son and I just came back from Yesler High School, Mom says. Jeffrey, this is Ethan. Ethan, this is my friend, Jeffrey Seaholt. He writes op-eds for *The Seattle Times*.

The columnist laughs.

You skipping a grade, Ethan?

Just trying to secure a spot, Mom says.

Jeffrey pulls out a chair, setting his satchel on the back of his seat, sitting down without asking.

You know, he says, I'm doing a column on Yesler this week.

That's quite the coincidence, Jeffrey. What's it about?

As it turns out, some of the students have a certain divisive nickname for the school. Have you heard it yet? Ethan, have you heard this?

When they say nothing, Jeffrey leans over the table, almost whispering.

They call it the Slave Ship, he says.

The Slave Ship? Mom says.

Some parents call it that too. Isn't that outrageous?

What's their reasoning?

Well, certain sources tell me the Advanced Placement classes are held on the top two floors of the school, and the regular program is held on the bottom two. White kids enroll in A.P. courses while Black kids take regular courses. White on the top, Black on the bottom. Hence, the Slave Ship.

That's terrible.

I agree. And, in my opinion, it's well past time that we force the issue.

Force the issue?

The culture issue. Some cultures don't value concepts like math or showing up on time. Or showing up at all. And that's okay. But it's unfair that these kids have to see their peers run ahead of them every day. Consider the envy and resentment that builds up. I propose we do the right thing. No more school within a school. Instead, I propose we have two schools for two kinds of student.

You mean like segregation? Mom says.

Don't act so fragile, Nora. This would be for the benefit of everyone. Everyone would be where they want to be. Maybe some learning could finally get done.

Do you hear how racist this sounds? Mom says. Are you insane?

No, I'm not insane. And I'm not racist either. I don't have a racist bone in my body. Now, if you feel so strongly about it, what's your solution, Nora?

I don't know, Mom says. Have you talked with anybody at Yesler? Sat down and chatted with someone like Chief Gbagbo, or any of the parents you're writing about? Or did you come up with this solution out of your own benevolence?

Jeffrey scoffs. He leans in his chair.

We miss you in our writing class. Your spunk. Word around Hugo House is that you're in Logan Rivers's workshop now.

So?

You always pick the winner, don't you? Man commits armed robbery at eighteen, reinvents himself as some sensitive novelist, lands on the bestseller list, and everybody just looks the other way. Logan Rivers stepped out of the jailhouse and into your heart, huh?

Jeffrey, you need to leave.

She does not raise her voice, and she does not need to. The columnist stands up, takes his satchel, and departs, his clean-cut figure melting into the crowds along the vertical mall's pavilions, taking something from our mother that Ethan is not meant to see.

The dim sum cart arrives with steamed dumplings, rice noodle rolls, and barbecue pork buns. Without emotion, Mom begins picking items. Ethan wants to tell her how Mr. Finnegan is assigning one of Logan Rivers's novels in the spring. He wants to be excited that they know each other.

MOM LEAVES ETHAN in the house to teach a piano lesson in Ballard. He wants to see me in the studio, but I've been on the hard stuff since noon.

He sits in front of the living room television, alone except for Pepper. Homework will come after dinner. He looks at the piano. Our grandmother's, Lilith Jamestone's. The baby grand. Mom won't touch it.

There is so much my brother and I will never know.

I TELL HIM what I can.

She first arrived in Seattle by train, traveling across the Rockies and Cascades. Because she was fifteen, she was assigned a point person to shepherd her journey, a man who told her he could take care of her like a real woman if she wanted him to. She was a ranch girl, who said yes when she needed to, but who disappeared at Union Station at her earliest opportunity. With her rolling suitcase, she crept across the wet asphalt of South King Street, marveling at Chinatown's immense gate, searching for the bus that would take her to the University District.

Seattle was dismal then: the Seattle of the Boeing Bust, the Seattle of the '70s, the unemployed loggers on the waterfront. Drizzle falling like saliva from the roof of a cold mouth. Decayed leaves clogging the storm drains. Decayed men.

At the U-Dub, an admissions officer told her that, between her test scores and piano skills, she qualified for early acceptance. Her homeschooled background would be no impediment, perhaps even an advantage. The admissions officer shook her hand, looking into our mother's adolescent eyes a moment too long.

Twenty minutes later, Mom was on the Ave, walking to the dress shop where she would rent a sparkling red gown and an imitation pearl necklace. She waited at a nearby bus stop, waiting in the U District of Ted Bundy, blocks away from some of his first femicides. She boarded for Lower Queen Anne and arrived at the Seattle Opera House, where she performed for the city's most discerning cultural patrons. With impeccable skill, our mother played every note of Frédéric Chopin's Nocturnes with a concentration that, as one reviewer described, looked like communion.

When she stood up and curtsied, she received a three-minute ovation.

That night, in her hostel near Pike Place, the director who invited her to Seattle came knocking at her door. He did not leave until dawn. Our mother boarded a train for Montana later that day.

Three years later, at the University of Washington, she met Dad.

A year after came me.

Now, everything she once put into that baby grand piano, into that concert, into her scholarship—the genius in her fingertips—has been reduced to after-school lessons in Ballard. Every now and then, a version of her tries to break away. I see it and she sees it. The wild, reckless self, running, always running. In every way, I am her son.

PERHAPS THIS IS why she can see what is impending between me and Isadora. Perhaps this is why she tries to warn me.

Hungover, I sit with her on the porch where Ethan and I have been holding our afternoon conversations. April is settling into the city. Robins sing their gorgeous scales, songs I remember from mornings when my bedroom skylight was cracked open. A seaplane passes by.

Isadora has been calling the house, Mom tells me. Asking where I am, asking for advice. My fiancée is serious about relocating to Seattle. But she does not believe I believe her.

You need to support Belinda, Mom says. Every decision needs to be for her.

I laugh.

Cut the bullshit, Mom says. This is about your little girl.

No, it isn't, I say. You don't get to say that.

I'm your mother.

Are you?

We'll pay for counseling, if that's what you two need.

I get up. Without saying goodbye, I saunter down the stairs. I need to return to the studio, where nothing is going right, where the engineer has been greeting me with increasing exasperation.

Mom looks down.

Every crossing of the Fremont Bridge feels final.

· Seven ·

Bering Strait Blues

THE VESSELS OF the North Pacific Fishing Fleet bask in the sunlight of the late afternoon. Framed by the Ballard Bridge, the towering ships are at rest now, waiting for the summer fishing season in the Gulf of Alaska. Bright-colored buoys hang against the massive hulls, eye-catching from inside the Fisherman's Terminal.

Our table at Chinook's is long tonight: Mom and Dad and Ethan, Belinda and Isadora, Holly and her parents, Mr. and Mrs. Johansson. Baskets of focaccia float from hand to hand as we wait for entrées of salmon pot pie, Dungeness crab fettuccini, rockfish tacos, and pan-fried oysters. The restaurant, with its metal-pipe interior, is loud, the kitchen bustling with shouted orders, sizzling, chopping. Fishermen drink at the bar, telling stories to waitresses or losing themselves to the basketball game on television. In our party, the conversation is cheerful.

For the most part.

Spring break is here for the middle schoolers. Mr. and Mrs. Johansson thank my parents in advance for taking their daughter with them to British Columbia. The vacation is attached to a conference Dad is attending for his new law firm, networking with reps from the mineral extraction and natural gas industries. The same week, the Johanssons will be overseeing the opening of a cocktail bar connected to their oyster house, which was recently profiled in *Seattle Magazine*.

Tonight is also a celebration for Isadora.

With an acceptance letter from the U-Dub's School of Social Work, she will be matriculating in the fall, committing to Seattle for good. While my parents and Ethan are in Vancouver, we will be staying at the house, searching for an apartment. Tomorrow, I'll be down in Oly, helping Izzie and Billie move out of the cottage.

As everyone else talks, I mix liquor into my coffee. I came here straight from recording in Fremont, and I will be going straight back. My guitar case rests in its own chair, a placeholder between me and Mom and Dad. For good reason, nobody engages me in conversation. Only when Holly's parents begin asking Isadora about her master's program do I speak.

New Orleans, I say. N-ew Or-le-ans.

Isadora takes my hand.

What's that, dear?

That would be a good place to call home, I say. Le Vieux Carré. A French townhouse by the Mississippi. Gas lamps by our front door. I could work on Bourbon Street, play the clubs. How would you like to live on a rue in New Orleans?

She makes herself smile.

We're in Seattle, babe, she says. Isn't that a marvelous thing? That we get to raise our daughter in the city where we grew up?

I stand up, swaying.

I got a cab coming. Think I'll take a walk first. Mr. and Mrs. Johansson, it was an honor to meet y'all. Holly…

Instrument in hand, I salute and walk out. They all watch as I stop at the kitchen to say hello to the hardworking line cooks, then disappear out the front entrance. Outside, I pay my respects to the Fisherman's Memorial, to the metal mariner on top of the column hooking an enormous halibut. I continue to the commercial docks, staring up at each vessel.

Inside the restaurant, I picture my daughter looking up from the kids menu where Holly has been teaching her how to sketch sea creatures and mermaids. I picture Belinda seeing her father removed from her family, pining after the fortress ships as though he were about to stow away to Alaska. Nobody could tell her she's wrong.

OVER THE WEEKEND, I drive to Olympia. Izzie and Billie are already there, catching a ride last night from a friend. Traffic is light. I sip coffee from a thermos like a trucker. In the rearview mirror, stubble grows on my jawline like a rash. Suburbia passes outside, then the refineries outside Tacoma, then the sprawling installation of Fort Lewis.

Malls and military, military and malls.

In Thurston County, the estuarine mud of Nisqually is the last open vista before hills swallow up the road again. Taking the exit for Highway 101, I absorb my surroundings as though they are dissolving.

Marjorie is waiting in her driveway. Billie is running around in denim overalls, back and forth and back and forth, brandishing a tree branch like a weapon. I step out.

What's going on? I ask.

You should talk to her, Marjorie says.

She excuses herself and hurries inside. I tell my daughter to come over, and when she ignores me, I strike a rare tone of demand. My girl shuffles over, holding the sharp stick behind her.

Tell me what's wrong, I say. What's got you all worked up?

Belinda looks at the damp soil.

Why are we moving?

I crouch down.

Because, I say. Mommy is going back to college.

Why?

So she can get better jobs.

But I want to stay here.

Look. We can visit Aunt Marjorie anytime we want. Right now, we gotta move along. That's what we do, Billiebat. It'll be good for all of us. We're gonna get you in a new school.

Do we get to live in a house?

For a little bit. Grandma and grandpa's house. Then, we'll see.

I want my own room.

We'll see, sweet girl.

I don't want to move back to Texas, she says.

Well, I say. Good.

I stand up. Marjorie comes out, telling me Isadora wants help folding the laundry. In the meantime, she wants to meditate with Belinda. When she tries to take my daughter by the hand, my daughter takes off running.

Inside, Izzie is sitting on the couch with an overwhelming amount of clothing, handwashed and air-dried. Her hair is a mess. I can tell she has not slept.

She looks at me.

Out back, our daughter hurls her branch like a javelin. She leaps onto a rotting stump, threatening to tear out the pulplike bark. Before Marjorie can get to her, Billie is running through fern fronds, trampling earthworms, screeching, screeching, screeching. She touches the chicken wire that protects Marjorie's vegetables from deer and raccoons, then bolts towards the woodshed. Marjorie ties to compel our daughter to stop, to take some deep breaths and count to ten.

Isadora yawns.

At some point, she says, I suppose we should plan our wedding.

ON SUNDAY, WE bid farewell to Mom and Dad and Ethan and Holly. They wave their goodbyes from the curb below 91 West Etrusca Street. Pepper plays with Billie along the porch. Isadora and I wave back as they depart.

This is the last time they will see us like this.

ONE DAY, MY brother will tell me how they experience it.

The Jetta crosses the border at noon. Traffic across the provincial highway is swift. In Vancouver, they are staying at the Canada Place Hotel, a waterfront tower overlooking Burrard Inlet. A valet in a red jacket takes Dad's car keys and summons a bellhop. The four of them ascend a luxurious elevator to the lobby, where broad windows frame the North Shore Mountains, snow glazing their dark crests. Dad strides to the check-in counter. Mom avails herself of the currency exchange. Holly and Ethan sit by a gigantic fountain map of the Pacific Rim. Clean water swirls around granite nations near and far. Holly's attention drifts to Southeast Asia.

What are you looking at? Ethan asks.

Nothing, Holly says.

Mom, who has completed her business at the currency exchange, beckons them over. Dad and the bellhop are ready. Leading everyone across the glistening lobby, Dad mentions that rooms here are already booked for the 2010 Winter Olympics. Near the guest elevators, three totem poles representing Vancouver's First Nations rise out of the granite floor, cordoned off by a velvet rope: the Squamish, the Tsleil-Waututh, and the Musqueam.

They look like hostages, Holly whispers.

Huddled in elegant coercion.

IN A RESTAURANT in Japantown, the four of them sit behind a sliding shōji door. Ambient music plays on hidden speakers. They dip tempura into soy sauce: gently fried potatoes, zucchinis, shiitake mushrooms, eggplants. When Dad isn't at the conference, Vancouver is their playground. The seawall at Stanley Park, the belugas at the aquarium, the treetop suspension bridge. Holly hopes to visit a few Asian beauty stores, maybe also the market at Granville Island. Her parents want maple candy.

The waiter comes by with udon, yakisoba, and ramen, rich and hearty. Mom and Dad drink too much saké. Mom hiccups. Dad looks at her with a bleary smile. They hold hands under the table. Happy.

After dinner, they walk back to the hotel. Amid the dense tenement buildings of Hastings Street, they pass men and women coalescing around a teal-colored storefront with a white syringe painted on the glass door, the only legal heroin injection site in North America. In Gastown, antique lamps glow in the evening, the narrow streets lined with art galleries and pubs. Like Pioneer Square, but with less strife. Holly asks my parents to take her picture by the steam-powered clock. Dad takes out his disposable camera, telling Ethan to join her. Flushed, my brother stands at her side. Holly's smile falters.

Dad turns around.

A man is speaking with Mom, a man commanding her complete attention. He is built like a football player, huge, with thick black hair, wearing a professorial sweater vest, blue jeans, and sneakers. He places a hand on Mom's shoulder, removing it when he sees Dad.

Mom's smile—giddy like a teenager's—vanishes.

Hunter, this is Logan Rivers, she says. He leads the Monday night writing workshops at Hugo House.

It's a real pleasure, the author says. Your wife is very talented.

She is, Dad says.

I credit the fact that she's also from Montana, Logan Rivers says. There's something in the air where we come from.

Yes, Dad says.

Logan's doing a reading at the Central Library, Mom says. *Three Shots in Great Falls* got shortlisted for the PEN/Faulkner Award. Isn't that incredible?

Yes, Dad says. Congratulations, Mr. Rivers.

With that, Dad walks away. He crosses the street as the light turns from yellow to red, leaving Mom, Holly, and Ethan on the other side. Mom whispers something into Logan Rivers's ear. For a moment, my brother believes he sees her kiss him, perhaps on the cheek, perhaps not at all. The author disappears, plodding down a cross-street of puddles and unanswered questions.

When it's safe to cross, Dad is almost three blocks away.

EMPTY BOTTLES OF red wine sit on the table, desolate and useless. Mom and Dad are in the master bedroom, door shut, their agitated voices leaking into the room like carbon monoxide.

On the television, the CBC babbles away. Ethan and Holly are spread out on the pull-out bed with their sketchpads. While Holly's is a flourish of manga cityscapes, Ethan's is blank. He is staring into Burrard Inlet. A gas station floats in the middle of the water like a piece of surrealist art. For reasons my brother cannot explain, he wants nothing more than to be down under the blue and white sign, snacking on potato chips. A moment of convenience, something routine and uneventful in the unlikeliest gas station in the city.

Hey, Holly says. You want to rent a movie? Your mom said not to worry about the charges.

Okay, Ethan says.

Holly takes the remote control, pulling up the on-demand service, selecting Still in Theatres. She taps my brother's knee, almost frantic. On the screen, a movie poster shows an old anime woman in a blue dress and red shawl looking to the sky, hunched on a steep path of rock and grass.

Howl's Moving Castle, Holly says. It's been out in Japan since November. It's subtitled. Is that okay?

Sure, Ethan says.

She orders the movie. As Studio Ghibli's reassuring Totoro logo lights up the living room, Ethan listens to Dad's rising voice. Mom's voice answers. Distinct words are beyond reach. Just tone.

What's wrong? Holly asks.

They don't care, Ethan says. They know we're out here, and they don't care.

We can turn the volume up, Holly says.

Terrell taught me to stay out of it, Ethan says. I have to be the calm one.

Ethan, Holly says.

What?

I don't know. I'm sorry.

Do your parents fight? my brother asks.

Not really, Holly says. They go silent. Sometimes, I'll ask if they think of me more as a white girl or a Hmong girl. They pretend they haven't heard me.

The opening credits of *Howl's Moving Castle* play against backgrounds of distant lakes, mountains, fields, and war machines. On the pull-out bed, Holly rests on my brother's chest. Their breathing is gentle.

EUROPEAN OR ASIAN—as the film comes to a close, Holly cannot tell what the characters are supposed to be. As the end credits roll, she disappears into her bedroom. In the morning, she is silent. Hiding without hiding.

MOM AND HOLLY and Ethan visit the market on Granville Island. Scents of curry and fish 'n' chips mingling, they stand in line to pay for a box of maple candies. As they approach the register, Mom takes out her phone, frowning. She steps away to take the call. By the time Holly has paid for her candy, Mom's off the phone.

They need to return to the hotel.

Nobody argues.

On the walk to the car, Mom calls Dad. She calls three times. Glass condos towering behind her, Mom yells that they need to get home immediately. She won't say why. She tells Ethan and Holly to wait in the Jetta. As they buckle their seatbelts, my brother can make out only one of the phrases yelled into the phone.

Because he's your son too.

THE INTERNATIONAL BORDER takes three hours to cross. Queues of vehicles waiting, engines idling. Mom and Dad don't talk. The radio is not on. The chic cosmopolitanism of Vancouver has been relegated to something like a false memory. When they advance into Whatcom County, Mom tries the home phone again.

Isadora picks up.

DESTRUCTION IS EVERYWHERE: family portraits knocked off walls, a coffee table tossed over, a corner chipped off the baby grand, six wine bottles bleeding on the floor. A 100-year-old window lies shattered.

Isadora sits on the porch, saying, He wasn't trying to hurt us, saying, It was like he was trying to hurt the house itself. While it was going on, she hid with Billie in the first-floor bathroom, running the shower so our girl couldn't hear. He was living something out.

For now, the two of us—the three of us—are over.

For the foreseeable future, Izzie and Belinda will be staying in Beacon Hill. Sunshine Madera is on her way via taxi, arriving any second. Isadora does not wish to impose any further. Dad passes inside, dumbfounded. Holly and Ethan linger by the rhododendrons. Mom sits with Isadora, trying to talk.

I'm so sorry. Terrell shouldn't have done this.

Nobody should've done this, Isadora says.

Her voice is like a stone.

Upstairs, Billie is beyond control: laughing, racing up and down, her unnatural energy part of the mess. Eventually, she runs onto the porch, trying to fly down the twenty-seven steps. Before anyone can intercede, she skins her knee on the concrete landing, tearing her overalls. Clutching her wound, tears pour down her cheeks. Isadora tries to console her, but Billie pushes her away. She rocks, screaming.

Papa! Papa!

Into this scene, a taxi pulls up. Sunshine Madera comes out in a maroon pantsuit, luxury heels, and designer sunglasses, wearing a dispassionate expression. She does not move as Isadora escorts her crying granddaughter into the vehicle. The driver, a middle-aged man, tends to their baggage while Izzie's mother scolds her: How could you ever think this could work? I raised you to have more self-respect than this. How could you allow yourself to be such a fool for this man?

Isadora yells. She almost breaks down. Her mother, at last, takes her in a hug, close and tight. Without saying goodbye to my family, the Maderas are off.

THIS IS THE last time my parents see Isadora and Belinda for six months.

Holly's parents pick her up.

In school, she and Ethan begin their long drift apart.

IN CONVERSATIONS MY brother is not supposed to hear, our parents talk about me. He hears my name, and nothing else.

Not long after the window is repaired, Tina, the riot grrrl turned A&R rep, comes by, banging on the front door. When Mom answers, Tina demands to know where I am. After failing to deliver the album, she says, I ran off with a not-insignificant amount of Sub Pop's money. Dad steps in, telling Tina that I have been gone for weeks. No contact. Nothing. Tina says the matter will now transfer to debt collectors. Until my debt is paid, nobody in the music industry will be willing to work with me. Not in the Pacific Northwest.

My brother suspects this is what I wanted.

HE DREAMS ABOUT me sometimes. We're in Discovery Park, Ethan and I, hiking the Loop Trail. We begin at a grove of maple trees and redcedars. Suddenly, I pull away, so far away I end up alone in an open meadow, the white geodesic dome looming in the distance. We rendezvous at a new grove of trees, a trailhead overgrown with roots. I disappear again. Ethan goes down the rough wooden stairs along the Magnolia Bluff, a muddy and unstable path. Hard raindrops biting. Madrones groaning and whining. He reaches the brooding shore, the seamud. Over the waves, the rushing air forms into my voice, telling him I'm sorry. I am already back at the meadow, delegating my apologies to the wind.

· Eight ·

To the Plains

JUNE 2005.

Ten years after my first summer in Montana, Ethan and Dad visit a park in downtown Missoula, watching college students surf the rapids of the Clark Fork River. The Jamestone men are in town for an hour, taking a break between Seattle and Tanner Ranch, where they will be staying with Uncle Rod and Aunt Dottie. For reasons my brother could not hear over the late-night drone of his television, Mom stayed home.

Right now, Ethan's attention is on the cartoon emerging from his pen: a parody travel ad, featuring a pile of broken surfers, their bones sticking out, with the tagline: See Missoula—Now With 20% More Mangled Limbs! Dad is concentrating on the strivers in their wetsuits, failing and failing and trying again. His gaze turns to the rising scalp of the Northern Rockies, glacial floodlines still visible in the grass above town.

His phone rings. He picks up and listens, his expression turning from perplexed to uncomfortable. He looks over his shoulder before hanging up.

Uncle Rod's in town, Dad says.

What? Ethan says.

He wants to meet at the Hellgate Diner. We passed it on the way here.

Why is he in Missoula?

I don't know, Dad says. Just put away your sketchbook. Okay?

Dad turns from the river overlook and walks towards the spiral staircase leading to the Higgins Avenue Bridge. Ethan puts his pen and sketchpad in his backpack. Trailing our father, he dodges a pair of adolescent skateboarders as they veer by. Our father's movements are nervous like a teenager's.

UNCLE RODERICK OCCUPIES a window booth by himself, curving the diner around his presence. He is a fourth-generation cattle rancher, and anybody looking at him would know it. He seems legendary the way a grizzly bear is legendary. The genuine article. Upon his arrival, more than one customer must have gossiped about his denim jacket, his boots, his jeans, his silver belt buckle, his cream-colored hat. His thick neck and mustache endow him with permanent seriousness. He sips from a mug of coffee, waiting.

Dad and Ethan slide into the booth. Uncle Rod glances at Ethan. They have not seen each other since he was in kindergarten. Reassessed now, Ethan does not know if he comes across more as a boy or a man. To prevent embarrassment, he keeps quiet.

What brings you to Missoula? Dad says.

Uncle Rod grunts.

Ethan, why don't you step out?

No, Dad says. We were out the door at the crack of dawn. We've been talking about this trip for months. You can tell him what's going on too.

Uncle Rod looks at the roughneck bar and crystal emporium across the street.

Dottie and I talked it over, he says. We don't think you should visit.

Dad turns red.

Where is this coming from? he asks.

Never sat right with us, how you and my sister treated Terrell, Uncle Rod says. We don't want you to get the notion that we'll take Ethan off your hands too.

That's not what this is, Dad says. We just want him to see the ranch. He's never been.

Uncle Roderick shakes his head.

Y'know, he stopped by, he says. Terrell did. Before he went to Texas. Told me about the deal he had to strike to keep you two from involving Ethan in your nonsense. Your tantrums. My sister is a lot, I know, but it ain't just her. Sending your kid away doesn't get at the root.

Terrell visited you? Dad says.

Couple months back.

Do you know what he did? To his fiancée and daughter?

We talked about that, Uncle Rod says. That conversation is between us. My concern right now is you. Me and Dottie, we can't be a part of this anymore. We decided the decent thing was for me to meet you. Thought you deserved to hear this in person. Sorry we didn't do you the courtesy sooner.

My uncle takes out his wallet, paying for his coffee with a couple dollar bills before maneuvering out of the tight seat. He looks down at my father, inviting him to speak in his defense.

Those were hard years back then, Dad says. When Terrell was a teen. You don't know how those law firms can be. It's a constant scramble to prove yourself. The senior partners dangle all these rewards. Everyone's fighting over territory. There were no guarantees for my career. And your sister, my wife, she just— she just couldn't—neither of us could—

Uncle Rod puts a hand on Dad's shoulder.

You never took stock. You should've, and you didn't.

After several seconds, Uncle Rod walks out. Ethan looks around, anywhere but the booth. At the counter, college students flirt and chat. A couple speculate about the imposing man. Nobody sees the mess he has left behind. A waitress drops off a pair of menus.

Dad scans the hot sandwich section.

You ever try buffalo beef before, Ethan? he asks. They have a bison burger. I'm curious how it differs from regular beef.

Ethan and Dad sit on the same side of the booth as though Uncle Roderick will return.

THROUGH THEIR SHARED wall in the hotel, Ethan can hear Dad yelling. Sometimes, he's sobbing, voice thick with remorse. From his king-sized bed, Ethan watches a loud, uncensored broadcast of *Scarface*, three hours of cocaine melodrama playing out in Miami. The movie ends, and he watches late-night informercials. With his curtains closed and his sketchbook shut, he surrenders.

EARLY IN THE morning, Dad knocks on Ethan's door. Today, he is dressed like an elite professional, in a charcoal-gray blazer, slacks, polished black shoes, and a leather-banded wristwatch. His new appearance claims distance from his surroundings. To visit Big Sky Country is to indulge it, to be amused by it.

After breakfast at the hotel buffet, they return to their rooms to pack, check out, and depart from the underground garage. Driving eastbound out of Missoula, my father does not tell Ethan their destination, or how far they will travel before turning back for Western Washington. They could be gone for days, passing through every square mile of the open range if they want to. Every square mile, except for Tanner Ranch.

I-90 CURVES BENEATH the mountains, shafts of light pouring from behind steep peaks. Campgrounds sit in shadowed isolation. In the breaks between summits, the horizon is golden and great. Protected by the windshield and comforted by the heater, Ethan experiences the scenery as cinema. For the first few hours on the road, he and my father hardly speak, remarking only upon Our Lady of the Rockies, the giant archangel casting her beneficence over the mining town of Butte.

Crossing the continental divide, the mountains cede to the Great Plains.

My father is ready to talk.

Things were never easy in your mother's family. Your grandfather, Silas Tanner, could be a real son-of-a-bitch. In some ways, he was like the Hutterites, the traditional communities out here. They live in colonies. Anyway, your grandfather…his values…well, he never saw the point of your mother having ambitions, for example. And Uncle Roderick, he was always predestined to take over the ranch. He carries his own hurt. That's why he always showed Terrell so much kindness.

Ethan bundles his hoodie into a pillow.

Is Terrell coming back? he asks.

Yes, Dad says.

When?

Couldn't say.

What's going to happen to Billie and Isadora?

We'll take care of them.

Why did Terrell leave?

Dad turns on the radio. Static crackles over the airwaves. He turns the dial over and over. Hundreds of miles go by. Towns come and disappear.

THEY DRIVE ACROSS the prairied bosom of the Apsáalooke Nation. Trailers and teepees dot the outskirts of Crow Agency. Dad exits for a truck stop, where outdoor stalls sell frybread and crafts. He parks near the entrance, saying something about a souvenir for Mom.

Inside, Ethan looks at a community bulletin board listing events around the reservation: bingo night for groceries, Shakespeare in the Park, rodeos and powwows, a public meeting of the Tribal Leadership Council. In the center, a black-and-white photograph shows a great elder standing at a podium, adorned in a feathered headdress. Beneath the statesman's image, the flyer advertises:

LITTLE BIGHORN COLLEGE PRESENTS: DR. JOE MEDICINE CROW SPEAKS! WORLD WAR TWO VETERAN & LAST LIVING PLAINS INDIAN WAR CHIEF.

Posted on a second board is a series of mugshots, angry young men wanted for a litany of violent felonies. Beneath the mugshots are pictures of missing women, some teenagers, some missing for months.

Dad opens the door to the gift shop: coffee mugs and figurines, dreamcatchers and horseshoes, bleached buckskins and t-shirts. Plastic ponies for girls, plastic tomahawks for boys. Posters capture the Battle of Greasy Grass, Sitting Bull and Crazy Horse staring down the Lieutenant Colonel of the Seventh Cavalry.

While Ethan drifts through the store, Dad approaches the wares by the counter. Behind the cash register sit two women in prairie-yellow dresses, a mother and a daughter. Dad smiles, picking up a turquoise necklace from a tray.

You two visiting the battlefield? the mother asks, gripping her cane.

No ma'am, Dad says.

On your way to Mount Rushmore?

Too crowded, Dad says.

You could visit the Devil's Tower. You heard of the Devil's Tower?

Is it in Wyoming?

We call it the Bear Lodge, the mother says. The Great Spirit lifted the rock out of the earth to protect a woman as she was chased by a grizzly.

Unprompted, she tells the story, which her daughter takes as a signal to pour out the day's receipts and count revenue. When the older woman finishes, she invites Dad to tell her something about where he and Ethan come from. After some thought, Dad reproduces the myth of Seattle: a metropolis summoned out of a remote isthmus by entrepreneurs and philanthropists, where innovation is harnessed for the greater good. Innovation, the creator of the city's wealth.

Seattle used to be a man, the mother says.

Dad nods.

Ethan sets down a blanket. Blue and yellow trapezoids with a black background, laced with spiritual geometry, machine-washable. Forty dollars. As Dad pulls out his credit card, my brother notices the tag: Made in Malaysia.

WYOMING OPENS INTO high valleys of grass and creeks. In the distance, the Bighorn Mountains tear at the underside of a purple thunderhead, a land-locked mesocyclone, a rotating horror. Dad pulls them onto the shoulder of the interstate, keeping his eyes on the supercell as though it has exposed something in him. Something weak. Before the storm's fury can roar out, Hunter Jamestone turns the car around. He and Ethan ride the road until the prairies and Rockies collapse into the streets of Queen Anne, where the fright in my father's eyes can retreat behind Victorian doors.

2012

· Olympia ·

· Nine ·

Canal Street Dreams

SHE PLACES THE dry seaweed onto her tongue, laughing as the square sheet dissolves. She takes a new square and snaps her jaws shut, crunching it like a potato chip. Her skin is pale and pink, her hair a ponytailed flare of orange. Her eyes are gray, overflowing with self-amusement. She is dressed in a soft and stylish chocolate-colored coat, denim blue jeans, and black-and-white sneakers. Handcrafted earrings glitter from her ears, seashells swirling in imitation gold.

Across the laminated table sits my brother, insomnia ringing his eyes. He wears hiking shoes, jeans with frayed cuffs, and a black hoodie. His hair is still rust-colored, uncombed but fashionable. He is twenty years old, a sophomore at The Sword Fern State College, set to graduate in June 2014. His girlfriend,

Bailey Voclaine, is twenty-one. She will be graduating in ten weeks. Winter quarter, her last at Sword Fern State, begins tomorrow.

Tonight, they are riding the *Wenatchee* from Bainbridge Island to Seattle.

The ferry is almost empty, the upstairs cafeteria closed. A few stragglers hang out between the empty rows. Though the ride is smooth, the rumble of the engines and outer darkness contribute to a feeling of hurtling. Ethan jiggles his right leg, his hands plunged into his kangaroo pocket. Sometimes, his hands reappear over the table, just long enough to trigger concern.

Bailey puts down her seaweed.

Hey.

Ethan looks up.

You scratched your palm, Bailey says. What's going on, Jamestone? Are you nervous?

Why would I be nervous?

Gee. I don't know. Because you're visiting a maximum-security prison tomorrow? Because you're visiting a maximum-security prison every week for the next two quarters?

Dale Raven told me not to worry. So I'm not.

Fine. What else is on your mind? My parents found you hilarious, by the way, in case you were wondering.

Hilarious?

Highly. My dad will never get over the fact that he's been working with your dad in the same law firm this whole time.

Oh. Right. I can't believe he commutes from Bainbridge.

He's too comfortable to leave. I was lucky to be raised there.

You were.

Okay. It's not prison, and it's not my parents. But you're still a wreck. I want to clear this up before we get to Olympia. Is it…don't tell me.

What?

Is it because I mentioned polyamory again?

I don't want to talk about it.

Most guys would be thrilled to have a girlfriend who wants to fuck other bitches. But you say you have boundaries, so I say I'll respect them. You don't need to be so insecure.

Thanks.

My goodness, Jamestone. We'll be living together by spring break. I promise I won't bring any saucy ladies into our new home. Agreed?

Ethan looks away from her. Bailey tells him to give her his hands. She locks their fingers.

Talk to me, you emo doofus. What is it?

It's my dad, Ethan says. He's putting in fourteen-hour days, six days a week, all for Lockhart-Brisbane. Defending them from a lawsuit by the victims of drone strikes. Mom says his drinking is way up.

Bailey scoots out of her seat, thin-strapped purse around her shoulder, and slides next to my brother, wrapping him in warmth. She points at their reflection glistening over the black waves, telling him to be grateful for what he has.

Outside, the darkness begins to shift: hills of lanterns, then hills of streetlights, the metropolitan area arriving like a starlit iceberg.

Let's go outside, Bailey says. See your city.

DOWNTOWN SEATTLE SOARS above Elliott Bay, towering over the double-decked viaduct, the docks and piers. A helicopter motors over the ferry, local news capturing the city at made-for-television angles. The skyline seems to run the length of the Cascades, all the way to California.

On the outdoor deck, Bailey grips the freezing metal rail. My brother hugs her from behind. As the city scales up, she looks at him.

I love you, Ethan says.

They kiss.

I like you too, Bailey says.

She leads my brother back inside, down a white metal stairwell that could have belong to an ocean liner from a century ago, to the vaulted vehicle deck where the dark blue Volkswagen Jetta awaits. He passes her his keys, which she takes with an eyeroll. She sits behind the wheel, watching my brother buckle himself into the passenger seat.

We need to build up your confidence, Bailey says.

Ethan yawns.

I only got three hours of sleep last night.

Confidence is sexy, Ethan. I want you to be confident. I want you to drive your own car. I'll do it tonight, but not next time. Seattle to Oly is not that far.

Hold that thought. Dale Raven just texted me. He says Justin's in one of his weird moods.

When isn't he?

They're at the Reef. Dale Raven's asking if we can come by. He thinks Justin might do something stupid.

You two can play babysitter if you want, but I'm dropping myself off at campus.

I won't be long.

I've got an early day in the woodshop. And if Justin is in the type of mood I think he's in, you'll be dealing with him for a while.

I feel like I should try.

Try all you want, but that boy needs help. Like, real therapeutic intervention. We only dated for three weeks, but he cried every time we kissed. He's manic-depressive or something. I keep my distance for a reason.

We've been friends since the beginning of freshman year, Ethan says. All those months in D Dorm should count for something.

You and your big heart, Bailey says.

The *Wenatchee* docks at the terminal. Trucks and passenger vehicles begin rolling into the city. As Ethan texts Dale Raven, Bailey blows a kiss through the window.

JUSTIN BRAUN SITS with a steaming plate of chicken and waffles and a mug of coffee, which he drinks despite the late hour. Tonight he is styled in his signature leather jacket, an expensive green turtleneck, designer jeans, and shoes handcrafted from fine Italian leather. His hair is black and gelled. He is a strange sight to behold in Olympia, stranger still with his companion, Dale Raven Buford. Dale Raven is tall and lanky, dressed in a plaid gray flannel long-sleeve, denim jeans, mudboots, and circular glasses. Born and raised in Grays Harbor, and looking every bit like it. He keeps his hair, as black as Justin's, in two thick braids. His plate is empty.

This quarter, Justin may or may not still be enrolled in his gender studies program. He will neither confirm nor deny it. Many details of his current existence are unclear, except the major ones: his twenty-first birthday was about two weeks ago, on Christmas Eve. He now enjoys unfettered access to his trust fund. And the first major purchase from his trust fund was the black, brand-new Dodge Challenger parked out front, which my brother passes on his way into Reef.

Ethan makes his way to a booth near the secretive door to the dive bar. As Justin sees him, he shouts out.

Ayo, E.J.! Where's my girl, Bailey? She around?

Ethan sits with Dale Raven, faking a smile.

She wanted to get a good night's rest. Trying to set a good example for the other girls, you know, her being an R.A. and all.

Bailey is one bad bitch. That's all I know. You sure are lucky, E.J. Unlike some people at this table. Take you, for example. You're the unluckiest guy I know, Dale Raven.

How's that? Dale Raven says.

Come on. Look at you. Who names their kid after a crow?

I'm Nisqually.

You mom looked white to me.

She is white. But me and my sister's dad is Nisqually. We've been over this.

Don't be so passive-aggressive.

How is that passive-aggressive?

Everybody on the West Coast is so full of themselves. Let me tell you. The other night, I saw this big group of people on the corner waiting for the light to turn green. There was no traffic, but they were just waiting. Some sucker shit if you ask me. Everybody out here needs to take what they want and keep moving.

I'm sorry, you're pissed off because you saw a group of people who didn't want to risk getting hit by a car? Do I have that correct?

Justin laughs.

Speaking of getting hit by a car, I'm about to take my new ride for a spin. You boys up?

We can't, Dale Raven says. We got orientation tomorrow.

Justin grins.

Yeah, tomorrow you do. But what do you got going on tonight? Tonight, you got nothing but swag. Swag, and YOLO.

Excuse me?

Look, we're not gonna live forever. The Mayans say this is the year the world ends. I believe them. Steve Jobs is already dead. We could get a Mormon in the White House. I say we go out with a bang. I'm gonna take a piss, then we're hitting the highway. Okay boys?

Justin downs his coffee. Sticking a hundred-dollar bill under his untouched plate, he cuts through the kitchen for the restroom. A tattooed waitress swings past the table, timing it for Justin's absence.

In the minute before Justin comes back, Dale Raven and Ethan debate what to do. They agree it would be cruel to leave Justin to the mercy of his own nature. He meets them at the cash register, laughing like a kid at a birthday party.

As the boys leave, a woman yells out, Hallelujah!

PESO COMES ONTO the stereo for the twelfth time in a row, and for the twelfth time in a row, Justin raps along to every word. He maneuvers his Dodge Challenger like a raft, veering from one rain-soaked side of the interstate to the other, passing eighteen-wheelers as though jumping across eddies. When he isn't mimicking A$AP Rocky's uptown slick talk, he laughs at the rain storming across the windshield, and laughs as car after car clears out in front of him. Entering Lewis County, the rural countryside gives way to the Chehalis-Centralia micropolitan area. Near the highway, Moss Hill School—surrounded by barbed wire fences, operated by the Juvenile Rehabilitation Administration—is set to welcome Ethan and Dale Raven in sixteen hours.

Ethan holds his phone out, prepared to dial the state patrol. He waits for Dale Raven's signal, who will only call the police as a last resort. Seated in the back, they grip the ceiling handles, trying not to slide into each other across the red leather seats.

Up front, their driver is babbling.

Lord Pretty Flacko is the King of New York. He's too jiggy, too trill. He's got that Comme des Fuckdown swag. But 50 Cent? Is the greatest rapper of all time. *Get Rich or Die Tryin*? Classic. Should've got Five Mics. Nothing but the truth in that title. That's the code, boys. I've been into Fifty since before Supreme put a hit out on him. Look it up. You kids don't know about that. My dad used to take me to Canal Street every week. I snapped up every mixtape I could. Those bootleggers could negotiate, greedy motherfuckers. I can't believe he's dead.

Who's dead? Dale Raven asks.

My dad, Justin says. Didn't I tell you about that?

No, you did not, Dale Raven says. I'm so sorry, Justin. When did he pass?

9/11.

What?

9/11. I was ten years old. What? You don't believe me?

Justin glances in the rearview mirror.

He used to work in the North Tower, alright? The one with the antenna. He was with Cantor Fitzgerald. His office was on the hundred and fourth floor, same as WNBC. I always got a kick out of that. Whenever I visited, I felt famous, like we were a famous family. Everybody on that floor died. See, the thing with the North Tower was, the airplane destroyed all the elevator shafts and stairwells. With the South Tower, some people above the impact zone could get to the lobby. You couldn't do that in the North Tower. People went up to the roof, hoping to get rescued by helicopter. They died anyway. I don't know if my dad tried to escape up there. I'll never find out, probably. I always thought it was the stupidest shit how they made everyone from 9/11 into a hero. Ritchie Braun was no hero.

Why do you say that? Dale Raven asks.

Let's see. He was a coke addict. He felt up all my nannies and tutors. To top it off, the Feds were closing in on him for fraud. The SEC kept harassing my mother for years after he died. Swear to God, if Osama bin Laden hadn't destroyed Manhattan, my father would be in the penitentiary with Bernie Madoff at this very moment. But, shit. His money kept my mother living well. His money paid for this car. Maybe he was a hero.

Is all that true? Ethan asks.

Justin slaps the steering wheel.

This thing's got power, he says. I bet we could drive across the entire West Coast by morning. You boys ever been to L.A.? Or San Francisco? How much you wanna bet we could drive to California and back before sunrise?

That sounds like fun, Dale Raven says. But we need to be back at our apartment by midnight. Do you think we can do that?

Why would anyone want to go back to Olympia? Justin says. Tell you what. Let's compromise. Let's go to Oregon.

Justin. No.

But the debate is over.

The road carries them into Cowlitz County, bending around the Columbia River. Waterfalls burst forth from volcanic buttes, threatening rockslides. In less than an hour, they will be in Portland.

HE PARKS THE Challenger in the garage at Naito and Davis. The rainstorm is relentless, blurring the night, blurring everything. Descending to the sidewalk, Justin bursts into the Rose City. He waves his arms, howling, his keys falling out of his pockets. As Ethan saves the keys from getting swept into a storm drain, Justin runs down Naito Parkway, parallel to the Willamette River, Dale Raven in pursuit. A chaotic minute later, they all catch up at a streetcar stop beneath a bridge. Justin is doubled over, hands on his knees as though he were in transformation. He taunts Dale Raven, claiming that the only reason he was running was to get out of the rain.

As the three boys shelter, a huge homeless man emerges from the shadows. A second, smaller man is at his side. In the darkness, they approach a third homeless man, sprawled out where the filthy sidewalk meets the brick façades of Old Town.

The smaller man shouts: Lay him out, son!

Then—

BOOM.

Something explodes, the sound reverberating everywhere. The man on the sidewalk scrambles away. The giant reveals an exploded paper bag. The smaller man toddles off in contempt.

Gunshots don't scare me no more. I heard too many of 'em. Anyone out in these streets needs to get used to it.

As the practical joke becomes clear, Justin cries Bravo! He takes out his wallet, distributing a ten-dollar bill to the giant man and a five-dollar bill to the smaller man, ignoring them when they ask for more. He puts his arms around Ethan and Dale Raven, leading them out from under the bridge, telling them he's heard Portland has the most strip clubs per capita of any major city in the United States. He's also heard that, unlike in Washington, you don't need to be twenty-one to hang out in a bar. Both Ethan and Dale Raven are only twenty. Justin wants a couple of drinks before the night is over, maybe in the Pearl District. He says something about partying like Somali pirates. Ethan and Dale Raven are too stunned to argue.

HE SEES ME.

He sees me, and he doesn't.

He's looking through the glass of the Portland Outdoor Store, a three-story emporium of saddles and boots and rancher apparel. Somebody is at the microphone, playing an acoustic guitar on a makeshift stage, telling jokes. Somebody skinny, somebody with a prairie-yellow hat, a denim shirt, long dark hair. Outside, parked under the store's peeling wooden sign, is the brown pickup truck with Montana plates, dust embedded on the windshield.

Unmistakable.

But how many brown pickup trucks are there in the city of Portland? How many from Montana? He homes in on the license plate, but hesitates before taking a picture. Truth be told, he doesn't know what's worse: confirming I'm in the Pacific Northwest or confirming that he wants me to be.

While Ethan stands and wonders, Dale Raven and Justin are in a nearby bar. Their hijinks find him quickly. Out of nowhere, Justin is running towards the Willamette River again, missing his leather jacket. Dale Raven is behind him, punching my brother in the arm as he runs by, asking for help. Though Ethan doesn't know it, tomorrow he'll find out Justin tried to steal a velvet painting of a mustang. In the frenzy to escape, he dropped the kitsch art and his jacket, which he will never see again. He is banned from that bar for life.

Ethan finds them at the river, arguing on the sandy embankment, Dale Raven holding an orange medicine bottle above Justin's desperate face. He unscrews the lid and scatters the pills into the water. Justin begins to undress to retrieve the pills. Before he dives in, Dale Raven seizes him under the arms, telling Ethan that Justin is high on molly, that he will drown if they don't stop him.

A police cruiser rolls up, lights flashing.

NOW ETHAN IS the one driving the Challenger, taking everybody home. The digital clock reads 3:30 a.m. The rain has calmed to a drizzle. South of Tumwater, my brother realizes this is the most he's ever driven in one shot.

Justin is in the backseat, head resting in Dale Raven's lap, released of his spell. Peaceful, unaware. He has been asleep since they crossed the Columbia. The cop who responded to the boys gave them a ride back to Naito and Davis. He knew what it was like to have a rowdy night on the town. But the fun was over.

Dale Raven yawns.

I'm done enabling him, he says. He's just getting worse. We did what we could.

The first exits appear for Oly.

I think I saw my brother, Ethan says.

Dale Raven frowns.

In Portland?

Yeah.

I didn't know you have a brother.

I do, Ethan says.

Downtown is coming up, where Justin lives off Sylvester Park. Ethan activates the turn signal, preparing to return to where this impossible night started.

Ten

Two Bricks, Part II

LUIS ROSALES IS cheering as his fellow coordinator for Unlocked Youth, Diana Johnston, struts down an imaginary runway in the seminar room. Dressed in an oversized dark green sweatshirt and jeans, Diana has rendered the curves of her body invisible. Her brown hair is tied in a frizzy bun. Her olive skin is absent of makeup. Her piercings are removed. Her tennis shoes are white and unremarkable.

Lady mentors need to show up in outfits like this, Diana says. Moss Hill is mostly a woman-free environment. It's also an environment filled with raging hormones. We encourage you to take every precaution.

Some students laugh. Some don't.

From his place by the heater, Luis speaks next. With his buzzed hair and goatee, he seems endowed with maturity beyond his years. He's dressed in a gray sweatshirt, gray sweatpants, and gray sneakers. Neutral, neutral, and neutral. We men also need to be mindful of our choices, he says. Hoodies are not allowed. Neither are undershirts, t-shirts, or shorts. All mentors need to be careful with colors. No reds, no blues, and no sports logos.

Obey the rules. You'll be fine.

As the mentors enter Moss Hill, they will need to leave their keys, wallets, and phones in the van. They should only bring in their IDs and prescreened materials. As an example, Dale Raven holds up the photo essay he is bringing for his mentee, Trevonte, which the coordinators approved before winter break.

Diana and Luis are three-year veterans of the program, entrusted by Sword Fern State to conduct the weekly visits and most of the workshops. One of the college's bolder alternative pedagogies, Unlocked Youth supplements in-person prison mentoring with studies in sociology, behavioral health, psychology, criminal justice, and civil rights. The class has fourteen students, including Luis and Diana. Eight men and six women, twentysomethings to fortysomethings.

Something else you may notice about these boys, Luis says. Their hygiene is not always great. I won't lie. Your mentees might smell a little funky. But we advise against giving grooming tips. We don't know how tough it is to stay clean in prison. Some weeks, they don't get to use the showers. When it comes to how the mentees handle their day to day, we aren't qualified to speak.

Correct, Diana says. Another thing to keep in mind is that a lot of these boys are institutionalized. The time you spend in the visitor center will feel like a big deal to you, and it is, but they're used to people dipping in and out. Our roles are super limited.

Keep in mind that, while these young men ain't angels, Luis says, they are hungry for the opportunities we provide.

Unlocked Youth attracts the best of the best, Diana says. These are the guys trying to rise above it all. But all of them are tough. That's another thing. We've seen so many mentors, especially male mentors, get insecure and try to act hard. Sorry guys, it's true. Just be who you are.

Talk how you talk, too, Luis says. We hear a lot of mentors slip into accents they don't have and use phrases they wouldn't use while speaking to anyone else. Slang-jacking is discouraged at all times.

The last, most important thing to remember about your mentees, Diana says, is that society defines their lives by the worst thing they've ever done. In a lot of cases, that one worst thing is all that separates us.

She asks if there are any questions. Nobody responds.

Diana hands out a stack of papers outlining the schedule. For the first hour of the visit, mentors and mentees will decide their academic goals. For the second hour, everyone will come together as a group to establish the rules for their learning community: rules of respect, rules of safety. In fifteen minutes, the van will arrive to take the Ferners to Chehalis. For now, new mentors are encouraged to break the ice with returning mentors.

As the room begins chatting, Diana taps Ethan's shoulder. She and Luis need a word in private.

YOU LOOK TIRED, Luis says. Not to pry, but you went hard last night, huh?

The two coordinators sit behind the desk in Unlocked Youth's office, looking at my brother. The office is windowless. Concrete walls and white paint. Fluorescent lights hum in the ceiling. Every small word sounds loud.

Ethan yawns.

I'm okay, he says.

Trouble sleeping? Diana asks.

My brother nods.

Hopefully, our debriefings will help with that. Our first workshop is about how the parasympathetic nervous system interacts with trauma. You'll get a lot of support from us.

I appreciate it, Ethan says.

Luis and Diana exchange a glance. Neither of them has said yet why they need to speak with him.

Okay, so, Diana says. There's been a changeup. It's out of our control.

This happens a lot in prison, Luis says. Just wait til the first lockdown. We may be put in the cold for weeks.

Luckily, that's not the case today, Diana says.

True, Luis says.

The mentee we had for you dropped out at the last minute, Diana says. He got a new job in the kitchen. He's very excited about it. Your spot is still secure. One of our mentors, Herbert, also dropped out due to a family emergency. Everything is balanced. But the mentee who was working with Herbert, the one we have available, is not someone we would assign a newbie.

He's a big boy, Luis says.

His name is Loto, Diana says. This is his fourth year in Unlocked Youth. He's about to age out of Moss Hill. He's very…how do I put this?

He's very open about his affiliations, Luis says. The other boys look up to Loto, take their cues from him. He sets the tone, so to speak. If you don't feel up for it, we could pair you with Dale Raven and Trevonte. I'd be happy to work with Loto one on one. He knows me. We get along.

How do you want to play it, Ethan? Diana says.

They wait.

I'd like to try with Loto, Ethan says.

Diana claps her hands in excitement.

We'll introduce you today, she says. He'll try to get you to call him by one of his nicknames. Nicknames aren't necessarily off-limits, but we try to keep things professional. It's good for boundaries. And boundaries are good for everyone.

Since you're the same age, Luis says, you'll be able to meet him as a peer. With Herbert, there was some tension because he used to teach high school up in Tacoma. He was an authority figure. My advice is just to take Loto as he is. Try to work on some objectives, but if Loto just wants to talk, let him talk. He's a smart guy. Very thoughtful. Think of it as a chance to strengthen those active listening skills.

Still think you're up for it? Diana asks.

Ethan nods.

Luis imparts one last bit of advice.

Loto's gonna tell you he's Mexican. He's not. He's Samoan. When he comes at you with the fake Spanish, call me over to translate. That way, he'll know you know the deal. It won't stop the pranks, but it'll show him we got your back.

My brother thanks them. He tries not to yawn. The meeting is over.

The clock strikes two.

Five minutes later, Luis and Diana shepherd the twelve mentors into one of The Sword Fern State College's official white vans. They board, one by one, in the January drizzle. After everybody figures out their seatbelts, they settle in for the forty-minute drive to Chehalis.

MIST FILLS THE yard, shrouding the brick housing units. Each building reflects a different type of incarcerating offense: drug possession and drug distribution, theft and fraud, violent crimes, sex offenses. Murder. The units are named for subspecies of salmon. The Chinook Unit, the Coho Unit, the Sockeye Unit, the Steelhead Unit, the Chum Unit.

Everything but Cutthroat.

The Secure Housing Unit almost has no name, a place unspoken of unless there is an incident, a chamber in the cracks between work facilities. Work is most of what Moss Hill is about. The prison is a local jobs engine, a haven of union pay in a county of fast food joints, gas stations, and strip malls. Moss Hill School enjoys the most acreage of any institution in Chehalis, extending up to I-5, where signs warn that Hitchhikers May Be Escaping Inmates.

In the central yard, Canadian geese come and go. Unbounded. Everyone else's movements, mentors included, are under tight regulation.

But not everything will be contained.

Rumors hang in the air. Rumors, and some truths. Throughout the quarter, Diana will tell the mentors never to type the names of their mentees into a search engine. Some of their crimes have made headlines. You don't want to deprive yourself of the opportunity to build an independent relationship.

Inevitably, stories come through anyway.

There is the former high school basketball star who robbed a medical marijuana dispensary in Everett, pistol-whipping the clerk; the wannabe comedian recruited to burglarize a pawn shop in Fife, who took a security guard hostage and got into a shootout with the police; the chess player, ranked at the eighty-eighth percentile in the world, who slept in an abandoned butcher shop in Oakville, who got too close to a homicide one night and was convicted of accessory; and the most prolific car thief in the Tri-Cities, who stole hundreds of vehicles before his sixteenth birthday, whose case almost went federal when prosecutors tied his thefts to chop shops across the river in Oregon.

Some of the boys will try to psyche mentors out by overstating their crimes.

Early on, one mentee will confess that he is a government-registered sociopath, his name kept on a list the President of the United States reviews during his morning briefings. Teens locked up on marijuana charges will bullshit about being killers and OGs. Still, mentors shouldn't make any assumptions about who they're talking to.

Bloods, Crips, Norteños, Sureños, Vice Lords, Gangster's Disciples, MS-13, Calle 18.

Unlocked Youth welcomes them all.

For the most part, the learning environment will be constructive, on-task. Mundane. Prison, new mentors learn, is mostly mundane. Residents on the highest privilege level can look forward to a television in their cell and pizza delivery twice a week. D&D is a popular past time, though corrections officers tear up the maps during searches, sometimes labelling them contraband. Anything can be contraband to a C.O.

Don't ever pass your mentee something we don't know about.

Last year, a student anarchist tried to convince his mentee to incite a violent uprising inside Moss Hill. In exchange for distributing pamphlets advocating revolution, the anarchist promised to secure the recording equipment his mentee needed to jumpstart a rap career. The mentee played the anarchist, saying he was down but throwing out the pamphlets the moment he got them. When Diana and Luis uncovered the scheme, they ejected the anarchist within the afternoon. If the mentee had done what the anarchist wanted, he would have been placed in solitary confinement, perhaps for months, and hit with a new wave of charges.

Punishment is always heavier in there than out here, Diana and Luis say. Never forget that you get to go home.

THE COORDINATORS STAND by the yard entrance to the visitor center, preparing to greet the incarcerated youths one at a time. Behind them sits a plain-clothes guard named Conner, dressed in running shoes, cargo shorts, and a light brown t-shirt, a badge pinned to his collar. The mentors are seated in white plastic chairs along rows of gray plastic tables. Cheap furnishings made out of materials least likely to be weaponized. There are no barriers between mentees and mentors. In case of crisis, posters on the backwall provide lists of coping skills.

Out in the mist, officers take mentees from their units and escort them across the grounds. Soon the visitor center will be alive with learning: small business management, beat production, how to apply to college, reading comprehension, Islamic studies.

Before the mentees are allowed in, they are strip-searched.

TREVONTE FISTBUMPS DALE Raven with a big smile, an energetic nineteen-year-old with short braids and angular cheekbones, ready, as always, to get to work. Wearing an orange jumpsuit from his job picking litter off the highway, he stands out from his peers, who are all in Moss Hill's green and white uniforms, which bear an unnerving resemblance to Sword Fern State's official apparel. The orange jumpsuit is required for every outing from the prison grounds, including doctor's appointments, which, when combined with their shackles, seems to convince civilians they're all big bad serial killers. Trevonte keeps his on for amusement as much as individuality.

Upon his release, Trevonte dreams of working as a photojournalist, capturing underground musicians and scenes in their ascendancy. For now, he's soaking up everything Dale Raven can pass about the trade. Today, they will look at photographs of Occupy Wall Street, deconstructing the stories the images tell, and how the media uses mass movements to influence opinion.

My brother waits for Loto.

After fifteen minutes, Diana comes over. Per administrators deeper in the prison, Loto will not be in attendance today. She can't say why. She sends Ethan to Dale Raven and Trevonte. Though they welcome him with grace, Trevonte stares with strange intensity.

Hey, my bad for asking you this, Trevonte says, but who are you supposed to be working with today?

Loto, my brother says.

Oh wow. Good luck with that. What did you say your name was, my guy?

Ethan.

Right. Okay, Ethan. I couldn't tell you where Loto is. But I got another question for you.

What's that?

Who built Yesler with two bricks?

Dale Raven raises his eyebrows.

You did, Rick, Ethan says.

Trevonte grins.

Thought I recognized you. That red hair in those narrow Yesler hallways. I'm Class of 2010. Or, I would have been. What about you?

Same. Class of 2010.

Wait, you two went to the same high school? Dale Raven asks.

Looks that way, Trevonte says. Not that we knew each other. Say, Ethan. You ever hit up Ezell's for lunch? With the spicy wings, right across from the Medgar Evers Pool?

Yeah, sometimes.

Twenty-Third and Jefferson. That was the spot, huh? It's all about that Ezell's. I know I saw you around there. That's crazy. Do you remember seeing me?

I don't think so. Sorry.

Trevonte laughs.

For a few minutes, everything is on pause.

Trevonte remembers those Yesler days. He remembers those spirit weeks, when each graduating class took over a hallway, cutting the lights and covering the corridors in purple and white streamers. Someone always set up a DJ booth, bumping hyphy music, mostly Mac Dre. The Thizzle Dance was mandatory, everybody wilding out with stank faces. Tell Me When To Go was also mandatory, E-40 and Keak da Sneak's lyrics printed on school t-shirts.

The assemblies were wild too. Even the abstinence one. Trevonte still remembers the former professional football player who told the boys to keep their dicks clean and told the girls to keep their legs closed. The ex-linebacker then demonstrated his strength by curling a frying pan with his bare hands. Then there was the Veterans Day rally where an old man screamed that if it wasn't for him, they'd all be speaking Japanese. The last assembly Trevonte remembers was a somber presentation about child soldiers in Africa. The speaker ended the presentation by saying, This child was a soldier, and he was a boy. You could say he was a soldier boy. Get it? The speaker then played Crank That, causing everyone to jump out of the bleachers, dancing to Soulja Boy and immediately losing the point.

See, they wouldn't do something like that at a school like Ballard, Trevonte says. It's 'cause we were in the Central District. So disrespectful. But then, maybe we disrespected ourselves responding like that. You know?

I remember that, Ethan says. I can't believe the principal thought that was a good idea.

Hey man, Trevonte says. Even though Principal Carson is Black, he's hecka racist. Did you know that?

Dale Raven presses a finger to his lips.

What do you mean? Ethan asks.

It's like, respectability, Trevonte says. Principal Carson was always getting in every Black kid's business about sagging their pants or cussing. He was getting us suspended for being five minutes late. But...I don't know. The night I got locked up, he came by. Asked how he failed me. I didn't know what to say.

When his grandmother visited, Trevonte reveals, she asked the same question.

That felt worse.

Trevonte asks Ethan if he's ever been by Twenty-Sixth and Jackson. Down on Twenty-Sixth, Trevonte's grandma lives in an old cedar shack next to a row of new townhomes. That's where she raised Trevonte while working as a shift supervisor at the Red Apple, where Trevonte has a job as a grocery clerk waiting for him. Though her income is boosted by his deceased grandfather's pension, times are lean.

One time, as a gift, Trevonte built a fence around his grandma's property, cobbling together ad hoc pickets and two by fours, trying to keep it from being too crooked. As a finishing touch, he painted the fence a bright, vibrant yellow.

She thought it looked like sunshine, Trevonte says. She loved it. But then I heard these white kids calling it a ghetto yellow fence. No respect for a working family. They don't want to see us on Jackson Street. To them, we're just ghetto, with a ghetto yellow fence. Shit.

He apologizes for cussing. He checks the time. He and Dale Raven return to their work. Ethan says nothing.

Day One.

CENTRALIA'S OUTLET STORES illuminate the dusk on the ride back. Luis drives the van with the radio tuned to the Spanish channel, to ranchera and cumbia music, saying, This has got to be the strongest signal in the Pacific Northwest. Gotta reach those workers in Yakima somehow.

From the passenger seat, Diana gives everyone kudos. She leans in, telling Ethan they'll reach out to Loto to confirm whether he's still interested in being part of Unlocked Youth. By the end of the week, they'll have an answer.

THESE YOUNG MEN are the judged, Luis says in seminar. One day in late February, after a shooting in Florida, Luis will come in wearing a black sweatshirt for the #MillionHoodieMarch.

DIANA LEADS A workshop on California's Three Strikes Law, enacted when she was a toddler in Oakland.

With the Three Strikes Law, you could get twenty-five to life for a misdemeanor. Anything from public intoxication to stealing twenty dollars. Just one misstep, and you're locked up for life. Just one.

Eleven

Belinda's Song

EARLY ONE AFTERNOON, the rain thins over Olympia. Dale Raven sees his opportunity. Enlisting my brother and my brother's girlfriend, he rents a canoe from the student recreation center, a vessel constructed from plastics and fiberglass.

It'll do.

He and Ethan and Bailey hoist the canoe upside down over their heads, carrying it into the on-campus forest. As a part-time groundskeeper, Dale Raven is intimate with these eight-hundred acres, the bright red torii gate near the organic farm, the shells encircling the Coast Salish Longhouse, the rusted remains of a flatbed truck, the clearing where he stumbled on a bluegrass trio fiddling under the stars at midnight. Down through the moss-draped hemlocks, past the wetlands and burrows, Dale Raven leads Bailey and Ethan to the shore.

High tide. They set the canoe in the water, clamoring into position. The boys sit on the ends. Bailey sits in between.

Ethan and Dale Raven take their paddles.

Out into the Salish Sea they go. The grayscale expanse. Clouds shift in and out of the rain. A great blue heron soars across the sky, pterodactyl-like, her wingspan defiant to the wind. The Black Hills rise over Thurston County, former mountains eroded by forty-million years of precipitation. This used to be a sea of Chinook Jargon. A sea of Lushootseed, Nooksack, Klallam.

A sea of many languages.

The canoe passes the ruins of a sailboat, brown and barnacled, anchored to rocks underneath the waves. After about forty minutes of paddling, they begin their long arc to shore, transformed in ways they cannot yet articulate.

INSIDE HER APARTMENT, a white bandana covering her orange hair, Bailey tends to a pot of lentil soup, bubbling with celery, onions, carrots, paprika, olive oil, tomatoes, and spinach. She insists on organic ingredients. As my brother struggles to peel some Yukon golds, she loses her patience and does it for him. We need to get you cooking more. No more microwave for you, mister. Didn't your parents teach you any cooking skills?

Nope, Ethan says.

Bailey kisses his cheek.

My emo doofus.

Dale Raven comes out of the shower, clean and sore. Ethan's phone vibrates in his jeans. He checks the number, and looks at Bailey. He asks if he can go into the spare room. As the residential advisor for this building, she shares her home with four other girls, formerly five, until one dropped out because of her seasonal affective disorder. In the sad girl's empty room, Ethan picks up.

Mom.

Belinda—now a seventh grader—is in trouble.

Crammed into Beacon Hill with Isadora and Sunshine, her behavior has crossed from eccentric to disturbing. For the last month, she's refused to eat any meal unless it is drenched in teriyaki sauce, a demand met with indifference until she lost eight pounds. She's been writing *Hail Satan!* on her forehead and etching upside-down crucifixes on her arms. She's cutting class right to the edge of criminal penalties. One day, when her grandmother swept her bedroom for paraphernalia, she discovered an unopened pack of condoms under her pillow. When confronted, my daughter said the condom fairy must have paid her a visit.

Now, things are even worse.

Late last night, Billie cut off all her hair with a pair of kitchen scissors, then took a disposable razor and shaved off the remainder. The combination left cutmarks in dozens of places. When Izzie discovered the disaster, she kept her out of school to buy a wig. When Sunshine shouted that the last thing her spoiled granddaughter deserved was a day of shopping, Isadora shouted back that if they sent Belinda to school looking like that, they could expect CPS on their doorstep by the afternoon.

Desperate to get Belinda on track, they want her to visit Sword Fern State this weekend.

Why? Ethan says. She's only twelve.

Isadora wants Billie to envision a future for herself, Mom says. She told me Billie is beginning to remind her of the kids she works with. The ones at the inpatient facility, the foster kids. She wants to try everything before sending her to a psychiatrist.

Ethan agrees to play host for his niece, aunt, and whatever-Grandma-Sunshine-is.

When the call ends, he returns to the kitchen, where Bailey is asking Dale Raven the best methods for smoking salmon. Ethan interrupts, relaying the latest on Belinda, asking if Bailey could serve as a tour guide in her official capacity as a Sword Fern State employee.

You know, Bailey says, if you were an R.A., you could do this yourself. Both me and Dale Raven have jobs. Why don't you?

Ethan looks down. Bailey tastes her lentil soup. Yes, she will guide the Maderas around campus. But for now, dinner.

One by one, they ladle the soup into bowls, sitting at the round table in the living room. Like her parents did during her upbringing in Bainbridge Island, Bailey forbids television. Instead, she shares a photo on her laptop sent by an artist couple named Rupert and Klarissa, who are serving as advisors on her final woodcarving project. On their sprawling Orcas Island property, the husband-and-wife team have upgraded an old van into a paragon of comfort and livability, renovating it with a set of cabinets, a bedframe, and a kitchen nook. Bailey is excited to see it in person. She has stayed with Rupert and Klarissa before, and wants Ethan to visit with her over spring break, maybe after they sign the lease on their apartment.

See, now that's interesting, Dale Raven says.

What? Bailey asks.

Rich folks living in vans for adventure versus poor folks living in vans out of necessity.

Rupert and Klarissa are excellent at their craft, Bailey says. Don't judge them.

Does all their money come from woodworking?

If you must know, Rupert's family used to own an emerald mine in South Africa. But they sold it off in the '90s.

South Africa?

South Africa has white people too.

Trust me, I'm aware. Did they sell off their mine before or after the end of apartheid?

We're done here. Who wants wine?

Alcohol is prohibited in on-campus housing, but Bailey keeps a bottle in her R.A. tote bag. She retreats to her bedroom, coming out with the illicit vino and three plastic cups. She pours one for Ethan, one for Dale Raven, and one for herself. Ethan doesn't drink and he never will. Something she already knows.

After a few sips, Bailey takes his cup.

Red wine, earning his own money, and sharing his woman with other women, Bailey says. What are three things Ethan Jamestone is afraid of?

Dale Raven keeps an eye on him.

THE MOTHER OF my child is now the first one in her family with a driver's license. Leaving from South Seattle, Grandma Sunshine criticizes Izzie the entire way to Sword Fern State. The heavy traffic is somehow her fault, as are the reckless eighteen-wheelers, as is the entire reason for this intervention. During this tirade, Belinda sits in the back of the sedan with an iPod, protected by the dream pop of the Chromatics. For their visit, she is wearing a black, cat-eared hoodie over her orange-highlighter wig. Stylish as always.

Bailey and Ethan wait for the Maderas by the concrete clocktower off Red Square. Bailey, in her Residential and Dining Services jacket, is bright and respectful. Grandma Sunshine ignores her handshake, silent under her sunglasses. With her silver pantsuit and heels, she is ever the businesswoman. As Bailey begins the tour, Grandma Sunshine asks about the student groups. Who are they? What do they do? She purses her lips as Bailey lists the Hip-Hop Congress, the LGBTQ+ Caucus, and the Democratic Socialists of America.

After this, we should visit a real college, Grandma Sunshine says.

Isadora hangs back with Ethan. Now in her thirties, she has solidified into her personality, tender but assertive, dressed in a pink sweater, a floral-print skirt, and tights with sandals.

With her master's degree, Izzie works as an assistant supervisor at a subacute behavioral treatment center in North Seattle. Her unit houses children ages five to eight, the littlest on campus. With teams of therapists and caseworkers, the residential staff respond to everything from bedwetting to domestic violence reenactment. Case files include accounts of meth flakes found in hair, animal torture, and pre-psychotic paranoia. Diagnoses range from reactive attachment disorder to fetal alcohol syndrome to oppositional defiant disorder. Almost all the patients have PTSD. Kindergartners stow knives in toy bins to defend themselves from their caregivers.

Violence defines most of Izzie's shifts: dangerous escalations and physical restraints, some of which last hours. Izzie participates in a dozen restraints a week, pinning children to walls and carpets, sometimes to the street outside. Street holds are the worst, especially when neighbors involve themselves. The children scream, always scream. Sometimes they hallucinate. Lighters burning knuckles, spiders crawling up legs, adult lips where they should never be. Staff concussions are a regular occurrence. So are blackeyes. With sad regularity, Isadora sends her employees to the urgent care clinic in Lake City, sometimes the emergency room.

Turnover last year was seventy percent. Wages are only a dollar higher an hour than flipping burgers at Dick's.

In response to her stress, Izzie has taken up smoking, excusing herself once every couple hours for a cigarette break. This, after reminding me over and over of the cancer and blood pressure risks. Despite advancing to management, she cannot afford to move herself or her daughter out of her mother's house. Not in Seattle. Even though she has her degree, she is still many thousands of dollars away from earning her therapy license.

Her only advice for my brother, should he continue down his career path, is to prepare himself.

For the last portion of the tour, Bailey brings everyone back to the library building, the basement classrooms where students have access to rotoscoping equipment and professional-grade recording studios. Belinda asks about the poetry scene.

Grandma Sunshine cuts in. Poets are junkies. Screwed up as Billie already is, poetry should never cross her mind. Olympia is a town of obvious freaks.

Bailey asks who wants lunch. Belinda asks if the cafeteria serves teriyaki. The tour is concluded.

IN A STUDIO next to the cafeteria, the student-run radio station, KFRN, hosts its shows on the bottom floor of the College Activities Building, or CAB. Before they pass inside, Belinda halts at the station's outdoor speakers. An acoustic song is playing, a voice she knows, singing in a convincing if affected drawl about a coastal village called Taholah, a night spent in a van.

Brotherhood and peace.

The performance ends. A live audience erupts in applause. The singer, young and confident, speaks in a playful cadence. He launches into a slurred monologue about how great it is to be playing in Ballard, U.S.A., how, living in Texas the past few years, he's been missing the Pacific Northwest's sparkling waterways. As the monologue fades, KFRN's midafternoon DJ cuts in, stating the name of the album: *Live at the Saint Rose.* Recorded in 2011 by Seattle's very own Terrell Jamestone, released on Sub Pop. The DJ repeats my name, telling his audience I may be the most important working musician in the alt-country scene today. He hopes I swing by the studio the next time I pop up in Oly.

Billie screams.

Snot running from her nostrils, eyes shut in fear.

Isadora tries to take hold of her. Her daughter slaps her. Grandma Sunshine calls her insane. She threatens to call the police. Bailey steps in, gripping Belinda by the arm and, in a kind but strong whisper, leads her inside the CAB to the nearest restroom, where she can melt down in privacy.

Outside, nobody moves.

SHE HEARS ME, my lost girl.

My voice sounds laidback. That is what devastates Belinda the most. That I sound so unconcerned.

BAILEY COMES OUT fifteen minutes later. Isadora, Sunshine, and Ethan are waiting at a picnic table. KFRN has moved on to Delta blues.

Belinda is recovering. But she asked Bailey if she could stay overnight in her apartment's spare room, if only to get a better sense of life at Sword Fern State. Bailey is open to the idea. Sunshine signs off without second thought. Isadora takes some convincing, then agrees. If only for one night, everybody in the Madera household can have peace.

Ethan tries to be useful. He tells everyone how he thought he saw me in Portland, putting on a show in Old Town. He has no corroborating evidence other than the pickup truck with Montana plates. The Maderas receive his report with blank expressions.

A deadbeat is a deadbeat, Grandma Sunshine says. He could be living up the street and it wouldn't matter. He's a miserable coward.

She spits.

Isadora puts out her cigarette. She never agrees with her mother. But she agrees.

THREE CUPS OF licorice tea sit on a polished wooden table, illuminated by dim red lamps. Tonight, Bailey and Ethan have taken my girl to SIZIZIS, the twenty-four-hour tea and coffee shop a few blocks up from Oly's downtown core. A den of potted ferns and decorative glass doorknobs, hosting K Records artists and one a.m. showings of obscure black-and-white films. At their table, Billie is reading a chapbook published by Sword Fern State's poetry society, underlining favorite phrases with her pen, writing truncated verses of her own in the margins.

Putting down her mug, she asks where the bathroom is. Bailey points. Billie strides across the creaking floorboards, her sherbet-colored wig bobbing like a ball of lightning. She closes the thick door. Bailey turns to Ethan.

You should stay at your place tonight.

Why?

Girl talk, Ethan. Girl talk. This is Belinda's sleepover, not yours. You can't be lurking in the background like some weirdo.

Ethan shakes his head.

A few minutes later, my daughter reappears. Before she sits down, she takes off her wig, revealing her five o'clock-shadowed scalp.

Do I look like a lesbian? Billie asks.

IN THE MORNING, Isadora knocks on the door to Bailey's apartment. Belinda is inside, sitting at the table with my brother, devouring scrambled eggs and toast. No teriyaki sauce needed. Our girl is smiling with authentic cheer, something she hasn't done in months.

Izzie holds back tears. When her daughter leaves for a shower, Isadora asks how the night went. Fine, Bailey says, though there wasn't much of a heart to heart. Mostly, they hopped around YouTube, Belinda sharing performances of her favorite musicians, mostly Grimes.

Isadora shares some news.

Last night, with her mind clear, she decided the main issue is Seattle itself. For her daughter to thrive, Izzie will apply for jobs in less expensive parts of the state. Probably in Eastern Washington, though she won't be revealing any of this to Billie yet. Until she has a solid lead, she has a proposition for Bailey and Ethan. How would they feel sharing their phone numbers so Belinda can text or call when she needs a lifeline?

Everyone is on board. When Belinda comes out of the bathroom, she exchanges her number without hesitating.

She gives Bailey a tight hug goodbye. She hi-fives my brother.

At home, the success of the overnight visit is conspicuous. Billie is more poised. She stays in school. She has a relief valve now, and though she does not use it immediately, she keeps it in mind.

WHEN ETHAN IS alone, he searches for me on Sub Pop's online store.

He finds me on the page for rarities and limited editions. *Live at the Saint Rose*, recorded last August and released in October, is sold out. The product description is minimal. He searches for video of the show on YouTube. There I am, center stage, taking shot after shot, playing song after song, courting a crowd only ten minutes from 91 West Etrusca Street.

He calls Mom, leaves a message. When she calls back, he hears a man's voice in the background. Mom has been housesitting Mr. Rivers's condo near Green Lake. She does not have much to say.

If Terrell wanted to be in our lives, he would be.

Ethan tries Dad.

He struggles to understand. His mind is sloshing. He's now leading the defense against the lawsuit. He cannot believe what his client's missiles do to their targets, superheating and sucking the air out of lungs before obliterating the rest of the bodies. He cannot believe how skin chars against desert sand.

We're bombing seven countries now, Dad says. What are we even doing in Yemen? His client, the defense contractors Lockhart-Brisbane, are sociopaths. But that's tuition money. Retirement money. Some of it will be put into a nest egg, a gift for Billie on her eighteenth birthday. She will always be taken care of.

I still love Terrell, Dad says.

He hangs up.

HE VISITS MARJORIE.

She welcomes Ethan into her cottage, remembering our visit from seven years ago. She is delighted to hear that he's matriculated at Sword Fern State. While Ethan sits down on the sofa, she lowers herself into her wicker chair. A septuagenarian now, she is careful with herself, though she still lives almost off the grid, with only some electricity and water. Over a ceramic bowl of coconut dates, my brother tells her everything.

He asks Marjorie if I've been by.

She saddens.

Yes. Terrell was here.

I swung by last year, right after the Ballard show, and stopped in last month for tea before the performance at the Portland Outdoor Store. Everything in my career is last-minute, a reputation built on murmurs. When I do tour, I do so unannounced. Marjorie isn't certain where I'm living these days. Somewhere in Northern California, maybe.

Do you want his number?

Ethan's heart skips.

No, thank you. Not now.

She understands.

Towards the end of the visit, Marjorie says a friend is coming to drive her to the Westside Food Co-op, where root vegetables are on sale this week. She sees Ethan off. As he crosses the garden path to the driveway, he looks at the pronghorn antelope on her woodshed. The ghost of the plains. The paint is fading under the heavy winter sky. He won't visit a second time.

· Twelve ·

Eye to Eye

PRISON DREAMS CREEP into his nights. He's in the yard at
Moss Hill, almost blinded by mist. Goose shit clings to his
uniform. Somewhere, a horn blares in a doomed tone. He sees
a man in an orange jumpsuit the same color as Belinda's wig.
The mist closes in, swallowing everything.

WEEK TWO.

Loto Posala arrives.

Welcoming him with respect, Diana and Luis point to
where my brother is sitting. Loto rubs his huge hands together,
flashing a mischievous grin. His jawline is wide, his eyes alert,
his hair in tight cornrows. He wears his Moss Hill rain jacket

like armor. He saunters through the visitor center in great deliberate steps. Everyone looks at him.

Before he and Ethan introduce themselves, Ethan takes in Loto's tattoos: three dots forming a triangle between his left thumb and index finger; five dots forming a quincunx on his right hand. Two teardrops fall out of his left eye. Over his throat, the letters S.O.S. are inked above the number 90. Everything is blue.

Loto regards my brother with kingly amusement. He nods with his chin.

What's crackin', cuzz? You my new Herbert?

I suppose so, Ethan says.

You suppose? Okay. Well, I suppose they call me Loto, a.k.a. Loco Loto, a.k.a. Lolo Loto, a.k.a. Big LP, a.k.a. Left Eye Loto, a.k.a. LL, a.k.a. Ladies Love Cool Posala. Two nuts hangin', big thing swangin'. What's up with it? What they call you where you from?

Everyone waits for his response.

Ethan, Ethan says.

Loto scrunches his face.

You got any other names? I could call you New Herbert.

Ethan is good.

Loto smiles.

Only right. Luis and Diana must have told you about me, huh? They tell you about the Spanish thing I do?

They did.

See, that's a punk move on their part. But that's okay. Anyway, listen. I heard a rumor about you. People are talking.

They are?

I heard you a bulldog. Woof woof.

What?

You really went to Yesler? Like, really really?

I did. Class of 2010. Trevonte told you?

Doesn't matter who told. Point is, I'm surprised. Where'd you grow up at?

I'd prefer not to talk about where I'm from.

Smart, Loto says. That's smart. I respect that. Tell me this though. They got Samoans where you from?

Yesler had a student group for Pacific Islanders, I believe.

But you never kicked it with the Samoans, right?

I guess not.

Figured that. Ain't too many of us on the Mainland. The few of us here, there's a pressure to represent our culture a certain way. But then there's guys like me, who got our own types of pressure. Feel me?

I think so, Ethan says.

Maybe you do, Loto says. Maybe you don't. You know who Ermias Ashgedom is?

Can't say I do. Who is he?

Someone I admire. Like a role model. He's out of South Central, Crenshaw and Slauson. But his family's from East Africa. Even though he's with the Rollin' 60s, he's handling the world in a different way because his pop took him to Eritrea to see his roots. Now he's using his businesses to invest in his neighborhood. That's, like, his activism. Truth be told, I've never seen much outside South King County. Everything could've been different if I'd stepped out more. Feel me?

I do, Ethan says.

Loto rolls his neck on his shoulders.

You a good dude. I can tell. We getting to business or what?

You got it, Ethan says. I hear you and Herbert were reading *The Four Agreements*. Would you like to continue with that?

Nah. This quarter, I want you to teach me how to rap. I'm talkin' bars for days, cuzz.

Okay, Ethan says. Who are your favorite rappers?

Loto laughs.

You want my Top Five? What're you gonna do, bring in a bunch of CDs with the clean lyrics? We about to do nine weeks of rap-alongs?

If that's what it takes.

This guy's crazy. What rappers you like? Eminem?

The *8 Mile* soundtrack, maybe.

Yeah, you like Eminem. No doubt. You got issues with your mom too or what?

Ethan starts laughing. Loto points at him, yelling, Ayo this guy's craaazy. From the guard station, Luis and Diana give the thumbs up. For their remaining session, Ethan and Loto move into their work.

Rapping is dropped as a subject of study. They settle on a field to which Loto is already attuned: acting.

LUIS GIVES A presentation he calls How the Other Half Bangs.

In contemporary entertainment, the gangbanger is the new Noble Savage. How do you really see the young men of Moss Hill?

PICTURE ME ROLLIN'.

One afternoon, when the visitor center is warm, Loto rolls up his sleeve, revealing the title of his favorite Tupac Shakur song in his skin, an affirmation of victory recorded after his release from Clinton Correctional Facility. Loto's always loved 'Pac, always loved the West Coast.

When I was a kid, I always wanted to run away to Cali, Loto says. You ever been?

Not yet, Ethan says.

I got some uncles down in Long Beach. They always used to send me pictures of their lifestyles. Lowriders with spinning rims, gold ropes, palm trees. Everything always looked like a party.

Sounds like it.

My people put in work for those nice things. You ever heard of Mr. Cartoon?

Who's Mr. Cartoon?

The world's greatest tattoo artist. His parlor is in downtown L.A. Hella celebrities come through. Calvin Broadus, all of them. My Uncle Tito paid Mr. Cartoon thirty thou to put his daughter's portrait on his shoulder. Took it from her first-grade yearbook. Looks just like her. Tito would have got one of his lady too, but then he got caught up. He's in San Quentin now doing a bid.

Sorry to hear that.

I used to feel jealous about that. Can you imagine that? Being jealous of San Quentin? Where they got death row?

Why did you feel that way?

Couldn't tell you. There's like a glamor to it. I heard you can see the Bay from the yard. Blue water and pretty hills. Sounds a lot nicer than this. Plus, you can get a college degree. Uncle Tito's on that grind, learning all types of skills, meeting all kinds of volunteers. San Quentin ain't what it used to be.

That's great, Ethan says.

Loto nods.

When I was first sent to county, all my uncles called me up. They took turns sharing their congratulations. They were proud, mostly. I'd proved I was about my business.

Family is complicated, Ethan says.

Don't I know it. First opportunity I get, I'm going to Cali. What about you?

Could be a good time, Ethan says.

Could be good. Could be real good. The Golden State. Shame we haven't been yet. But that's okay. We're still young.

We're still young, Ethan says.

Loto nods. They get back to work. My brother has brought in packets on the Meisner Technique, along with some monologues to practice.

Before they begin, Loto rolls ups his other sleeve, revealing a tattoo of the Seattle Mariners logo, the unmistakable white S and star. Ethan asks if he likes baseball. His mentee laughs so hard he almost falls out of his chair. He gestures at the others, repeating my brother's question. This guy said baseball.

VISIONS ACCUMULATE, INEVITABLE visions: officers running across the yard, hands on their pepper spray; photographs in the visitor center showing off the prison's ethnic study groups, boasting about the prison's diversity and inclusivity; a curly-haired boy sitting outside a processing office, wrists cuffed, nose bloodied; a sunny spring day, the young men outside playing flag football; the vapors, always the vapors, rising from the grass, but never rising over the razor-wire fences.

HALFWAY THROUGH THE quarter, Ethan and Loto are practicing monologues near a heavy blond boy named Chuck Chuck. Rocking in his plastic chair, Chuck Chuck holds his gut, childlike rage in his eyes. Rocking and rocking. Diana and Luis are with him, as well as the C.O., Conner. His mentor, a young woman from the D.C. suburbs, is keeping her distance. Something was said. Tension fills the room.

Loto turns to Ethan.

Chuck Chuck's feeling the pressure today, he says.

What's going on? Ethan asks.

That kid's fifteen years old, right? Came in here with a forty-year sentence. Only been down for two. Every time he thumps with the guards, he gets five more. That's straight from the judge. He's been in trouble eight times since getting here. Now try putting yourself into that situation. Forty years turning into eighty.

I can't.

You know what type of offender Chuck Chuck is? The type they put in Coho?

That's not my business, Loto.

You'd feel different if you knew.

I believe you. But we should move on.

There is no moving on for Chuck Chuck. Feel me? Chuck Chuck ain't with this no more. He can't stand being around these guys who got futures. Trevonte, for example. He's about to be out. He's got a plan, got somewhere to stay. Most of the guys, the mentees, they're like Trevonte. Me and Chuck Chuck got it different. I can take the years. But Chuck Chuck?

Loto gestures for Ethan to come closer. He whispers.

He's got an out. Wanna hear it?

What?

He's about to take one of those lip balm things, right? He's about to strip it down to the corkscrew and stick it into one of his eyeballs. He's gonna do that til he's blind. Then he's gonna do the other eye.

Are you serious?

You think I'm playing?

Why would he do that?

To speed up transfer to the Department of Corrections. He doesn't want to wait six more years. He wants that big boy lockup. Moss Hill will send him to the hospital first. They can't stand self-injury. After that, my guy Chuck Chuck will relocate to Walla Walla. Probably the only fifteen-year-old at the penitentiary. How do you like that?

At Chuck Chuck's table, a resolution occurs. Conner radios for support. Two more guards appear. Calmly handcuffing him, they lead Chuck Chuck out into the yard, headed towards the Secure Housing Unit.

Diana and Luis check in with the girl from D.C.

My brother asks Loto more about Chuck Chuck's scheme to self-mutilate. His mentee shrugs like he said nothing. He picks up his script.

IN THE PROGRAM office back at Sword Fern State, Ethan relays everything Loto told him to Diana and Luis. They confirm that Chuck Chuck is already in the custody of the Department of Corrections. He will be housed in the same facility as the Green River Killer.

ETHAN TYPES THE name into a search engine. He breaks the rule, and he regrets it immediately. A headline out of Palouse. A seven-year-old girl found in a beartrap, still alive, her clothes dumped in a highway litter barrel.

DIANA AND LUIS moderate a discussion about self-care. Chuck Chuck's mentor walks out in tears. She never comes back.

ONE DAY, LOTO is running his hand across his cornrows, over and over, disinterested in his script, disinterested in Ethan. Quiet.

What's on your mind? Ethan asks.

You sound like a psychologist, Loto says. Why something gotta be on my mind?

The guard watches.

I got a baby girl back home, Loto says. Four years old.

That's young, Ethan says.

She's already got a temper too. Already been thrown out of daycare twice. Ain't even been to kindergarten, but she's tearing up pre-k. Her mom ain't about to do anything. Four years old, and it's too late.

Sorry to hear that, Ethan says. If it helps, you should know it isn't too late.

How do you figure? Loto asks.

There are programs for kids like her, Ethan says. Early childhood intervention. Strengths-based, trauma-informed care.

That's the type of thing you're fitting to do when you graduate, huh?

Yeah, probably.

You're the type of dude I'd trust with my daughter. No doubt. But does it work, though? These programs?

In some cases, sure.

Don't they take the baby away, though? Put her in foster care and all that?

It depends.

Psssht. It depends? Okay.

Loto Posala cracks his knuckles. He twists in his seat, gripping the back of his chair to pop his back.

Hey, I forgot to tell you, he says. My mom wants to thank you for all you've done. You down to meet her?

I'd be honored, Ethan says.

Loto takes an extra moment to look out at the yard, the wet grass and drizzling sky. His transfer to Coyote Ridge is in less than a month.

ON THE VAN ride home, Diana tells Ethan that was the most she's ever heard Loto open up about his daughter.

OVER DINNER, DALE Raven points out that the furniture in Bailey's apartment was built by prison labor. It says so on the tags beneath the cushions. Bailey giggles like Dale Raven told a dirty joke.

Thirteen

No Sunset

WILHEM KUNST IS smirking on the front page of *The Seattle Times*. Nineteen years old, he's now living in Palo Alto, studying at Stanford. In the photograph, he stands shoulder-to-shoulder with his fellow computer science majors, all male, all wearing the same burgundy sweaters. An above-the-fold story describes how these ex-Seattleites are pushing the boundaries of artificial intelligence. Pioneering a new predictive algorithm, several of these luminaries, including Magnolia's own Wilhelm Kunst, are already fielding job offers from top companies.

Mom shares the story with Ethan and Bailey, sad-eyed. The other day, she ran into Wilhelm's mother at the Uptown Mercer Market. Mrs. Kunst is overjoyed. As much as Wilhelm loves California, he's probably coming back to Seattle after graduation. Amazon's recruiters are pushing hard to secure his future employment, though he needs to prove himself first with a prestigious internship. Not that he has anything to worry about.

Mom looks at Ethan.

I'm sorry you hated Yesler so much, she says. That extreme competitiveness. But maybe some competitiveness is good. You could always transfer out of Sword Fern State and change your degree. It's not too late, Ethan.

Bailey picks up the newspaper.

This was your best friend in middle school?

Ethan nods.

He looks like a douchebag, Bailey says.

Mom and Ethan laugh. It is an early Saturday evening at 91 West Etrusca Street. My brother and his girlfriend are staying the weekend. Soon, they will be out in the city, bouncing from excitement to excitement. Dad is still at the offices of Howard, Warwick, and Moore, combing through documents on behalf of Lockhart-Brisbane. He is finalizing the argument that, because the victims of these drone strikes were overseas—Iraq, Afghanistan, Libya, Syria, Pakistan, Somalia, and Yemen—the families have no standing to prosecute a wrongful death lawsuit in the United States. If this argument does not get the suit dismissed outright, he will then try the argument that his client simply fulfilled their obligations to the Department of Defense. Their responsibility begins and ends with manufacturing and supplying weapons. How the weapons are employed by the American military is immaterial to Lockhart-Brisbane's culpability.

Dad has never worked harder.

Mom would like to take a bath. She asks Ethan and Bailey to take Pepper on her evening walk. As they leash the capering black Labrador, my mother retreats with Logan Rivers's new memoir in hand. Every single book Logan Rivers has ever written sits on the end of the dining room table. When Bailey points this out, Ethan tells her about his mom's close friendship with the famous author. To this, Bailey does not say a word.

THE SHIP CANAL twinkles below the Google offices where Wilhelm Kunst's dad still works. Pepper rootles under bushes as Ethan pulls her leash, trying to lead her to the asphalt path by SMU's track field.

Suddenly, he and Bailey see a dark figure sitting on a bench, a man in a suit, his face in his hands. He looks like a downtown lawyer because he is a downtown lawyer.

Dad.

Bailey takes Pepper while my brother approaches. Dad looks up. He reeks of whiskey. His expression brightens in recognition. He does not perceive my brother's concern.

Ethan! he says. Bailey! What are you two doing here?

We're spending the night, Ethan says. Didn't Mom tell you?

Dad runs his hands along his pants. For the first time, Ethan notices the potbelly he's putting on. His beard seems thicker, more unkempt. His eyes are glassy. He does not respond to my brother, except to mumble that Mom says whatever she wants and doesn't care who she hurts.

Ethan kneels at his side.

Pop, what are you doing out here? he asks.

They share eye contact.

Ninety percent of drone strike victims are civilians, Dad says. Did you know that?

Is that from the lawsuit?

It's public information. Lockhart-Brisbane wants to countersue these families. I talked them out of it. If I do nothing else, I did do that. I did do that.

We should get you home, Ethan says.

Dad shakes his head. He places his hands on his knees, looking out across the Ship Canal.

Three-Fourteen, Sixteen, One-Fifty, he says.

What?

Title Three-Fourteen, Chapter Sixteen, Section One-Fifty of the Washington Administrative Code. No sale of liquor to intoxicated persons. The Nickerson Street Saloon is very good about that. It's not enough to be sober, you need to look sober too. I'll be fine.

Dad looks at Bailey. He tells her that her father is a helluva litigator.

Philip Voclaine is a cunning one, he says. So proud my son is dating a girl like you. I hope to see your art someday. Your sculptures.

You're welcome in the woodshop anytime, Mr. Jamestone, Bailey says.

Slowly, Dad stands up. He asks Ethan if he's heard my album.

Terrell sure can sing, Dad says. Hell of a guitar picker too. Wish I knew he was doing that show at the Saint Rose. I used to sing to Terrell to get him to sleep. I used to sing to you too. Remember that?

Ethan says nothing.

Our father staggers off in the direction of the Fremont Bridge, disappearing into the darkness like a corpse.

Bailey puts her hand on my brother's shoulder.

Ethan plunges his hands in his pockets, struggling. After a minute, Bailey nudges him. Your dad can take care of himself. We'll see him in the morning. We shouldn't let this ruin our evening, should we?

They take Pepper to the house. Mom is in bed.

IN A DAZE, Ethan drives them to Capitol Hill. Cruising down Broadway, passing the disorganized tents of Occupy Seattle. On Pine Street, the city's skyscrapers are incandescent and outstanding. The sidewalks are packed with drunks and heroic one-night stands. Kendrick Lamar plays from Ethan's silver iPod Classic, the nocturnal loneliness of A.D.H.D, connected via aux cord. This is Kendrick in his *Section.80* era, the indie debut before the major label debut, *good kid, m.A.A.d. city*, which will hit markets in October, an instant West Coast classic, rich with emotional intelligence and stories about growing up in Compton. Something Ethan will listen to over and over to better know the young men of Moss Hill.

Bailey, whose playlists involve Edward Sharpe and the Magnetic Zeroes, is unimpressed, laughing and throwing up mock gang signs.

Yo, yo, yo. Keep it ratchet, ho. Get that money, E.J.

The ride is almost over. As my brother struggles to parallel park near a private high school, Bailey gets out of her seat and practically carjacks him to finish the job, cutting K. Dot off in the middle of Ronald Reagan Era.

They walk to the Melrose Building, to Bauhaus Books & Coffee. Two stories of seating, the restless main floor and the study-session top floor. Ryan Henry Ward paintings decorate the soaring bookshelves, surreal creatures with bulbous eyes in melting landscapes. The menu lists everything from cappuccinos to Kool-Aid. Young women in PBR shirts vow that they're done dating musicians. Middle-aged men in berets debate Occupy and the Arab Spring. Outside, nightclubbers move in uphill waves: women in shining miniskirts, men with elaborate mustaches, glittering drag queens preparing to seize their crowns. Capitol Hill, parading in paint and sequins, paganistic and elated.

Ethan and Bailey sit on the second floor.

They talk. After she graduates, Bailey wants to move to Orcas Island. Her mentors, Rupert and Klarissa, are looking for ways to connect her to the local craft community, maybe get her an apprenticeship with one of their peers. She would love nothing more than to hone her skills in one of the most beautiful places in the Pacific Northwest.

What about our plans? Ethan asks.

We don't need to live together to be together, Bailey says. You need to have more faith in our relationship.

Sounds like you've made up your mind, Ethan says.

Rupert and Klarissa have done a lot for me. Especially Klarissa. She's such a hottie. Speaking of which, I have some photos you need to see. The last time we hung out, Klarissa tied me up with her homemade ropes. We did this erotic photoshoot. I was naked and—

What?

Let me finish. I was naked and she put me in all these wild poses. Tied me in all kinds of knots. It was one of the sexiest nights of my life. Want to see?

You cheated on me with Klarissa?

Holy shit. You emo doofus. We did not fuck. Klarissa's only kissing me in one picture. Why are you always trying to control my body?

Why didn't you talk to me first?

Because you would've said no. You need to see a therapist. This emo shit isn't cute anymore. Do you have any idea how exhausting it is for me to date someone like you? Someone with borderline personality disorder?

Excuse me?

Never mind. I'm lucky my friends are so supportive. Rupert got me this workbook on BPD. If you want, I'll pass it along to you.

Ethan stares.

You've been telling people I have borderline personality disorder?

Unbelievable, Bailey says. Way to miss the point.

She tells my brother she needs to use the restroom. When she finishes washing up, she waits by the entrance, expecting him to understand that he's supposed to come down and meet her. For whatever reason, he does.

On his way out, Ethan bumps into a hipster with sleepy eyes and a dollop of blond hair. In a raspy voice, the hipster apologizes. Turning to his sharp-jawed friend, he resumes a conversation about sobriety. In less than a year, the duo will top the Billboard charts, splitting Capitol Hill into either annoyance or pride at their independent come-up. Someday, my brother will share the story about that one Saturday night when he collided into Ben Haggerty and Ryan Lewis at Bauhaus, back when Bauhaus was open at Melrose and Pine, back when he and Bailey used to have a favorite coffee shop together.

ON THE NIGHT they first met, they talked for eight hours straight. When they began dating, Bailey told him he felt like a first love. Someone she could see marrying. She said he was the only boy who ever got her to climax. He remembers believing her.

THEY TRY TO salvage their night.

They drive to Pike Place, parking in Post Alley. Opposite the Gum Wall, street artists have plastered a collage of the avant-garde: menacing babies, three-eyed mystics, cosmic demons. Slogans like Keep Seattle Hostile, My City is Filthy, 206ness. Bailey poses under the art, trying to appear pensive as Ethan takes a picture on his phone. The result is grainy and underwhelming.

Bailey deletes the photo.

She wants bubble tea.

My brother takes her to the International District, to Oasis Tea Zone, right across from Uwajimaya. Inside, speakers blast techno remixes of J-POP hits. The late-night crowd swarms the arcade games and pool tables, trading manga and magazines. Bailey orders taro milk tea with tapioca balls, then rushes off to claim a table. Ethan puts in an order for deep-fried chicken gizzards, something he tried and liked in high school, and waits by the pickup counter. When he sits down, Bailey is upset. How, she asks, could he order something so thoughtless? She won't want to share that. Rather than put in her own food order, she sucks down her milk tea, ignoring him, scrolling through her phone.

Driving back to Capitol Hill, Ethan looks up at the new condominiums, noticing how far they rise above him.

Returning to Broadway, they pull into the mobbed parking lot at Dick's. 1:30 a.m. This month, Bailey is a vegetarian, so my brother places an order for fries. Standing at the stainless-steel counter outside, he looks out at the massive construction site across the street, slowly evolving into a new transit hub.

Bailey pokes Ethan. She wants to hear one of his stories about growing up in the city.

He tells her one.

In his Yesler days, he used to ride the bus from Rodgers Park to 23rd and Jefferson, passing through Belltown, Downtown, First Hill, and Pill Hill. He remembers all the eccentric personalities that came on and off, mostly in the Free Ride Zone. The most memorable was a red-nosed man who regaled his audience with a recipe for something he called Boat. Boat, the man said, was the greatest drug he'd ever smoked. To make some, you pour everything from your pantry—hot sauce, bleach, vinegar, glass cleaner, everything—into a bathtub. You let the mixture sit for three days until it hardens. You take a ballpeen hammer, break the solid mass into chunks, then smoke up. Best high of your life.

Everyone who rode the Route 3 or the Route 4 in that era has some version of this story. Ethan laughs as he plucks the details from memory.

Sounds like that man had a serious addiction, Bailey says. What is wrong with you?

To boot, she hates the fries at Dick's. Too greasy. She tosses them in the trash. She wants to return to Queen Anne.

Ethan scratches his palm with his car key, almost breaking the skin.

KERRY PARK AT 2:00 a.m. The skyline at its most famous angle, the Space Needle in the center. Ethan and Bailey are on the mansion end of Queen Anne Hill, the part where everyone assumes we grew up. Bailey shivers, asking for my brother's hoodie. He removes his outer layer with an audible sigh. Fine, she says. She tosses his hoodie into the abstract metal sculpture that all the tourists like. The hoodie lands in a puddle.

2012 IS THE line in his memory where Before slams into After. Before is belonging. After is moving on.

ON SUNDAY MORNING, Belinda calls Bailey's phone. Bailey tells Ethan to take the call. She needs to shower.

Billie's voice is shaky. Isadora just accepted a job offer in Spokane. They will be moving at the end of the school year. My girl would rather hole up in one of those shady Aurora motels than move to Eastern Washington. She cries and cries. Ethan tells her he's sorry. He says her mom is trying to do what's best. He tells her he hopes to see her soon. He hopes she's reading poetry. My girl thanks him for listening. Being there.

When Bailey comes out of the shower, she does not ask why Belinda was trying to reach her. She barely speaks to Ethan.

This is the last time she will ever stay at the house at 91 West Etrusca Street.

· Fourteen ·

Belinda's Song, Part II

IN MID-MARCH, A rare snowstorm smothers the South Sound under five frozen inches. City snowplows clear downtown, but fail to reach West Olympia, where the roads are soon impassable. Several conifers collapse onto the powerlines, cutting off electricity to Sword Fern State. All classes and extra-curriculars are canceled for the week. The first few hours are a party of winter amusements. On the big field, on-campus residents build giant snowmen. Lovers hold hands. A set of diesel-powered generators brings electricity to the hub where students collect mail and do laundry. Scores of Ferners sit inside, charging phones and laptops, gaming.

The Coast Salish Longhouse collapses into itself, the roof unable to take the snow. My brother snaps pictures of the damage and forwards them to Dale Raven, who is saddened but not surprised.

Ethan waits alone for the bus at Red Square. Without boots, he does not want to risk the walk to the apartment. On the thirty-minute ride, a ride that would take ten minutes without snow, my brother has never felt so cold.

WITH POWER STILL out a few nights later, Dale Raven and Ethan take their studies to the Reef, spreading their books over the counter, taking notes for their collaborative term paper. Around them, regulars dig into heavy comfort foods. The jukebox plays punk and dream pop. Outside, dirty snow lines the curb.

The boys take a break, sipping coffee, shooting the shit.

Any plans for spring break? Dale Raven asks.

Might visit that married couple on Orcas, Ethan says. The ones with the van.

I remember. The white South Africans who used to own an emerald mine. Probably owned a few miners, too.

Bailey's thinking about moving in with them. You know, when she graduates.

Weren't you two going to move in together?

We were.

Is everything okay? Dale Raven asks.

Ethan looks into his mug.

Bailey's telling her friends I have borderline personality disorder.

Jesus, why would she do that? Dale Raven says.

Because I'm moody.

Did she diagnose you or something? Is she an expert on the *DSM-IV* now? Even if there was a diagnosis, why would she spread it around like that? I hate to say it, but this feels like bullying to me. It feels like she bullies you a lot, actually.

It feels like she's looking for an out, Ethan says.

Is she?

I don't want to talk about it.

Then we don't have to, Dale Raven says. You know what? Here's something. Have I told you that my sister keeps inviting me to stay with her in San Francisco?

Down in the Bay Area, Cheryl Raven Buford is living the painter's life by day and tending bar at night. She loves her home in the Mission District, and Dale Raven would love to see it. He also wants to visit Alcatraz, not to participate in carceral tourism, but to stand on the Ohlone island once reoccupied for nineteen months in the '70s. But to save money, he'll probably spend vacation in Oly. He'll see.

Suddenly, Dale Raven and Ethan turn their heads.

Justin Braun reappears, a half-remembered dream in overpriced clothing.

Swaggering to the counter, Justin asks why these two jerkoffs are at the Reef. When Dale Raven tells him about the power outage, Justin laughs. The West Coast can't handle snow for shit, he says. Him? He's glad to be done with Sword Fern State. He can't stand all these oversensitive douchebags. Last week, the professors in his gender studies program kicked him out for the new tattoo on his neck that says Pretty Motherfucker.

They said I was creating a hostile learning environment, Justin says. Or something. Blah blah blah. I said the bitches need to know. I be that Pretty Motherfucker.

Now what? Dale Raven says. You going back East?

California, baby, Justin says.

What's in California?

Silicon Valley, dumbass. Do you know how easy it is to make a fortune down there? All you gotta do is teach yourself coding, come up with an idea, and get some investors. One-two-three, boom. Just like that. I'm already looking at apartments. Looks like I can get a nice one-bedroom in San Fran for four-thousand a month. Smooth, right?

The waitress comes over, resentment in her eyes. She tells Justin to cover up his tattoo or get lost. Justin takes a red cloth napkin, tying it around his neck like an ascot. He slides off his stool, drops his menu on the floor, and leaves. Dale Raven stoops and picks up the menu, apologizing. The waitress tells him that Justin got kicked out of Jake's last night for trying to start a fight.

That boy's money is eating him alive, Dale Raven says.

He wishes he and Justin could share a real conversation. He too lost his father. Never knew him that well in the first place, but he identifies with the pain, the directionless ache.

His name was Harold Raven Buford.

Right after Dale Raven's birth, Harold Raven visited Canada. Coinciding with his arrival, a series of explosions took out multiple drilling rigs in Alberta's tar sands region. Despite circumstantial evidence, the Canadian government announced Dale Raven's dad as a suspect, placing him on a list of eco-terrorists. Harold Raven was a wanted man until his death in the 2000s. The rumor is that he passed away from pneumonia on the islands of Haida Gwaii. Rumors are all Dale Raven has. He someday hopes to visit the remote village where his father breathed his last, honoring the people who gave him sanctuary.

You're lucky you still have your father, he tells Ethan.

Ethan nods.

The tattooed waitress asks if they would like more coffee. Dale Raven orders a slice of huckleberry pie. Outside, a muddied semi-trailer hauls bark-stripped logs down 4th Avenue, carrying timber through the drizzle.

EVENTUALLY, THE SNOW melts. Up in Seattle, Belinda runs away.

An early Wednesday afternoon.

Gray and bitter.

She ditches at lunchtime, a strategy in mind. She was always so smart. Fifth period is an aging substitute who won't report absences until the end of the day. Hopping a bus from Beacon Hill to downtown, Billie conceals herself in her puffy black jacket. 3rd and Pine—they call it The Blade—teems with strangers, gnarled and volatile. Police patrol the crowd. Here, the city is not iconic. Here, the city is an intersection of fast food and weed smoke and seagull shit.

Billie comes to a three-sided schedule board. She memorizes the routes out of town. She does not know where her ultimate destination lies. Portland is a possibility. But so too are even greater possibilities, by turns fog-drenched and sun-drenched.

Before she takes her case federal, she turns off her phone, taking out the battery so nobody can contact her, or track her. She will keep the battery out for three days.

The bus pulls up. Sitting near the back, she minimizes her presence, putting up her cat-eared hood. For her escape, she pulls up *Born to Die* on her iPod, playing it like she has every day since late January. Rolling out of Seattle, my girl's sole accomplice is the self-described gangster Nancy Sinatra.

NOBODY KNOWS HOW to pursue a twelve-year-old girl who doesn't want to be caught. Everyone converges at 91 West Etrusca Street.

My father takes a day off. Over the decades, his standing in the legal community has netted him contacts with city police and the FBI. He leverages them all. Notices go out to the Port of Seattle, the train stations, ferry terminals, the airport.

King County Metro is harder. Greater Seattle has more public buses than almost any other metropolitan area in the country, a frenetic system serving tens of thousands of passengers a day, operating in an environment of total unpredictability. Three years ago, a mass murderer rode on the Metro after executing four police officers in Lakewood, evading the largest manhunt in state history for two days before being identified and killed in South Seattle.

Anyone could hide.

Over the phone, Ethan asks Mom whether he should come up to the city. Mom tells him to stay put. So he does.

LOTO POSALA IS silent today, his personality sealed with his lips. On most visits, my brother knows better than to ask. But with Belinda missing, everything feels wrong. Even the fortified walls of the visitor center seem porous. The rules are not the rules.

What's up? Ethan asks.

Can't be sure, Loto says. Can't be sure.

He sits up as though preparing to offer something in trade.

You know how it is, Loto says. There's weirdos in these streets, cuzz. I got stories on stories. You gotta protect the women. Feel me?

What do you mean? Ethan says.

Women, my guy. Girls. Girls who grow up too fast. Hanging where they shouldn't. Mixing with the wrong dudes. Where I'm from, some new girl comes through looking for a place to hide. Maybe she tricks to get by. Maybe a weirdo puts hands on her. My boys keep me up to date. There's a lot of missing girls out there. Some never come home. Feel me?

My brother sits up.

Loto, he says. What have you heard?

Like I said. I got stories on stories. Couldn't tell you most of them.

Loto holds his gaze. He tells Ethan he should start bringing in horror movie scripts. In another lifetime, if he could ever pursue acting as a real career, he would want to do horror movies most of all. Stories with monsters.

ON THE SECOND day of Belinda's absence, Dad plans to get the Department of Justice to issue an AMBER Alert, turning my daughter from a runaway to an abductee. He'll tell the DOJ that I kidnapped her, possibly across state lines. That way, every cellphone in the Pacific Northwest will light up with her name and a description of my pickup truck. Nobody could ignore that.

Isadora convinces him to put the phone down.

ON THE THIRD day of Belinda's absence, Bailey reveals her masterpiece.

The Salmon Girl sits in the center of the woodshop floor, six feet tall, a startling accomplishment worthy of its exhibition. Carved out of yellow cedar, the Salmon Girl is naked, her hair in an elegant bun, her hands holding the back of her head. The tail and fins on which the Salmon Girl sits are varnished, sleek. Compared to her marine qualities, the human surface is almost coarse.

The mermaid keeps her eyes closed. By a trick of craft, the lips seem to tremble.

The happy artist is chatting with Rupert and Klarissa, who have come to Olympia in their famous van. Rupert stands with upper class confidence, dressed in CEO casualwear, an off-white button-down shirt, blue jeans, loafers. His wife, Klarissa, sports glossy black hair. She, like Bailey, is in an earth-tone dress of brown and green, and, if not for her golden sandals, would personify the eco-boutique aesthetic. Bailey giggles, batting her eyelashes.

Ethan keeps his distance.

A new woman joins Bailey's club, a long-lost friend whose arrival elicits screaming. Her name is Evelyn, blonde and dreadlocked. She once lived on the school's organic farm, and is also wearing an earth-tone dress and sandals. Bailey gestures for Ethan to come over, introducing Evelyn, telling him she's invited them to her place for an after-party. Unfortunately, Rupert and Klarissa can't stick around.

Ethan says sure.

The South Africans bid everyone good night. They tell my brother how lovely it was to meet him, and how they look forward to hosting him sometime on Orcas Island.

EVELYN LIVES IN the basement of a house near Pear Street. Already graduated, she's working part-time at Rainy Day Records, and recently apprenticed under a famous papercutting artist. Some kind of dream.

Tonight, Evelyn and Bailey are drinking candy-flavored vodka, laughing and falling off the sofa. Around the basement, the landlady's sewing supplies take up almost every surface, yarn and spindles and plastic boxes of beads. Ethan sits in a wicker chair, staring at the wall. When Evelyn asks if he's okay, he says he only got three hours of sleep last night. When Evelyn offers her mattress for a nap, Bailey laughs.

This may be the only way to get him into another woman's bed.

Ethan admits a nap may be in order. Before Evelyn sends him to her bedroom—a storage closet within the basement—she produces a record from her vinyl collection. Because Rainy Day can't sell bootlegs, one of the perks of her job is she can take home whatever illicit merchandise comes their way. She passes Ethan a black disc encased in light brown parchment paper and a see-through sleeve: *Live at the Saint Rose*.

Bailey told me Terrell Jamestone is your brother, Evelyn says. Customers rave about him. I hear he's living in a bookstore. Somewhere in San Francisco. Is that true?

Ethan holds the vinyl.

Bailey whispers in Evelyn's ear, fingering one of her dreadlocks. Evelyn looks at Ethan with sympathy. Before he knows it, the women are smoking weed in the backyard.

He needs a break, any break.

Setting down the record, he goes up the cellar steps to the garden. From the stone bench where they sit, Evelyn and Bailey don't notice him. In the shadows, Bailey appears to be sitting on Evelyn's lap, a pair of statues about to kiss.

Ethan compresses himself between the house and a fence overgrown with vines. Escaping to the sidewalk, he strides in the night towards SIZIZIS, just a few blocks away. His phone vibrates. He picks up.

BELINDA HAUNTS THE doorway like a displaced spirit, her short hair unkempt, her clothing muddy, her eyes gaunt and tearful. She drops her backpack, now with an unexplained rip on one of the straps, and throws her arms around her uncle, weeping.

Ethan takes her inside.

Ordering a mug of licorice tea, he sits with Belinda at a dim table. Eventually, she takes a sip, calming. She does not want to talk, but my girl knows she should.

Do you need to see a doctor? Ethan says.

I don't know, Billie says.

My brother needs to call everyone, tell them she's here. He tells Belinda every law enforcement agency in the State of Washington is looking for her. A minute passes.

Okay, she says.

Belinda has one last request. Before returning to Beacon Hill, Billie wants to know if she could be dropped off at the house in Queen Anne. Just to brace herself. Ethan can't make any promises. He phones Dad and Mom. Mom speaks to Belinda. When they hang up, Billie tells Ethan that Mom offered to let her soak in the master bathtub. She loves her uncle, loves the Jamestone half of her family. She regrets she does not say so more.

Then Ethan sees something. A discolored bruise swirls on her neck, purple and black rings.

What's that? Ethan asks.

Billie covers it immediately, her eyes wild, seizing her throat as though strangling herself. Her breathing intensifies. The table lamp lights her face like votive candles.

Hey, you're not in trouble, Ethan says. Not with me.

Lowering her hands, she looks ready to bolt. She doesn't believe him.

Ethan rolls up his sleeves, pointing to the razormarks still visible on his forearms. This is from when I used to cut myself, he says. I was thirteen. I was in pain all the time, and I couldn't talk to anyone. Your father was the only one who helped me. You aren't alone. Remember that.

He rolls his sleeves back down.

Belinda doesn't say a word.

Eventually, they collect themselves. They leave SIZIZIS. Belinda won't tell anyone how she got the bruises on her neck until high school, when she tells the story to a therapist in Spokane. She will always remember that, when my brother noticed the injuries, he shared his scar tissue in return. She will always remember what he said about me.

BEFORE LEAVING OLYMPIA, they stop in the basement to retrieve his keys. Bailey and Evelyn are sleeping naked on the couch. Bailey is spooning Evelyn from behind, clutching her bare breasts.

What the actual fuck? Belinda whispers. Your girlfriend's a lesbian?

Come on, Ethan says.

Ethan takes his niece by the arm, rushing her outside. In the backyard, she tells him she's kissed a few girls herself. She'll protect Bailey's privacy if Ethan protects hers.

They leave for Seattle.

TONIGHT IS THE most she's ever talked to him: about the fights between Izzie and Sunshine, about how bored she is in school, and about those girls, girls, girls she loves to kiss. Boys too. That's what confuses her the most. She thought she was a lesbian. Lesbianism—in Billie's mind—is a tidy concept. This rush Belinda feels from both girl lips and boy lips, it's so messy. She's not sure if she likes one more than the other. She doesn't possess the vocabulary to talk about it.

You could be bicurious, Ethan says.

Belinda repeats the word: bicurious. The concept fills my girl with joy, the same way poetry fills her with joy.

Bicurious.

With her uncle's permission, she plugs the aux into her iPod, playing the first track off *Visions*. The music is like a demonic rave sung in a lisped falsetto. The artist, Claire Boucher, is a magnet of Belinda's attention, irresistible in her art-student allure. A subject of great bicuriosity.

When the song Oblivion comes on, my girl sings every word of the chorus. On the third replay, she turns down the volume.

Do you know where my dad is? Billie asks.

Somewhere in San Francisco, Ethan says.

Do you have his address?

Nope.

Well, Belinda says.

They cross into South King County. The Pacific Highway stalks a course parallel to the interstate. Belinda turns up the volume, playing Oblivion for a fourth time.

91 WEST ETRUSCA Street stands above them like a beacon. For the last time, Ethan looks up at the elevated Victorian structure and sees comfort.

· Fifteen ·

Overfamiliar

SHIVERING AND SILENT, cold outside and cold inside. Hanging out in her on-campus apartment for the second to last time. She dumps a cylinder of high-sodium lentil soup into a bowl, microwaving it for two minutes without ceremony. Ethan sits at the dining room table, holding a shoebox of miscellaneous items belonging to him. A charger, a sock, a toothbrush. An unopened pack of condoms. With the quarter almost over, most of Bailey's possessions are in cardboard boxes. She is on her way out, hurrying. Sick with a bad cold most of the week, she and Ethan have not discussed the night in the basement. As she sits with him, her roommates gossip.

Bailey slurps her dinner in silence.

How is it? Ethan asks.

Good.

I thought you were against microwaved dinners.

Not everyone has time to prepare elaborate meals. Not like you.

Ethan looks out the window, thinking about the first time they talked about getting married.

Are you applying for any jobs next quarter? Bailey says.

Probably not, Ethan says. Unlocked Youth is keeping me pretty busy.

Sure, Bailey says.

Sure what?

Sure, you don't need a job. Who needs a job? Everyone else is a sucker.

I'm a full-time student, Ethan says, doing what I'm supposed to be doing. Why are you getting on me about this?

God, you are so sheltered.

What is with you tonight?

It's this cold.

Do you still want me to drive you to Anacortes?

Bailey shrugs.

Evelyn can drive me.

The dinner lasts ten minutes. Bailey and Ethan sit together in a non-place with no past and no discernible horizon. Though neither will say it yet, they are already anachronisms, resisting the hour that has already come.

BEFORE ATTENDING SEMINAR, Ethan and Dale Raven sit in a forest treehouse. Despite the precarity of the shelter, nailed into the canopy of a big leaf maple, they are at peace, listening to the soft dialect of water on bark. Justin Braun climbs the crude ladder, joining them, grinning. His hair is shaved, and though he still wears designer clothing, none of it fits. He has been losing weight. He is finished with the West Coast. Really, the West Coast is finished with him.

After hosting a three-day party in his apartment with molly dealers he met in Seattle, Justin found an eviction notice pinned to his door. Upset with his passive-aggressive landlord, he took his Dodge Challenger out for a spin. A Thurston County sheriff's deputy clocked him speeding through downtown at eighty miles per hour, running several stoplights and nearly hitting multiple pedestrians. Arrested and charged with reckless driving, Justin appeared before a judge the next morning, who, after reviewing his situation, told him he could receive a suspended sentence, pending completion of a drug program. A few phone calls later, his mom's new boyfriend secured a spot for him at a detox center and spiritual retreat outside Princeton, New Jersey. The minimum stay is six weeks.

Justin expects to be there longer. He hopes to come out knowing how to love himself. He hopes to do something about his nightmares, too. But he won't get Pretty Motherfucker removed from his neck. Not just yet. The bitches, in his words, still need to know.

The boys laugh, but the laughter fades. Justin settles into the sounds of the forest. For a few minutes, he sits still. The last conversation he will ever have with Dale Raven and Ethan is over, less than half a mile from the simple dorm where they first met. He does not say what is on his mind now. Perhaps, he is thinking about the Dodge Challenger, still impounded outside the county jail. Perhaps, Justin is remembering his father, reading the *Wall Street Journal* at the dining room table, picking through eggs benedict slathered in hollandaise. Perhaps, he is beginning to understand that, in some ways, adulthood is a process of statistical reduction, a sorting out of what-can-pass from what-will-never-pass. Perhaps, Justin will be sobering up for as long as he is alive.

Perhaps, someday, he will still find his way to San Francisco.

THE JUVENILE REHABILITATION Administration pushes Loto's transfer to the Department of Corrections up by a week. At a preset hour, the DOC will collect Loto for transportation to his new cell in the high desert.

Today's visit will be his last.

In good faith, my brother drives to Moss Hill an hour before the rest of Unlocked Youth, allowing time for a goodbye. Ahead of the move, Loto is wearing the same orange jumpsuit Trevonte wears for his community service.

Today, the young men are joined by Magdalene Posala. Sitting in her blue and black TSA uniform, Loto's mother came straight from her job at the airport, where, by the grace of God, she was hired three months ago. Aside from Conner, the guard, they are alone.

The conversation is slow, halting. Magdalene Posala smiles nervously.

Thank you for coming in like this, she says. I always wished my boy could have had a role model like you.

He ain't no role model, Loto says. We're the same age. Matter of fact, I'm older. He's just here to help with my ca-reer. My ca-ca-ca-reer.

Stop that, Magdalene says.

He doesn't know what that means. Do you, Ethan?

My brother looks away.

The clock near the security station ticks.

Well, I'm still glad you had someone like him, Magdalene says. Look at where he's sitting. Look at where you're sitting. You're a man. You need to learn to be responsible. Ethan, can you keep visiting?

That won't work, Loto says. This is strictly a Moss Hill-type thing. He's done his part and I've done mine. He's like those Mormon kids that take a trip to the hood and build houses for the poor. I'm your good work, ain't I, Ethan?

Magdalene Posala glares.

With fifteen minutes remaining, Loto is done indulging this conversation. He gestures for Ethan to stand up with him. When Ethan does, his mentee seizes his shirt, clenching the collar, pulling him close. The guard screams.

Hey!

Loto leans into Ethan's ear, almost hissing.

I killed five boys. Killed them one by one. The judge gave me two-hundred years. What it is, cuzz? What that Rollin' 90s like? What that S.O.S. like?

He releases my brother just as Conner rushes over with his pepper spray. In an instant, Loto is in handcuffs. The guard puts a hard hand on his neck, practically shoving him out of the visitor center. Backup comes running from the yard.

Loto winks.

Don't let them catch you slippin', my guy. See you in Cali. Stay dangerous.

Magdalene looks at Ethan in fear. She follows the C.O., trying to maintain closeness with her only son before he is taken to the maximum-security bus.

Ethan leaves.

The guard at the main entrance unlocks the steel doors, letting him out. Returning to his Jetta, my brother turns on the radio and closes his eyes. He will wait like this until the van arrives from Sword Fern State, when he can debrief with Diana and Luis.

IN TOTAL, MY brother and Loto Posala spend fifteen hours together. Slightly more than half a day.

BEFORE ETHAN DRIVES back to Oly, Bailey sends a text, asking him to swing by her apartment.

SHE TELLS HIM he's the most wonderful boy she's ever dated. Maybe someday they will work out. But for now, they are over.

What if I agreed to try polyamory? Ethan asks.

My emo doofus, Bailey says. I need to focus on my art now. Get closer to my family.

How am I keeping you from doing that?

Look. In a few years, after we've established ourselves in the world, maybe we can be together. Okay?

Are we breaking up or not?

Bailey sits with him on the bed, resting her head on his shoulder, forcing a final moment of peace. She asks if he can take the recycling on his way out. He tries not to run out of her once-welcoming door.

IN THE LIVING room of the house in Queen Anne, he watches television with our parents. Takeout from Pandasia steams on the coffee table. Spinach pot stickers, Mongolian beef, yellow curry chicken. Pepper, the black Labrador, circles with covetousness.

Tonight is an emergency movie night. Dad's home early. It is not clear how much he's already had to drink.

He and Mom sit on opposite ends of the leather sofa. The television is tuned to a Martin Scorsese marathon. Mom doesn't like Scorsese, and spends the evening on her phone. Sometimes, she'll tap Ethan on the shoulder, asking either a practical question, like does his car need an oil change, or if he's heard the latest about Belinda, who is hellbent on enrolling in an alternative middle school.

Dad drinks beer after beer. Mom texts nonstop with Logan Rivers.

In the intermission between *Goodfellas* and *Raging Bull*, Mom and Ethan clean the dishes. Dad takes Pepper to the wood-chipped enclosure on the side of the house for a final bathroom break. Then Mom excuses herself for an early bedtime. When Dad comes inside, he goes into his home office behind the laundry room. When he reemerges, he marches straight upstairs.

The yelling begins.

Pepper hops on the sofa. As she always does during fights, she paws at Ethan.

On the TV, the boxer Jake LaMotta descends into Hell, pounding the hard wall of the Dade County Stockade, screaming, infantile and horrific. By the end of the film, my brother is ready for bed. He turns off the lights, goes up to his room with Pepper.

Down the hallway, Mom and Dad are still fighting.

Under the covers, Ethan looks up at the nighttime ceiling, the same skylight view from his childhood. He sleeps a few hard hours.

HE WILL BE astonished by his memories.

Hiking with Mom and Dad in the Methow Valley. Lazy weekends at home, reading the Sunday paper. Annual tickets to see *The Nutcracker* performed by the Pacific Northwest Ballet, the sets and costumes designed by Maurice Sendak. Mom and Dad taking my brother around the University of Washington, showing him the Drumheller Fountain, where a study session turned into a first date. Mom, remembering how Mount Rainier's alpenglow resembled the cherry blossoms.

He will be astonished.

AT 3:16 A.M., Dad slams the front door, slams it so hard a window shatters, the same one I broke seven years earlier with a bottle of wine.

He pounds down the twenty-seven steps.

His hybrid screeches down the hillside towards Nickerson, hurtling towards the Ship Canal before taking a sharp U-turn towards the top of Queen Anne Hill. His outburst is the only sound in the neighborhood. Coldness seeps into the house. In his bedroom, fear passes through Ethan like ionized particles.

Forty-five minutes later, they get a phone call.

THE COLLISION TAKES place a block from Maynard Middle School. The homeless man is lying in a pool of blood, his body crooked almost beyond recognition. But for the police officer assigned to this safest of neighborhoods, he is easy to identify. Eugene, the old man who always claimed Grandpa Hugh fired him, is dead.

Dad killed him.

A bank security camera recorded everything. The relevant footage—the moment of impact, the body rolling across the asphalt, our father stepping out of his car, our father returning inside, our father attempting to drive away—is only eleven seconds long.

Dad is already booked into jail, mere blocks from his downtown office. He does not want to speak. Everything the family learns, they learn from the police.

Manslaughter in the Second Degree.

Felony hit and run.

Driving under the influence.

For now, Hunter Jamestone will be placed in protective custody, at least before his preliminary hearing. Despite registering a blood alcohol level of 0.17%, he seems to comprehend what he has done. The judge will likely prohibit cash bail. His jailers consider him suicidal. This is why they called our mother.

THIS IS HOW we lose Seattle. The house in Queen Anne.

This is how.

Mom files for divorce and moves in with Logan Rivers. Ethan returns to Oly. Dale Raven does not leave his side. One day, Ethan will tell me he never missed me more than he did then. Despite the past, despite everything, he thought I would understand.

A FEW DAYS later, Ethan is sitting with Bailey inside the Anacortes Ferry Terminal, waiting for the vessel that will take her to Orcas Island. Outside, cormorants and seagulls jockey atop rotting columns of wood. Drizzle blurs the Salish Sea into the clouds. In the distance, my brother can see the silhouettes of the San Juans.

He is here because he owed her one last favor.

Bailey's father, Philip Voclaine, has agreed to represent Dad pro bono. Even with that support, the situation is bleak. Dad has been fired by Howard, Warwick, and Moore, who are now also suing him for breach of contract due to his gross misconduct. The Washington State Bar Association has already terminated Dad's license to practice law.

As my brother floats in a trance, Bailey taps his shoulder.

The ferry is docking. In his condition, Ethan failed to notice the arrival of the three-story vessel. One by one, foot passengers filter into the alcove, forming a line. Tossing her unfinished clam chowder into a nearby trash can, Bailey produces her ticket. Ethan slides off his stool. They look into one another's eyes.

My dad will not let this go, Bailey says. He's going to fight and he's going to win.

She picks up her suitcase.

Wait, Ethan says.

I need to go, Bailey says.

I love you.

Don't you get it? Bailey says. This was never supposed to last. I wanted some dick and I let things go too far. You spoiled me, and you had a car, and for a while, being with you was easier than breaking up with you. It's my fault. Is that what you need to hear?

She takes out her seashell earrings, placing them in his palm. She kisses his cheek, and vanishes into the crowd.

Gone.

Ethan leaves the earrings on a stool. Someone else's lucky find. He stumbles through the terminal, tears in his eyes, unbelieving. And yet.

After relieving himself in the restroom, he steps out of the broad wooden building and into the visitor parking lot. He looks at the hundreds of vehicles idling in the lanes, ready to board the ship.

Ready to go anywhere.

He returns to the Jetta. Driving towards the North Cascades Highway, his eyes drift over Fidalgo Island, the hills and farms of Skagit County. The clouds break over the mountains, revealing snowpacked peaks, a thousand-mile ridge. Merging onto I-5, Ethan wonders what lies beyond the end of the Cascades.

EIGHTEEN HOURS LATER, he will be on the streets of San Francisco.

· Sixteen ·

The Old Siskiyou Trail

Your eyes trace the Great Hermit like the moonlit end of the universe. Nine miles from the summit, you stand alone in a high-altitude village, looking up, your vision fusing with the stratovolcano, its alloy of glacier and rock, its hyper-dimensions, its enormity. The season is transitioning, winter becoming spring, the snowpack thawing into rivers, cycling into the roots of trees. As the tundra melts, the crevasses widen, crags exposing themselves to fresh oxygen. In your private audience with the colossus, you see a boulder slip from its angle of repose. Ceding a position held since the Ice Age, the boulder rolls and rolls, taking the shape of a house, a Victorian built in 1893, a house whose position upon its hill can never be reclaimed. Falling, falling, falling.

Falling forever into California.

You are interrupted by police lights. A small-town cop, blond and muscular, steps out of his SUV. As he saunters towards you, you realize you are standing in the middle of an intersection at two o'clock in the morning. He shines his flashlight.

Sir? Is everything okay?

You gesture at the Great Hermit. The cop peers at your eyes, checking your pupils. When he asks where you're staying tonight, you say you're traveling through.

Where is your destination this morning, sir?

San Francisco.

What's in San Francisco?

My brother.

Does your brother live in a house or an apartment?

He lives in a bookstore.

The cop shines his light on your Jetta, parked by a storefront displaying purple crystals. He notes your Washington plates, and asks if you need somewhere to rest. The police station keeps a few cots for when people get stranded during blizzards. You decline. He waits for you to return inside your vehicle before returning inside his. You turn the key in the ignition, activating your headlights. The cop resumes his patrol, cruising the backstreets. You begin navigating away from the town's main boulevard, resuming your abandonment down the West Coast.

THE INTERSTATE DESCENDS out of Shasta-Trinity National Forest. In Redding, strip malls flicker against three a.m. shadows. Palm trees and cacti grow in the dust of car dealerships.

Nobody sees you.

Nobody wants to see you.

Red Bluff passes. The terrain flattens. The Sacramento Valley is a dream. Deep soil churns with isopods and centipedes. This is land without a ceiling. Cottonwoods huddle like wraiths over rest stops. Grain mills cluster by warehouses and machines. This is the suboceanic plain, compressed by fifteen-thousand pounds of pressure per square inch. Your windshield strains, threatening to detonate. A thousand insects splatter against the glass.

Your momentum slows. In Tehama County—exurban homes, olive orchards—you pull into a gas station. Sitting on the curb behind the convenience store, a young woman in a magenta prom dress sits barefoot, weeping into her hands, high heels and phone lying on the asphalt. A man with chalk-colored skin circles on a bicycle. He veers down an unnamed road, jolted by amphetamine. The woman in the prom dress notices you. She tries to hide her face.

You refill your gas tank, paying by credit card.

Paying with our father's name.

ORANGE AND BLUE light melts into the East Bay. Melts like hot wax. The road curves and curves, undoing the linearity of north to south. Oakland's industrial shoulder shields itself under a yellow glow. Signs divert commuters to Berkeley, Vallejo, San Jose.

San Francisco.

I-80 expands to ten lanes. You pull into a toll plaza, a dozen booths wide, paying five dollars to the operator, a heavyset man with salt-and-pepper eyebrows. He inspects the bills before handing you a receipt.

Can I return this for a city of equal or lesser value? you ask.

Something I would say.

You drive on. Traffic reaccelerates. After traversing nine-hundred miles of mountain and river and drought-stricken valley, the final two miles are over the Bay Bridge, towering like a metropolitan skyline unto itself.

For three minutes, you glide.

Halfway across, a sign welcomes you to the City and County. But you are no nearer.

I am no nearer.

AT THE CORNER of Geary and Larkin.

Past the anarcho-tech promises of Market Street, past the luxury stores of Union Square, you come to a neighborhood of SRO hotels and fire escapes, liquor stores and street art. Mayhem and more mayhem. Here in the Tenderloin, a boombox is playing. A makeshift marketplace spreads out on dirty blankets, bins of boosted electronics and bootleg DVDs. The alleys reek of piss and shit, weed and alcohol. Brothers and sisters shout in recognition, laughing, pounding fists, embracing. Graffiti and stickers swarm every surface, an open rebellion of profane cartoons, civil rights martyrs, and sexual provocations. Taggers repeat their signatures in bold colors. On the corners, working women flaunt themselves, enticing customers. SFPD patrol cars rocket past, chasing down felonies, lights blazing. Subversive coffeehouses and collectivist galleries lease spaces next to nightclubs and sex stores. Young professionals stride by with gourmet coffee, averting their eyes. Post-dawn light touches every surface of the city.

You roll into a motel and turn off your engine. Iron bars protect the garage from the streets. Suddenly, you feel the last twenty-four hours in your body, pounding in your head. You get out and enter the lobby. A tired woman in a business suit looks up from a computer. She does not greet you.

I'd like to rent a room, you say. Do you have any nonsmoking singles?

Are you twenty-one? she says.

Yes, you say.

Let me see your ID, she says.

Your face reddens.

Can you recommend somewhere else around here I can stay? you ask.

Nope, she says.

You ask if you can sit in a nearby armchair. She shrugs and types. You sit and pull out your phone. You look through your contacts.

You call up Dale Raven, tell him where you are, and how you got here.

Holy shit, Dale Raven says.

He says he'll call his sister. Cheryl Raven, the artist in the Mission. He hangs up.

Cheryl Raven texts you. She's sorry for all you've been through. Her space is cramped but she has a couch. You can stay for a couple nights, or more. It's chill. Someone is modeling for her this morning. She hopes you're cool with naked women lol.

You text back. She sends the address. On Google Maps, you see she's forty minutes away on foot. You're so tired of driving. You send your gratitude, then call Dale Raven again. Despite this rendezvous with madness, you plan to be in Oly within a couple days.

You return to the counter.

Are there any decent parking garages nearby? you ask.

Ours is decent, the woman says. Park as long as you want.

Really?

Seven dollars an hour, thirty for a day. Cash only. You can use the ATM.

She points to a machine by the brochure stand. Resigned to your options, you submit your debit card, type in your four-digit pin, and withdraw two twenty-dollar bills. Next to you, tourist pamphlets advertise the Golden Gate Bridge, the Esplanade, the Palace of Fine Arts. Five miles down Geary Boulevard, North America comes to an end at Ocean Beach.

You pay for parking, receiving a ticket for the dashboard.

We are not liable for theft, the woman says. Take out all your valuables.

But your valuables are all behind you: your laptop, your phone charger, your toiletries, your change of clothes. All in the Pacific Northwest.

In San Francisco, you are only what you came with.

Not much more than a name.

You return to the garage, mulling over whether to purchase replacement items. These thoughts come to a halt when you notice a man peering into the back of your Jetta. He is young and pale, lean with muscle, dressed in a gray undershirt, black sneakers, a backwards snapback, and denim capris. A thin gold chain loops around his neck. He carries a cardboard box filled with picture books and children's clothing.

The skinny man sees you. He glares, then notices the keys in your hand. He smiles.

Hello, he says. I stays at Vacaville.

His smile widens.

Before you can say anything, he hurries off with his box, slipping into the conspiracies of the neighborhood.

You sit in the driver's seat, placing the ticket on the dashboard. Your cellphone vibrates in the pocket of your hoodie.

Mom.

THE ATM CHARGE triggers the immediate attention of the bank's fraud department, which contacts your mother to confirm the withdrawal. Mom asks where you are.

You tell her.

She breaks down crying. She believes you when you say you will come home, that you just need time. For now, our mother can muse about how both her sons are in San Francisco.

You ask about Dad.

Dad's attorney believes he can get the felonies reduced to misdemeanors. Footage from the security camera shows Old Man Eugene staggering into the intersection without looking, his movements erratic, his gait unstable. Philip Voclaine is convinced he can pull someone from the neighborhood to testify to the hazard Eugene posed. This was not the first time he endangered himself by darting into the road. Anybody who knows Queen Anne knows the risk he presented.

Misdemeanors are the good news. But Dad is still disbarred. Howard, Warwick, and Moore are refusing to compensate his stake in the firm or provide a severance package. That is their privilege.

You and Mom do not talk about the divorce. You don't ask about Logan Rivers.

Mom winds down the conversation, passing along a few other details. For now, Pepper is at a kennel in Interbay. Isadora and Belinda are in Spokane, touring apartments.

Until you come home, nobody from our family will visit Dad in jail.

FOR YOU, THE Mission District begins underneath Highway 101. In a city of architecture imported from across the globe— bay windows, gothic spires, guardian stone lions, pagodas, Islamic minarets, Art Deco vanity, the gold-domed splendor of

City Hall—the tents and tarps tell the most relevant story. You try not to stray too close. You look and you don't look.

Mission Street.

Bright colors popping against a sky of coastal fog. Palm trees soaring over terracotta apartments. Fruit stands and bakeries and quinceñera dress shops. Zoot suits and luchador masks. Taquerias and beauty parlors. Bubble tea and craft cocktails. Laundromats. A homeless crowd huddled around the entrance of the 16th Street BART Station, a pair of pale tech boys speeding through, grimacing at the feces and syringes, one commenting to the other about the dangers of public transportation. Nearby, a silver and red Muni competes with a pearlescent lowrider in traffic. The lowrider skates ahead on spinning rims, mesmerizing in their twenty-six-inch diameters. Outside a salon, a construction worker helps a gruff old man to his feet, grinning in fraternal warmth, asking the man if he is Indian.

Aztec, the man says.

Murals are everywhere: murals condemning the school-to-prison pipeline, murals celebrating refugees and domestic workers, murals dedicated to landscapes of desert and river. Mesoamerican priests, celestial goddesses. Art as activism, art as salve against the aggressive blandness of gentrification. On 24th Street, you pass an educator gesticulating at a portrait of César Chávez. Last night, the educator says to a journalist, gangbangers pumped the UFW flag with bulletholes, Sureños escalating tensions with Norteños, who use the huelga bird as a symbol. Decontextualized from the labor rights movement, the eagle is a proxy for territorial strife.

I killed five boys. Killed them one by one. The judge gave me two-hundred years. What it is, cuzz?

See you in Cali. Stay dangerous.

You reach the corner of 24th and Shotwell, where Cheryl Raven lives above a Central American travel agency. To the side of the orange building, a metal door protects the stairwell. Buzzing Cheryl Raven's sanctuary, you wait, yawning.

She bounds down the stairs, barefoot with rolled-up jeans, a white smock, and a white t-shirt. Unlike her brother's tall and gangly frame, she is petite. Her hair his thick and black like his, but shorter, tied in a bun. Like Dale Raven, she also wears circular spectacles.

Ethan?

You nod.

Cheryl Raven throws her arms around you in a deep hug.

On the way up, Dale Raven's sister describes her living situation. Tenement style, sharing one toilet with six other units. The shower is out of order, and her kitchen is nothing more than a microwave, a hot plate, and a mini-fridge, which she shares with her roommate. The rent is nine-hundred per person, the best she can hope for. Her home is her studio.

She opens the door.

Her roommate looks at you, fiery yet Zenlike. She is naked, her dark hair free-flowing, her back muscular. She sits on her knees, hips and posterior compacted, strong arms plunging into her bare thighs. Her pose is a concentration of power. Discipline.

Cheryl Raven closes her door, giggling. She introduces the model: Sheila Delgado, born and raised in the Mission. Her best friend. At night, they tend the same bar, a nebulous place where coders and streetworkers commiserate. As San Francisco spins around them, their labor and joy are their tethers to the city.

As Dale Raven's sister takes her place behind her easel, you plop onto the purple couch beneath the window, and plug your phone into a spare charger. You sleep at last. Sometimes, you awaken to car horns, jackhammers, arguments. A neighbor down the hall screams at telenovelas. Sunlight and shadows pass over you. Sheila does not seem to move, an idol of restraint. When the painting session ends, the model clothes herself in blue dungarees, a pink t-shirt, a pink bandana, and pink shoes.

Cheryl Raven invites you to see her work.

Sheila's likeness is unmistakable, transposed to a stormy coastline off the Olympic Peninsula. Her lower body sits in a tidepool, a silver glittering mermaid tail nicked by barnacles, calloused by saltwater. Rough winds batter the rainforest behind her. Out in the waves, a rugged rock looms, piercing the sky as albatrosses circle their colony. The rock and the mermaid are twins of mineral and myth. Indestructible. Not even a squall could tear them apart.

I call her the Salmon Girl, Cheryl Raven says. Honest opinions only.

You say nothing.

Cheryl Raven winks.

She asks what you need now. She has the afternoon free. Sheila too.

GOLDEN BEER BOTTLES lie scattered across the steps of a cathedral. Homeless men sleep in the doorway. Schoolchildren run past, chasing and taunting each other, backpacks bouncing. Adjoining the cathedral is a small pueblo: La Misión de San Francisco de Asís, the European entry point for Yerba Buena. A modest white building, accented by a slight wooden balcony, a wooden crucifix on its roof. A small cemetery provides the final resting place for two and a half centuries of San Franciscans, thin slabs of concrete commemorating Indigenous souls, Californio souls, Mexican souls; American souls. In the center of the burial grounds, a thatched hut recreates the traditional homes of the Ohlone and Yelamu peoples.

After lunch at Taqueria Cancun, you stroll by the pink duplex on Lucky Street where Sheila grew up, where her parents still reside. Her father is a history teacher at Mission High School, and a local union leader. Her mother works as a special-needs educator. Many of Sheila's childhood friends have moved away, either inland or to the Pacific Northwest. Some have been deported.

In Balmy Alley, she consecrates them all.

The three of you stand in front of a masterpiece painted across somebody's garage door, protected by Precita Eyes. Two versions of the artist float above two versions of California, staring at each other across a vast gulf. The Sheila Delgado on the left is heartbroken and nude. In the Golden State beneath her, families huddle under mounds of post-earthquake rubble, flames engulfing the streets, babies coughing under smoke. The Other Sheila is blonde, blue-eyed, and white, clothed in a business skirt and jacket embroidered with startup logos. Under her computer-chipped heels, the Other California is prospering, citadels filled with silicon businessmen. Refugees from the destroyed California try to immigrate across the Bay Bridge, only to be blocked by a tollbooth named Encomienda. Underneath the bridge pulses an enormous *Lotería* heart. A ribbon around the heart says:

Mi Corazón es un Terremoto.

Lingering in appreciation, you relocate to the soccer field across the street, sitting on benches beneath a dripping eucalyptus. Cheryl Raven leaves for the restroom. For the first time, you and Sheila are alone. The muralist has long since transfigured herself from the unspeaking muse you first met.

She studies you.

Your brother lives in City Lights, Sheila says.

What?

The bookstore in North Beach. Rumor has it Lawrence Ferlinghetti is letting him stay in a room on the second floor. Your brother's Terrell Jamestone, right?

How do you know that? you say.

I got a friend who works at a teashop in Chinatown. Your brother comes in all the time, when he's not getting drunk at Vesuvio. He strums his guitar over Kerouac Alley. Tourists love him.

You run your hands through your hair.

Are you certain?

This city kills certainty. But I'm certain.

Sheila takes out a pack of cigarettes. Cheryl Raven returns. You take out your phone, typing on a map.

3.7 miles.

You stand up to use the restroom.

On your way in, you notice two spray-painted figures. A shirtless man in baggy jeans and boots, wearing a bandana with the corners tied over his forehead. A teenage girl, a flower in her hair, an infant in her arms. In scrawling letters, the artist mourns them both:

Lesane & Brenda.

Rest in Paradise.

YOU STEP INTO City Lights.

From the outside, the store defies the steep incline of Columbus Avenue, leveling out its hardwood floors and inventory of literature. Every form of fiction, art criticism, countercultural dissent, radical histories, and alternative economics fills the main floor, aisles crammed with shoppers, some in reverent awe.

You hike up to the Poetry Room.

Behind the shelves of verse, a dark wooden door stands almost hidden in the corner with a sign: Private Residence.

You put your hand on the knob. You try to turn it. Your hand slips, then slips again. Your palms are drenched. When you find your grip, the door won't budge. You could knock, but you don't.

You sit in a rocking chair.

Nobody else sets foot in the Poetry Room.

You stand up. You leave.

On the stairwell, you stop at a series of black-and-white photographs. In one, Allen Ginsberg, balding and bearded, hangs out with the poet Michael McClure and a baby-faced Bob Dylan, sharing cigarettes. In another, Neal Cassady shaves over a sink, a drawing taped to the mirror, a naked woman and the words, Clothed or Nude: We Are Not Obscene. Ginsberg reappears in another photo, sitting shirtless in his kitchen, eating cornflake cereal out of a dog dish. The photos are by a college student named Larry Keenan.

Suddenly, you get why I'm here. To be canonized. This is what I want.

More than my family, more than my daughter, more than you.

This dream of myself.

You step outside, hurrying beneath the fire escape where I am rumored to play guitar. You stumble into Chinatown: lanterns strung between dense buildings, upturned roof eaves, business signage in Cantonese. Restaurants and seafood wholesalers, tea shops and retirement homes. Hoodies and robes wave on a clothesline. You cannot hear any distinct noise, only the crowd. But for a moment, you think you hear my drawl singing over an acoustic twang.

Three more years pass.

2015

· Aberdeen ·

· Seventeen ·

Death of a Meritocrat

HE DIES IN an instant on a narrow, steel-trussed bridge, his black hybrid hurtling into a logging truck bound for Port Angeles, glass and metal exploding over the Sol Duc River. State troopers descend upon the scene, canvassing and setting up roadblocks on either end of this remote stretch of Highway 101.

For such total destruction, WSDOT dispatchers estimate the hybrid must have been traveling at eighty miles per hour. The truck driver confirms that, somehow, the collision felt intentional. Right before the moment of impact, the decedent's vehicle seemed to have been accelerating.

State troopers take a statement. No charges will be filed. By the luck of the angle, the logging truck has sustained minimal damage. But the remains of the victim and his machine are collected piece by piece. Eventually, a wallet is recovered. A driver's license is found intact.

An identity assembles itself.

He was a software development engineer at Amazon, a position held for only two weeks, overlapping with the conclusion of a part-time internship at a solar panel startup in Bremerton. Three months out of college, the young man had been living in Seattle while commuting back and forth across Puget Sound. His excursion to the Peninsula was supposed to provide a reprieve between the end of one opportunity and the beginning of another.

A provisional timeline is created of his last twenty-four hours. On the last half-day of his internship, he visited the hot springs near the restored Elwha River, soaking in solitude, absorbing the late-summer woods. Trekking into Port Angeles, he spent the night alone at a motel, perhaps taking an evening walk along the Strait of Juan de Fuca, looking out at vast stacks of timber in the harbor. He turned in early. Rising in the darkness, he seemed to time his departure so that he would arrive at the Pacific Ocean by sunrise. But his calculations, somehow, were off.

He died a minute after dawn.

His next of kin is notified. This is when the grief begins. *Queen Anne & Magnolia News* runs a notice about the death, which is also picked up by *The Seattle Times*. His alma mater— from which he received a Bachelor's in Science, earning a Joint Major in Computer Science and Linguistics, with Distinction—also receives word. The student newspaper, *The Stanford Daily*, runs his obituary. Former peers from the Class of 2014 remember his agile intellect, his astounding work ethic, his ability to balance his studies with his secondary career as a competitive chess player.

A public vigil is held in Magnolia. A private funeral takes place for family and friends at the First Unitarian Church. In public and private, the stated cause of the accident is sleep deprivation.

Seconds before dying, the story goes, he fell asleep behind the wheel.

As the months pass, his parents set up a memorial website in his honor. They petition Clallam County to rename the bridge for their child, and team up with driver safety advocates to spread awareness on the dangers of driving while tired. They start an internship in his name at Stanford for students who are majoring in two subjects, and have an interest in competitive chess.

For those who knew him only for his successes, the life of Wilhelm Kunst culminated in a starting salary of $100,000 a year and a two-bedroom luxury apartment in South Lake Union. The rest belongs to the rainforest.

FEBRUARY 2015. MY brother steps into the lower residential hallway at Queets Recovery House. He is here, at 11 p.m., to relieve the assistant supervisor from the folding chair outside a client's open door. Smiling as Ethan switches him out, Mr. Josiah, a slight and balding New Orleanian, whispers some quick advice.

He's only pretending to be asleep. Don't let that knucklehead fool you.

Ethan nods.

I'll be back at six-thirty for the transport, Mr. Josiah says. Jens will be working a double through the afternoon. You can clock out when Eliza gets here. You need anything?

I'm good.

Did you pack a meal?

My brother holds up a brown paper bag. Mr. Josiah nods.

You'll do fine, he says. If things get out of control, call 911. Jens has your back. Remember to stay calm. We haven't had a level-three in years. Hopefully, this is the last overnight I need from you for a long time.

The assistant supervisor ascends the stairs to the office. Jens, the full-time overnight staff, has taken his station at the computer. Bearded and surly, he surveys the two residential floors with dispassionate eyes, giving Ethan a curt nod before attending to his emails.

Inside the bedroom, a seventeen-year-old client named Eddy is on suicide watch, requiring staff to be within three feet of him at all times. Cutmarks were found on his wrists, along with an illegible farewell note on his desk. Until his transfer to a more secure facility, he is only allowed to wear hospital scrubs, so that if he escapes, he will be easy to identify. Per the fire code, the window to his room cannot be locked. If he opens up and runs out, staff are not allowed to pursue. An alarm will notify police, who will chase the runaway through the wet night.

For his protection, staff have removed everything from his room except the furniture and a framed picture on his dresser: county fair caricatures, drawn before his painkiller addiction, of Eddy and his best friend, a boy who looks just like him, but blond.

Ethan unwraps an energy bar. Eddy snickers. He rolls over on his thin mattress, a chubby-cheeked kid with a shaved head. In a theatrical whisper, he calls out, Hey…Hey!

My brother watches him in his peripheral vision.

Can I tell you a story? Eddy says.

Picking up the framed caricatures, he taps on his best friend.

See this guy? Eddy says. He's a pig fucker. Literally.

Ethan says nothing.

The FBI was tracking him, Eddy says. For months, he was posting pictures of himself fucking pigs on his family's farm. We got these drawings at the Kitsap County Fair a few weeks before the arrest, so he was already doing it then—fucking the pigs, I mean. He never told me about it. He used to be my best friend.

The seventeen-year-old sets the caricatures back down.

All I ever wanted was to be normal, he says.

My brother clears his throat.

Jens's eyes dart up.

But the teenager soon falls asleep. Jens returns to his paperback novel. My brother stays seated in the uncomfortable folding chair. His mind flits to the periodic creaks of the house we grew up in, 91 West Etrusca Street settling on its foundation. He hears the reassuring grunts of Pepper as she sleeps on the living room couch, the occasional hum of buses on their early routes.

The night is uneventful.

MR. JOSIAH RETURNS at six twenty-five a.m., cheerful in his soft-spoken way. When he comes downstairs, Eddy is at his window, looking at the dripping pine boughs, dark circles under his eyes.

How'd he do? Mr. Josiah asks.

Chatty at first, Ethan says. But he stayed safe.

Good, good. Eddy, your mom is waiting. We've already packed your stuff. Are you ready to say goodbye?

The seventeen-year-old turns around.

Is it true you survived Hurricane Katrina? he asks.

I did, Mr. Josiah says.

Is it true you've got a kid with leukemia?

Put on your flip-flops, Mr. Josiah says. We'll talk about it on the way to Fairfax.

Slipping on his footwear, Eddy shuffles past my brother and up the stairs, Mr. Josiah in tow. They are bound for the most intensive teen psychiatric care unit in the Pacific Northwest.

Ethan sets the chair against the wall. He does a final sweep through Eddy's room and notices that the framed caricatures were left behind on the dresser. He takes the memento to the office.

Upstairs, Jens emerges. A handful of residents come out of their rooms before rollcall, teenage boys in white t-shirts, black shorts, and white socks. They join Jens for morning exercises. Warm-up stretches, push-ups, and crunches, their movements synchronized to their thick and hairy leader. Towards the end, they sit in place, meditating, reclaiming their minds with their bodies, reclaiming themselves from the dependencies that brought them here.

Eliza—young and tough, with a lime-green pixie cut—comes through the front door at exactly seven a.m. She passes my brother on his way out. A short hello. She knows what she needs to know. Jens will update her on everything else.

RAIN RUSHES TO the storm drain near the Wishkah River. Dad and Dale Raven stand outside the cinnamon-colored house at 67 Simmons Street, drinking black coffee. Dad is in jeans, a white flannel jacket, and black boots. He is unshaven, his appearance both gentle and grizzled. Dale Raven's hair is in a ponytail, a ponytail he could never wear in the Aberdeen of his childhood.

Across the street, an ambulance idles in front of an abandoned house. Still charred from a fire, plywood boards cover every entrance, except for the front, which the emergency technicians have removed.

What happened? Ethan asks.

Overdose, Dad says. Someone called it in at dawn.

Fentanyl? Ethan says.

Probably.

An SUV for the Aberdeen Police Department arrives at the scene. A heavyset cop steps out. Should have torn it down years ago, the cop says, looking at the house. No one deserves to die like that.

How was your shift? Dad asks.

I got through it, Ethan says.

You staying with Holly this weekend?

Yup. I'm gonna try to sleep for a few hours first, then hit the road. My next shift isn't til Tuesday. I'll probably be back Monday night.

Say, friend, Dale Raven says. Mind giving me a lift to Montesano? I need to see my mom.

My brother nods. Dale Raven steps out of the rain. Before Ethan goes inside, Dad puts a hand on his shoulder.

Are you still doing that consultation with Mr. Robbin?

This afternoon.

One-hundred dollars for ninety minutes is a steal, Dad says.

The gas might add up, Ethan says. Driving out to Olympia and back every other week. But I'll make it work if it's a decent match.

Good, Dad says.

Do you have a meeting this morning? Ethan asks.

Every Friday, Wednesday, and Monday, Dad says.

A second SUV rolls up. The arriving officer assists in cordoning off the scene. My brother and father step into their home before the EMTs can haul out the remains of the overdosed. The body of a teenage boy, sealed in a plastic bag, protected perhaps for the only time.

· Eighteen ·

Mycelia

PER THE TERMS of his release, Dad is required to keep a permanent address within the State of Washington. After serving a reduced sentence in the King County Correctional Facility, he took a four-hour bus ride to Aberdeen, collecting the key to his childhood home from the deposit box I set up in January 2005.

When he unlocked the door, he expected the worst. Syringes, graffiti, a squatter or two. What he found instead was ecology: water stains on the ceiling; moss on the windowsills; mushrooms sprouting out of the carpet. Though unoccupied for over a decade, some invisible force had held destruction at bay. My father's childhood home was uninhabited, not uninhabitable.

Dad's probation officer scored him a part-time job at one of those big home improvement stores on the highway. Because he is no longer allowed to hold a driver's license, he commutes to and from his shifts by Grays Harbor Transit. When he has shifts, he aches, hauling slabs of granite for customers, operating saws, hoisting boxes up ladders, standing at the cash register. He has no control over the hours assigned to him, and has no prospect of moving to full-time employment until he's put in two years. Though he can't even count on working as a legal consultant these days, he holds onto the idea of something with healthcare, or paid time off.

His recovery meetings keep him grounded. He is still sober.

Mom lives in Montana.

Ethan was the second to arrive in Aberdeen. For the first six months after graduating from Sword Fern State, he was rejected from every position he applied to in his field. Behavior specialist, case manager, social worker, resource coordinator, life skills educator. Fast food joints and retail chains didn't want him either, his degree disqualifying because it was overqualifying. The irony, as Dad would tell him, is that Aberdeen used to be one of the best job markets around for a young man like him. In Grandpa Hugh's day, you just had to be able-bodied. Show up at a mill, a logging camp, the longshoremen's hall. That was that. If only Hugh Jamestone were alive to see his legacy.

Until Ethan met Mr. Josiah, every door was closed.

Dale Raven was the third to arrive. In certain circles, Dale Raven is now famous. In others, notorious. After Sword Fern

State announced plans to tear down the Coast Salish Longhouse rather than repair it, he led an occupation of the collapsed structure. A biology professor named Marc Visser sent out a series of emails across campus, ridiculing the tribes for needing taxpayer money to prop up their culture. Student protests erupted outside Professor Visser's classroom, leading to widespread condemnation. Jeffrey Seaholt penned a column decrying Sword Fern State's excessive tolerance of free speech. He proposed reclassifying verbal assault as a form of physical assault, and suggested Big Tech turn over the accounts of student organizers to the FBI.

In a viral response, Dale Raven called horseshit on the idea that speech was violence, or that free speech could even exist on a private platform. Social media is a machine to make profits, he reminded everyone. A dead end where the powers that be monitor and neutralize dissent. Social media is not a public square, and it is certainly not a foundation for effective or lasting activism. The greatest threats to public discourse in America are Silicon Valley, the Pentagon, and Wall Street. Until you challenge the power of those institutions, the Bill of Rights is irrelevant.

Nobody liked hearing that.

Eventually, police swept the protesters out with flash-bang grenades. Nobody was arrested. The Longhouse is still slated to be torn down. But Dale Raven got to meet his hero, Billy Frank Jr., who admired the young man's courage. Now he works for a furniture company, living with his best friend, planning his horizon.

Like the unyielding flows of the Wishkah and Chehalis Rivers, the three men move forward. With Dad's employee discount, Ethan and Dale Raven purchase cheap tools to upgrade 67 Simmons Street from livable to comfortable. Slowly, they are succeeding. Evenings are times of quiet reflection: conversation and reading, activities for which my father rediscovered his love in jail.

Most of the Jamestone family's Queen Anne belongings are in a storage unit in Seattle, too expensive to move. The only major possession that made its way to Grays Harbor was the baby grand piano, which now sits in the living room, unplayed.

AFTER RECUPERATING FROM his shift, Ethan visits the therapist, Mr. Robbin. The office is cozy, tucked into the brass-and-marble Security Building in downtown Olympia. Mr. Robbin, a late middle-aged man with thick arms and a silver beard, is a kind and patient listener. Prior to his career in mental healthcare, he served in the Coast Guard, mostly at Cape Disappointment. Applying the Hakomi Method of mind-body balance, he listens to Ethan talk about Aberdeen, his melancholy and his anxiety.

He tells the therapist about his work as an on-call residential drug counselor, filling gaps in the schedule. Queets Recovery House, which relies on money allocated from the state budget, is always underfunded, keeping open only ten of its fifteen beds. The juvenile residents are assigned there by court order, fulfilling rehab as an alternative to jailtime. Rough boys with rough stories. In a typical week, Ethan works between ten and twenty hours. Thirty is a blessing. The pay is $11.50 per hour. Before taxes.

Do you think about that number a lot? Mr. Robbin asks.

Yes, Ethan says.

He tells the therapist about Wilhelm Kunst. Not only his death, but the six-figure salary he commanded.

That's a lot money for anybody, Mr. Robbin says. I don't make anywhere near that. If it weren't for my Coast Guard pension, I'd be in the hole every month.

Ethan nods.

It feels like the recession never ended for my generation. Unemployment is low, sure. But nobody talks about if the jobs are gigs or part-time. Nobody talks about if the jobs are good jobs. Nobody in charge, anyway.

Why did you choose this career, Ethan?

Because I was unhappy.

He and the therapist talk some more about money. The subject changes. Mr. Robbin asks Ethan if he has any siblings.

No, he says.

What do you look forward to? the therapist asks.

Ethan smiles. Seeing his girlfriend. He tells him how they fell in love after reconnecting at Wilhelm Kunst's public vigil. She lives in a studio apartment in Lower Queen Anne, with a clear view of the Space Needle. He feels so lucky every time he's with her.

SHE OPENS THE door and pounces, pressing him against the wall, laughing. Dressed in stockings and a red flannel shirt, she flaunts her latest thrift store accessories: white oval-shaped sunglasses, a brown-and-gray fur trapper hat. Pulling my brother into her studio, she shuts the door. Her work station is by the window, where she keeps the tablet on which she creates digital illustrations for freelance clients.

Rent and utilities are fifteen-hundred a month, subsidized by her parents.

She pushes my brother onto the king-sized bed, climbing on top. She takes off her sunglasses and trapper hat, revealing the punkish Karen O bowl-cut she's rocked since college.

I missed you, Holly Johansson says.

They undress. After showering together, they wander into the city for date night. Dinner and a movie. Her treat.

IN THE UPTOWN Mercer Market, a Parisian-style deli serves steak sandwiches and pomme frites in paper cones. The organic produce section drips with artificial mist. At the seafood counter, fresh Pacific halibut and Dungeness crab sit on ice, awaiting customer inspection. There are refrigerated shelves of handcrafted cheese and cage-free eggs. Every variety of wine is available, merlots and cabernets and sauvignon blancs, along with wellness teas and granola snacks and homeopathic medicine. There's an in-house bakery, an in-house florist. Magazines on fitness, business, and real estate.

Twice a week in Aberdeen, Ethan visits the food bank.

Holly takes him to the soup counter, pouring tomato bisque into two containers. Taking their purchases to the express line, my brother fixes his attention on a flyer beneath the cash register. An entry-level position is open for a grocery bagger. Starting pay is $13.00 an hour. When Seattle's new minimum wage law goes into effect, the pay will be $15.00 an hour.

They sit in the dining area, watching late-afternoon traffic crawl past the most powerful philanthropic foundation in history. Taking out her phone, Holly searches the Cinerama's website. *Apocalypse Now: Redux* is playing. Tickets are twenty dollars each, plus tax, plus a convenience fee.

Or, the equivalent of four hours keeping opioid-addicted teenagers from killing themselves.

THE MOVIE IS attended by a few hundred members of South Lake Union's professional class. Well-dressed in stylish glasses, button-down shirts, khakis, and high-end footwear. Like the other expensive amenities of their neighborhood, the Cinerama is their playhouse, and by extension, so is Francis Ford Coppola's depiction of the Vietnam War.

On-screen, a jungle is napalmed, a schoolhouse immolated, a family shot to ribbons. Moviegoers return from the lobby with plastic cups of seven-dollar beer, spilling suds of barley onto the carpet. A man in the front scrolls through his phone. Dozens of side conversations percolate. The crowd is inattentive, bored. For twenty dollars a ticket, they may as well have come for free.

When the movie is over, Holly and Ethan wait on the street corner for their rideshare. Holly is unnerved, unamused.

A panhandler approaches with a cardboard sign. A combat veteran with post-traumatic stress. All he wants is a hot meal, a place to rest, maybe a few quarters. Holly and Ethan pretend not to see him, their eyes searching for their escape in the traffic of New Seattle.

IN HER APARTMENT, they stay up all night, talking. Anxiety pours out of Holly. Her clients are not paying their bills. Well, they are, but they're all overdue. Her father wants her to charge interest. Her mom wants her to get a real job. Holly spends at least ten minutes a day melting down. For weeks, she was waking up drenched in her own perspiration. Assuming it was hormonal, she went to see a doctor, who determined her night sweats were due to stress.

Sometimes, Holly wishes she'd stayed in Philadelphia.

In her best memories, she is like Karen O, jumping on cars, dancing, pushing roommates down sidewalks in shopping carts. Weekends were for breweries in Fishtown or hikes along the Wissahickon. Manayunk was her favorite place to party, a former small town that's held onto its small-town feel. She loves the Schuylkill River, where bullfrogs croak and fireflies flare. She misses her Drexel friends, who now live deep in West Philly, hosting indie shows in the basement of their rowhouse. She misses the sesame tofu at Lucky's, sold for five dollars behind bulletproof glass. She misses the dirt bikes roaring down Baltimore Avenue, a dozen Black teenagers commanding everyone's attention for a few transcendent seconds, popping wheelies. She misses dramatic Delaware Valley thunderstorms and strolling the Woodlands, the cemetery of mausoleums and Revolutionary War tombs. She even misses the top of the parking garage by the 30th Street Station, looking out at the blue façades of Center City.

Philly is great because it's where all the struggling artists who can't afford New York end up, Holly says. A rowhouse in Manayunk costs about $200,000. My parents could supply the down payment.

Babe, Ethan says.

He massages her shoulders. He can't leave the Pacific Northwest. No matter what, he has to stay here for Dad.

Holly exhales.

Truth be told, my brother is thinking about moving to Seattle anyway. He tells Holly about the open position at the Uptown Mercer Market, how it pays more than what he makes now. Holly gets excited. If he lived here, his commute would be a five-minute walk. If he moved in, her expenses would be so much less daunting. Gracious, that would be perfect.

Yeah, Ethan says. Perfect.

They kiss.

IN 2015, THE city of Seattle classifies any resident earning less than $67,000 a year as low-income.

AROUND SIX A.M., Ethan slips out of the apartment. The Uptown Mercer Market is open. My brother is here to purchase a Belgian-style cupcake for his love to awaken to. Costing six and a half dollars, the cupcake is the equivalent of thirty-three pre-tax minutes at work.

On his way to the baked goods, Ethan is seized by the headline from *The Seattle Times*.

LOGAN RIVERS RESIGNS OVER MISCONDUCT ALLEGATIONS.

In the lede of the story, the literary superstar, who served ten years in prison for armed robbery before reinventing the Western for the Twenty-First Century, has stepped down as the Director of Creative Writing at the University of Montana. A dozen current and former students have accused him of harassment and coercion, allegedly withholding career opportunities for sexual favors.

Ethan pulls out his phone. He calls Mom.

Hey, sweetie, she says.

I saw the story.

I suppose today is the day.

Are you okay?

I'll be staying at the ranch with Uncle Rod. He's here, helping me pack. I'm taking a leave of absence from the gallery. Figuring things out.

Do you think you might move back to Seattle?

A pause.

Mom tells Ethan she loves him. The call ends.

Ethan walks over to the checkout counter, where he asks for a job application, which he will take back to Aberdeen, pinning it to his bedroom wall.

· Nineteen ·

Cessation

METHMAPHMETIME IS RUTHLESS. So is heroin. So is alcohol.

So is money.

With Eddy's discharge, the boys are only nine now, sitting in a circle of chairs in the television area. One, named Harris, who always wears a tie-dye bucket hat, stands at a white poster-board, black marker in hand. Harris is my brother's assistant in a midafternoon drug seminar.

Today, the boys are listing the pros and cons of cocaine.

The cons: reckless behavior, job loss, alienation of loved ones, heart attacks. The pros are something else. Residents toss out enthusiastic suggestions—you feel invincible, you don't need to eat, you drive hella fast. Eliza shoots Ethan a glance from the kitchen. He nods, trying to redirect. The tone of the conversation simmers down. The boys agree that snorting cocaine helps with their ADHD, a diagnosis shared by all of them. Cocaine is the only time they can focus. That and videogames. The light stimulation. The meds they grew up on no longer work.

The discussion turns raucous again when one of the boys claims cocaine makes him better at sex. He's had threesomes he can't remember. Eliza comes out of the kitchen, holding a frozen slab of clam chowder.

I'm sorry, is this actually helping you?

Sure, Harris says. Cocaine is bad, mkay? Ethan is teaching us to be good.

I don't think so, Eliza says. I'm pulling the plug.

My brother is quiet. In the upstairs management office, Mr. Josiah taps on the glass, gesturing for him to come in. The boys hoot and jeer as he steps away, to which Eliza untherapeutically tells them to shut the fuck up.

Ethan closes the door. Mr. Josiah is at the computer desk, looking at a spreadsheet, eating beef and broccoli from Ocean Palace.

How are the knuckleheads? he asks.

Eliza's giving them a talking-to, Ethan says.

They don't respect nobody. Don't let it get to you. Anyway, I'm hoping to get you for some shifts. Are you available this weekend?

Of course.

Excellent. Tomorrow we're getting a new client. Private insurance, fifteen years old. Parents caught him abusing his mom's anti-anxiety meds. Could you be here to do intake?

Absolutely.

Have you done intake before?

Nope.

Eliza or Jens will walk you through it. Can I get you for Saturday, too? Might need you for a double.

As long as you don't make it a triple.

Mr. Josiah laughs.

It's going to be a bit unusual. You'll be leading a field trip.

A field trip?

You'll get to use the van. Our outing budget is tapped, so you're going to Ocean Shores. That's forty minutes each way. I'm hoping you can spend two or three hours at the beach. The tricky part is going to be the ratio. Eliza can't come in and neither can Jens. I'm gonna need you to be alone with eight of the guys.

Why? Ethan asks.

We're getting the carpets shampooed. Been trying to schedule it for over a year. Finally got someone affordable. We need it bad. One whiff of black mold, this whole place shuts down. I also need to be here to keep the med closet secure. I'm hoping to keep Tyler and Jaime. Can you handle the rest?

The official staff to client ratio, set by the state, is one to five. A double shift is sixteen hours. Before taxes, Ethan would net nearly two-hundred dollars.

Sounds great.

Mr. Josiah beams.

Before Ethan returns downstairs, he asks how his son is doing.

We got some bad news, Mr. Josiah says. Not about his health, but the bill. We're thinking about crowdfunding it. Accommodations in Seattle are expensive, too. There's nowhere really to stay near Children's Hospital. It's adding up.

Sorry to hear that, Ethan says.

The Pacific Northwest is still the best place in the country for a kid with a terminal illness. Better than Louisiana, anyway.

Mr. Josiah tries smiling.

Ethan leaves.

Downstairs, the boys are watching a nature show. For the next two hours, this will constitute their science education. If they want, they can retreat into their bedrooms to spend that time reading. Nobody leaves.

THE PRIVATE PAY, as they refer to the new client, is a boy named Leonidas. Small and shy, with a mop of light brown hair obscuring his eyes. He covers his diminutive body with an oversized hoodie, jeans, and sneakers. For the duration of intake, his mother—a rail-thin woman named Erin— accompanies her son and Ethan, peppering my brother with questions. She wants to know everything, from the daily schedule to the nutritional content of the menu. Ethan is reassuring. He answers every question. He tells her how the medicine closet is locked at all times, unless trained staff are administering prescriptions. All clients are protected by confidentiality laws and the highest standards of professional discretion. On weekends, they are required to participate in a communal deep clean. Queets Recovery House considers chores a key component of therapy.

Ethan does not mention that most of the residents are here by court order. When he leads them to Eddy's old room, Erin looks over her shoulder.

Are the other boys safe?

We've had no incidents since I started working here, Ethan says.

How long is that?

Since November.

Do you at least have a bachelor's?

Yes ma'am. From Sword Fern State.

Her eyes widen.

The college with all the free speech problems? The one that doesn't believe in grades? That Sword Fern State?

Ethan pretends not to hear her. Leonidas sits on the thin mattress of his new bed. His mother asks when her son's belongings will be brought inside. Since she is forbidding him from watching television—this is not a vacation—he needs his school books. My brother explains that his possessions will remain in the heat treat room for the first forty-eight hours, a sauna-like closet designed to neutralize any bedbugs or lice.

Erin is stunned. She approaches her son, putting her arms around him in a quick hug.

Make smart choices, she says.

Leonidas sits like a clay figure. His mother strides past Ethan without saying thank you or goodbye. She tracks down Mr. Josiah, audibly needling him about my brother's qualifications. With graciousness, Mr. Josiah takes her into his office.

Meanwhile, my brother tries to cultivate his therapeutic relationship with the client.

What part of Seattle are you from?

Queen Anne, Leonidas says.

No kidding. I grew up by Seattle Methodist University.

Leonidas pulls his hood over his face. He lies down, crumpling. The dim sky pours in through the trees.

LATER, MR. JOSIAH tells Ethan that Private Pays are the future of Queets Recovery House, a way to improve the budget. Clients from places like Queen Anne, with mothers like Erin. In a year or two, the less lucrative teenagers might just be sent to jail.

ON SATURDAY, ETHAN takes seven boys to Ocean Shores. Back at the facility, Mr. Josiah keeps three: the two he was planning on, plus a third sick with the flu. Leonidas is on the field trip, though he's not supposed to be. His mother insisted on it.

My brother has put him in the passenger seat, separated from the other clients. Against his expectations, the other boys have nothing to say to him. They are too caught up in their own stories: getting blowjobs at house parties; shoplifting cigarettes in suburbia; surviving fights on crowded buses. They can curse, and they can boast, and they can be lewd to a point.

The only prohibition is drug talk.

The closest they come to violating this rule is when one of them asks who thought it was a good idea to set up a recovery house in Aberdeen. There are junkies on every block. Aberdeen's most famous son is as well-known for his heroin use as for his music. If it weren't for the threat of jail, they'd be sneaking out every night, getting faded.

Leonidas has nothing to say.

The boys settle down as the van approaches the beach. Curiosity takes hold. Past a failing resort and grassy sand dunes, the ocean laps the surface of the world. Everything is visible. My brother drives to the edge of the tideline, skimming the saltwater mud. Slowly, he brings the van to a halt. Waves curl and roil, sent from as far away as the Sea of Okhotsk. Clouds jostle on the wind.

From the middle row, Harris leans forward.

Now what?

Now, we get out, Ethan says. You ready?

Fuck no, Harris says. It's all gross and shit. Can't we go mini-golfing or something?

Nope, Ethan says.

The boys grumble. Nobody is leaving. My brother turns to Leonidas as though he were co-chaperoning. He buries his arms in his sleeves.

Ethan turns on the radio. Southern trap booms through the speakers. Rattling hi-hats. The boys cheer. After a couple minutes, he sets the van in motion. This soon becomes the afternoon's activity: cruising with music, no one else in sight. Adhering to the speed limit is the only trick my brother will perform, despite the demands tossed out by the residents.

Ayo, Ethan, do a donut!

Stunt on them bitches.

You know how to ghostride the whip? Put this motherfucker in neutral. I'll teach you.

Amidst their revelry, Leonidas looks out at the horizon, the eerie simplicity of one-hundred eighty-seven-quintillion gallons of oceanwater. He seems at peace.

They pass dozens of trotting sandpipers. The rain picks up, pelting the van sideways. Ethan drives beyond the main section of the public beach, past a series of wooden signs listing unintelligible rules. The sand turns dark and wet. The van slows. And slows. And stops.

The van is stuck.

Ethan tries to reverse. But the vehicle is lodged in a substance like wet cement. Every turn of the wheel results in further entrenchment. The partylike atmosphere sobers up. The clients look at my brother, incredulous, ribbing each other.

Yo. Did you really just do that shit?

Ignoring his hecklers, Ethan pulls out his phone and tries to call Mr. Josiah. Between the weak signal and the noise of the carpet cleaning, the assistant supervisor can barely comprehend the crisis. When my brother's error clarifies, Mr. Josiah chuckles. Call a tow truck, he advises. Ocean Shores has an entire industry around pulling tourists out of the mud. If anything, he says, you've come up with a great way to ensure the clients stay out for longer. They can talk about the bill later.

As Ethan looks up low-cost towing companies, Leonidas unbuckles his seatbelt. He throws open his door, jumps into the thick sand, and runs. The other boys hoot and yell.

Little guy is going for it!

But he's not getting arrested, is he Ethan?

This Private Pay thing is bullshit. I wish I was Private Pay. Shit. I'd have run away in the first five minutes of getting to Aberdeen. Junkie-ass, punk-ass town.

Hey, Ethan, aren't you going to go after him?

My brother steps out. He phones Mr. Josiah a second time. Okay, the assistant supervisor says. Stay put. Mr. Josiah will call Leonidas's mother. Do not call the police, he tells Ethan. If he were to call the police on a Private Pay, he may as well call them on himself for negligence.

Leonidas runs and runs towards a block-like hotel, where he will charge into the lobby and ask for the phone. By bad luck, he will speak with his mother before Mr. Josiah can contact her.

My brother finally calls for a tow.

The other clients are getting restless. Under Harris's bucket-hatted leadership, they unbuckle their seatbelts and step outside, surrounding the van. Four take the front bumper, two take the back. They implore Ethan to return to the driver's seat and try again.

After fifteen minutes of trying, the van dislodges.

The clients whoop and dance.

On the return trip, they try to boost my brother's spirits. Thanks to him, they took charge of their circumstances. They worked together, and they saw the Pacific Ocean. None of them had thought about using for hours. But the Private Pay has still run away with Ethan's career.

THIS IS NOT a firing. Not unless my brother wants it to be. But Mr. Josiah cannot allow Ethan to work any shifts for the foreseeable future.

In his office, Mr. Josiah looks at Ethan like he's ready to cry. He blames himself for encouraging him to go out of ratio. That was his own poor judgment. But he also blames the budget for constricting supervisory options, and the carpet cleaners for their inflexible scheduling, and state regulations on mold contamination limits. But what is done is done.

A formal termination would allow him to file for unemployment benefits, which, in the best-case scenario, could net him one-hundred eighty dollars per week. The alternative is administrative purgatory, still on the books but not picking up any hours. This way, my brother can claim to be employed while applying for new jobs. Employers like candidates who are still working for someone else. Don't ask why. That's just how management makes decisions. Behavioral economics is the new clairvoyance.

Right now, pretending to be employed might be his best option.

Let's do that, then, Ethan says.

Use me as a reference, Mr. Josiah says.

He shakes my brother's hand. Would you like to pray? he asks. My brother declines.

On his way out, the residents say goodbye.

You don't deserve this shit, Ethan!

Harris warns him to be careful out there. Within a month, my brother could be an addict just like them, huddled in an alleyway somewhere, track marks on his arms. Harris wishes him the luck they never had for themselves.

DALE RAVEN MEETS up with Ethan at a Salvadoran restaurant, sharing a dinner of refried beans, tortillas, and fried plantains. Around the eatery, Aberdonians dig into pupusas and tacayas, burritos and tacos. Everybody looks exhausted.

Dale Raven says he can put word in for him at the furniture company, see if they could use an extra mover. Ethan says thanks, but he wants to stay in his field. To advance. It's the only way out of this. For the next few days, he's staying with Holly in Seattle, searching for jobs up there, seeing what bites. He'll take almost anything, as long as he can use his degree.

How will I tell Dad? he asks.

Dale Raven picks at his plantains.

Outside, by the transit center, a pickup truck pulls to the curb, depositing a group of workers at the end of their day, men who congregate in the home improvement store's parking lot for their gigs. Sometimes, Dad catches a ride with them. On his way into the Salvadoran restaurant, he looks at Ethan and Dale Raven with unaware joy.

ETHAN AND DAD talk at the kitchen table. Dad sighs over and over. He agrees that Seattle is his best option. Getting out of Aberdeen may be the only way to survive. Dad knows it's what he'd do. But his housing is virtually free right now. That's hard to give up.

There's another risk to consider.

If things don't work out with Holly, Dad says, you could be in the wind. Have you thought about trying Olympia again? Or Tacoma?

Renting an apartment on my own is too expensive, Ethan says. I'd rather risk being roommates with Holly than some random nutjob.

Dad nods.

Ethan looks at a copy of *The Daily World*, an interview with a young man planning to run for mayor. Born and raised in Aberdeen, trying to do right by his hometown. The candidate talks up his ideas on how to jumpstart his struggling community: attracting the so-called creative class with amenities like breweries, high-end coffee shops, and bicycle lanes. Nothing about improving the social safety net or increased funding for anti-poverty aid. As mayor, he promises to cater to a new economic reality. He is almost exactly Ethan's age.

When I was in seventh grade, Ethan says, why didn't you and Mom insist I take those classes at the University of Washington?

You didn't want to, Dad says.

You were in charge, Ethan says. Everything could have been different.

That's not true, Dad says.

Ethan leaves to take a shower. Alone, Dad walks over to the baby grand piano, touching its rich surface. Almost hearing it.

A FEW DAYS later, Ethan walks across Queen Anne Hill to the house at 91 West Etrusca Street. Just to remember. When he gets there, he finds me sitting on the steps. Drizzle drips from the brim of my prairie-yellow hat. Between my knees, I hold a bottle of liquor in a brown paper bag. For several seconds, he isn't sure it's me. But I'm sure it's him.

· Twenty ·

Malt Liquor Blues

COULDN'T SAY HOW I got through those years. Felt like I was putting them away on a shelf somewhere. Out on Tanner Ranch, I tried to sober up. Uncle Rod and Aunt Dottie tending to me. I tried to work up the nerve to call Isadora. Anyone.

That nerve never did come.

I went back to Austin, staying at a pay-by-the-week motel off I-35, pissing away the remaining advance from Sub Pop. Without a fixed address, my creditors couldn't find me. That worked for a while.

That summer, I hardly stepped out of my room, except to swing by the liquor store or get barbacoa tacos from the gas station. My unit was on the second floor. The place reeked of mildew and humidity. Hot moisture trickling in. Cockroaches crawling out of drains, climbing up walls in the blue glow of the television. The curtains were always closed, the lights mostly off. I put a Do-Not-Disturb sign on the door, banishing the cleaning service. I didn't want anyone looking in on me, least of all anyone with a mind for tidying up.

My neighbors were all kinds. Construction workers from Mexico, retirees waiting on nursing homes, foster kids waiting on group homes. You'd get working women, their pimps welcoming johns, laughing and smoking in the stairwells, playing music from their phones. Touring musicians would come through, taking all their gear out of their vans. One morning, I awoke to the sound of a mother in the parking lot, screaming that she had lost her toddler. When I ran outside to help, she told me to stay away. Don't you dare call the cops, she yelled.

Not that I would've.

I tried to be brave, venturing into the city. I recall tuxedoed thugs tossing me out of the Driskell Hotel, Santa Clauses tossing me out of Lala's, a small crowd of people keeping me from tumbling off the South Congress Bridge.

I tried to hustle up some cash, busking on the West Mall. I saw Isadora too many times.

Billiebat.

I couldn't venture up Guadalupe. Couldn't visit Spider House. Never tried to contact McKenna, or come near the house at Rio Grande and West 29th ½ Street. Eventually, I heard she sold it, and sold her tattoo parlor in East Austin too. The new owners told me she was engaged and had moved to the

Blue Ridge Mountains with her new fiancé. I almost called in congratulations. I remembered the hard luck she'd had with men.

One night, I texted Giselle. Don't remember doing it. She came straight from Kerbey Lane, still dressed in her apron. I was shirtless when I let her inside—I was always shirtless—thanking her for the stack of oat cream pancakes she snagged from work. She put the cakes in the refrigerator and came to the bed. She took in the squalor. The stained food containers, the fetid pile of unwashed clothing.

You're a sight and a half, she said. What'd you do, lover boy?

I fucked up, I said.

Looks like you're still fucking up. You got a gang of palmetto bugs in your kitchen and a second gang in your bathtub. It smells like feet in here. Why aren't you using your air conditioner? It's got to be ninety degrees.

Sweat's all I got now.

Why are you drinking like this?

Because I can't dance.

You shouldn't be in Austin. Get out of town, Terrell.

I want to. One of the last things I told Izzie is I wanted us to move to New Orleans. I told her we should live in a townhouse in the French Quarter.

Giselle sat on my bed, looking at me the way I deserved.

Bywater, she said. Someone like you would be living in Bywater. Hearing the freight trains whistle all night.

I would?

Sweetheart, you're so mixed up, you don't even know what your fantasies are.

Take me there.

I'm not taking you nowhere. Not until you get off the hard stuff.

She brushed my hair out of my eyes. She was tired and needed to get home.

Last I heard, Giselle moved to Houston to be with her aunties. After Hurricane Katrina, most of her family left the Seventh Ward, taking heavy losses. I heard she was enrolled in community college, earning a degree in social work, inspired by Isadora. Though she still says she'll never move back to the City That Care Forgot, Giselle will at least take her family to visit, if only every now and then.

FOR A TIME, I got off the whiskey. Kicked myself out of the Velvet Rut too.

Dripping Springs took me in. A new recording studio opened on a private ranch, sending out notices for session musicians. I auditioned and got hired fast.

That gig was alright. The best moments came when I was teaching other musicians how to play, up-and-comers who were all swagger til it came to laying down a track. Acoustic, electric, steel, banjo, bass, even the ukulele. I played everything. Taught myself the harmonica too. Also learned about sound mixing, hanging behind the boards, eventually qualifying myself as an engineer. That was a nice line of income to shore up.

I stayed put for years. I ended up adopting a dog from an animal rescue, a pit bull named Patsy, a sweet old girl who had the unfortunate habit of bonking my tear-ducts when she got too riled up. Me and Patsy rented a prefab house with a tin overhang for my truck. This was the closest I ever got to the stone home tattooed on my abdomen.

Me and Patsy spent a lot of free time watching public access shows out of Austin. I found strange comfort in the sincerity of the conspiracy theorists, who looked like they believed their own rants, like their voices alone counted as evidence. I thought there was something song-worthy about that.

Sometimes, we'd drive into the city. During a sale at I Luv Video, I picked up a copy of *The Whole Shootin' Match*, a movie I had never heard of, popping it into the VCR when I got home. For two hours, I got to see Austin and the Hill Country as they looked in the '70s, in Uncle Roderick and Aunt Dottie's day, replaying the tape til the film strip warped. Over all those reruns of Frank and Lloyd's polyurethane schemes, the old boys always ended up smoking cigarettes in the same fog. Sometimes, I felt I belonged with them, the secret third point in a trio.

Except for my pittie, I didn't feel like I belonged to anything most of the time.

Alcohol for sure.

Anniversaries, birthdays, and holidays knocked me out the hardest. I'd unplug my telephone and my answering machine, blacking out for a week. Finally, I missed too many sessions at the studio. I had to either take my skillset out of the Hill Country, or trade in another skillset.

I went back to ranching.

I got hired on the Luckenbach property of a nouveau riche expat named Mr. Ranjha, riding out his Texas dreams as a cigar-chomping, yeehawing madman. He owned a series of meatpacking plants in the Panhandle, and was the title-holder to a few oil wells in the Permian Basin. Out on his ranch, he set up a shooting range where he would line up pumpkins and watermelons, fill them with gunpowder, and fire automatic rounds into them from a modified AR-556. He did that once or twice a week, exploding the big fruit in all seasons.

I saw the sorts of guests he brought in. Ol' Dubya came for a weeklong retreat after his presidency. Jerry Jones. Joel Osteen.

My duties pertained to the livestock: his free-range Belgian Blue Bulls, who were almost immobile because of their extreme muscles. I also had to contend with a herd of zebras, who were like horses, only more skittish.

And then there were the emus. Those miserable emus. Seemed like Mr. Ranjha imported more every week, until he had a couple dozen chasing everyone. That's when the injuries began: cuts and bruises from adrenaline-rushed brawls. To Mr. Ranjha's credit, he kept several hundred extra dollars on hand for hazard pay. But a man can only get pecked so many times.

As the Hill Country suburbanized, the country roads lost themselves to strip malls and McMansions. Me and Patsy moved to cheaper pastures.

We made it to Alpine at last, renting a trailer off Highway 118. I hired myself out for saddle work, looking after horses and cattle in the high desert. On days off, I was more active than I'd been in Dripping Springs, taking Patsy up the unmarked trail behind Sul Ross State, availing ourselves of the desk on Hancock Hill. In anonymity, I contributed song lyrics to the journals in the desk, dedicated to those I'd wronged.

I visited Terlingua, jamming with strangers under the borderlands sun, just up the road from the emptiest corner in Mexico. Some days, everything was alright.

Then, on a job outside Marfa, a horse bucked underneath me.

I remember sailing in a great arc through the air and collapsing on the ground at an acute angle. The young hands laughed until they saw that my spine wasn't straight. To keep me from suffering, they plied me with mezcal. Took about three hours for someone to drive me to the hospital in Alpine. Health insurance was not something I had ever thought about.

A MONTH OF outpatient physical therapy left me jobless. The painkillers left me craving more. My discs slipped on a dime. My ranching days were over.

I owed $23,000.

The debt collectors found me.

I DROPPED PATSY off to live with a fierce old woman in an RV who loved pitties. She would be fine.

Evacuating my trailer, I took the last of my savings and bought a topper for my pickup. Slipping a mattress into the bed, I got on the road. From town to town, I played shows wherever I could, earning money to eat and get farther away. Some nights, I got paid in booze, some nights in pills.

This is how I ended up in Ballard to record a live album, fulfilling my contract with Sub Pop. Tina, the former riot grrrl, almost slapped me when I stepped into her office. And maybe she should've.

LEAVING SEATTLE, I hung my hat up and down the West Coast. After my residency at City Lights, I rode up Highway 101, living out of my pickup truck by the ocean. I busked in seaside towns, worked in kitchens, tried to work at construction sites. Drank all the time. Spent nights in the beds of women I don't remember, who probably don't want to remember me. I recall only slivers from that era. Singing to Paul Bunyan and Babe the Blue Ox. Seeing the redwoods. Running onto Cannon Beach under the moon, praying to Haystack Rock.

I got to Taholah to see Edwin Guthrie, only to learn he had moved to Forks. He had a lady-friend now, someone long-term. He was playing father to her two children, a boy and a girl. He still had his towing business, and also worked for an autobody shop. Their apartment was cramped, and to boot, his girlfriend didn't like me, but I was welcome to park my truck out back for sleeping.

My arrangement with Edwin almost worked out, until every part in my truck broke down at once. I had no money for repairs. I played in a couple bars but didn't collect anything past a tip jar. Since I couldn't get the truck to work, I couldn't travel to earn.

In Forks, it rains one-hundred and ten inches every year.

One night, someone left the door open to the town pharmacy. I sneaked inside, scooped as many pills as I could, and hightailed it out. I sold the pills off fast and paid Edwin enough to order new parts for my Montana clunker. Word got out that there had been a witness. Someone had seen a lanky stranger in a ten-gallon hat. Police had a physical description.

With my guitar and my duffel bag, I hitchhiked to the Kitsap Peninsula, stowing away on a ferry.

For the last two months, I've been on the streets, busking in Pike Place, hanging out on the waterfront and in Pioneer Square. Middle class folks laugh as I take swigs from brown-bagged bottles. Most of the money I take in, I mail to Edwin. Most nights, I get enough for a bed at the Green Tortoise too, or a motel room on Aurora. Sometimes, I sleep where I can. When I'm outdoors, my preferred hideout is behind the Fremont Troll.

THE MORNING WE reunite, we are pulling towards our shared past. Before arriving, I had been two blocks away, paying respects to Mr. Lavender. Then I came to the bottom steps of our childhood for solace.

My brother does not know where to begin.

Howdy, I say.

We agree to get coffee. On the way up the hill, I try to tell Ethan where I've been.

· Twenty-One ·

Decade Volcano

WE SIT IN El Diablo Coffee Co., sipping Cubanos in red armchairs, brown sugar and espresso on our lips. Though the second story is closed, El Diablo is still how I remember it. Behind us, a devil and an angel torment a matador, tempting him to drink more coffee, eat more cake. A black rooster squawks. Tricksters and cacti and flowers burst in pastel colors from every surface. Wu-Tang Clan rumbles on the soundtrack. White-collar professionals work on their laptops.

I want to be a smartass. I want to ask these affluent Queen Anne patrons what they know about pre-Castro Cuba, the mafia regime, the plantation feudalism. I want to joke about Che Guevara and *The Communist Manifesto*. I want to suggest that tension can be the best educator, even though it's not, even though I know better.

But my brother is telling me the hard news.

He tells me about the trial, the plea deal, the lenient sentence, the settled lawsuit, the disbarment, the return to Aberdeen. Every day, Dad wakes up in a town where men in dive bars still mutter Hugh Jamestone's name like a curse. A town where our grandmother's drowning remains an active subject of speculation.

He tells me how Mom ran away to Montana to be with Logan Rivers. Yes, he confirms, that Logan Rivers. He shares the allegations against the once-celebrated author, how their relationship has fallen apart, how Mom has retreated from rarefied Livingston for the ranch with Uncle Rod. She struggles to keep in touch, but last he heard, she's okay. Nora Tanner is as resolute as ever.

He tells me how the house at 91 West Etrusca Street is luxuriating as a financial instrument. Purchased by an anonymous shell company, the property is accruing spectacular value while nobody uses it as a home. Twice a week, a fleet of cleaners comes in to vacuum, dust, polish, and sanitize. The house is worth several hundred-thousand dollars more than its purchase price, which went to settling Dad's lawsuit. Most of the real estate agents who solicited my mother did so with the intention to tear it down and erect luxury townhomes. The only buyer who agreed to preserve it is keeping it empty in a city with ten-thousand nightly homeless residents.

With a heavy sigh, my brother updates me about himself. He recounts the underemployment and unemployment endured since Sword Fern State. He was supposed to be better than this. So much better. A high-powered graduate from a place like Stanford, living in a sleek new condo, taking in a six-figure salary. He isn't supposed to be living with his father between jobs, income always out of grasp.

Somewhere along the way, Ethan says, I failed. I'm sorry.

I set down my Cubano.

Bullshit, I say. I'm proud as hell of you, Ethan. You stuck it out when things got hard, not only with your career but with your family too. You might be the least fucked-up person I've met in a long time.

He looks at the floor.

What am I supposed to do?

It ain't over til it's over, I say.

Ethan nods.

Do you need somewhere to stay?

Always.

Are you on drugs?

Not really.

Dad will want to see you.

Well, if you're offering, I'm accepting.

Ethan stands up. He needs to make a couple calls. He steps out to the side patio to be on his phone. When he comes back in, he looks surprised I'm still there.

Where's your stuff? he asks.

Aurora, I say.

We bus our dishes and leave El Diablo, thanking the barista for her service. On the front porch, the drizzle has dissipated. Sharp sunlight is breaking out. His car is still in Lower Queen Anne. We begin our walk to the Counterbalance.

HOLLY AND ETHAN talk in the kitchen, waiting for the kettle to steam. Though she is courteous to me, fear radiates outwards.

In her clean apartment, I feel intrusive, raggedy. But it turns out I'm the least of her worries. From what I overhear, she is mostly concerned about my brother's job prospects. She wants him to look at an online application for a before-and-after school program at Maynard Middle School. My brother promises to apply. If he gets the job, he will be moving in.

Ethan kisses her on the forehead. He looks over.

Would you be okay if Holly comes to Aberdeen with us? he asks.

Sure, I say.

They decide they don't want tea after all. Holly turns off the stove and begins running around, packing her clothes into her bags, slipping her digital tablet into her backpack. She uses the restroom and stays in too long. She's under a lot of stress, Ethan tells me.

I see that, I say.

I end up waiting outside.

THE MOTEL WHERE I've been hiding out sits under the overgrown hillside just beyond the Aurora Bridge. The other rooms are a carnival of dealers and hedonists. Cars pull up at all hours, booming with trap music. Despite the traffic of Highway 99, I enjoy the views of Lake Union and the twinkle of Gasworks Park at night. On a clear day, I can see the Cascades.

In my room, dry blood stains the wall. A previous occupant has disabled the smoke detector. Ethan takes my guitar case while I hoist my bag. Carefully, we place my remaining possessions in the trunk. Holly sits in the passenger seat, looking around.

I take out a last cigarette. The road to Aberdeen will be jammed with traffic. My fingers are trembling.

IN THE CRAWL towards downtown, I whistle. The sky is clearing. The mountain is out. Always a pretty sight. We're so lucky, I say. Mount Rainier probably won't erupt in our lifetimes. The last stratovolcano around here to blow was Mount St. Helens. That happened a couple weeks shy of my second birthday. Ash fell on cars as far away as Boulder, Colorado. A Rainier eruption would be much worse. Seattle would be leveled, millions displaced. But today, the mountain is just pretty.

Ethan turns on KEXP. At the exit for Mercer Street, Holly taps his shoulder.

He already knows.

As he redirects the Jetta back to Lower Queen Anne, Holly apologizes over and over. It's okay, Ethan says. It's okay. He pulls in front of an upscale supermarket, where she asks to be dropped off. Holly takes her backpack and tells me it was lovely making my acquaintance again. She's sorry to delay me on my way to Grays Harbor.

She tells Ethan to call when we get there.

My brother does not complain. He worries only that Holly tend to herself. Holly worries that he might feel alone. And I don't worry about either of them.

ON THE ROAD to South Puget Sound, I take a brief nap, reawakening in Oly. It is the late afternoon now, dark and rainy. How about stopping for dinner? I ask. I'll pay. Sure thing, Ethan says. He takes a downtown exit, parking by King Solomon's Reef. We pass crust punks I don't recognize, who don't say hello back. The anarchist bookstore is still here, and so is the goth bar. Olympia is not yet overdeveloped like Seattle, but luxury apartments are on the way. Thank you, Walker John.

We sit at the counter. I linger over a bowl of chili and black coffee. My brother does not order anything. He has nothing to say.

Y'know, I say, I used to do that too.

What?

Clam up around people. I learned that if I talked first, I could trick myself into being comfortable. That helped a lot.

Do Isadora or Belinda know you're home? Ethan asks.

No, I say.

Shame will turn any good man into a coward.

Ethan swivels on his stool.

He tells me about their move to Spokane, how Isadora is working as a therapist but still struggling to make ends meet, how Belinda is in a high school for the arts, how my girl is writing and breathing poetry, how she dates girls and loves it, how she dates boys and likes it. Mostly, she stays out of trouble. The last scandal was when she got ahold of a DIY tattoo gun. Isadora was able to talk Billie out of using it on herself. They're at a point where talking is all it takes.

Ethan tells me how Belinda ran away from home, coming back with bruises on her throat.

I lean over. I press my hands into my face.

My brother pats my back. Finish your dinner. Izzie and Billie are okay. I won't reach out until you're settled.

My gratitude and my presence. That's all I can give.

BETWEEN OLY AND Aberdeen, I tell him my dreams.

There are three.

In the first, Mom and I sit at the dining room table. She is in a brown dress and boots, the daughter of Silas Tanner, looking out at the plains beyond the bay windows. You should leave, she says. We look in the kitchen. Belinda comes out from under the sink, four years old, giggling and screeching, wearing nothing but a diaper. Her hair is a matted tangle of black. She runs across the linoleum floor into the hallway, her toddler feet pounding the floorboards until she reaches the front door. You need to get her, Mom says. I bound onto the porch, shielding my eyes. Sunshine covers the grasslands. Belinda's movements are visible only in the parting of seed stalks. I hustle down the twenty-seven steps, pushing the prairie out of the way, struggling. When I turn around, 91 West Etrusca Street is a brooding thunderhead.

In the second dream, I am on a train, in a passenger car containing the interior of Pike Place Market, the golden-brown floor slick with mud. Between the stalls, men from the Great Depression stand in a breadline, wearing trench coats and fedoras, their faces shadowed. The unemployed pass a newspaper dated to December 7th, 1941, murmuring about the prospects of a wartime boom. Grandpa Hugh, tight-jawed and dressed like a conductor, is checking tickets, denying hot meals to anyone who can't present proof of purchase. Grandma Lilith plays a concerto on her piano, clothed in a black funeral dress, a veil over her face, a bouquet of red and white roses at her side.

In my last dream, I am in a jail cell, playing my guitar. Isadora twists in the San Marcos River, turning and turning in the clear blue water, responding to the chords of the song. If I stop playing, she can come up for air.

We drive into Grays Harbor.

RUNNING ACROSS THE lawn. Dad in the doorway, the light of the house behind him. Running across a lawn that took ten years to reach.

· Twenty-Two ·

Nursing Log Blues

DALE RAVEN GETS the call at seven in the morning. ProPublica has accepted his pitch. He needs to report to Kern County, California.

For the next year, he will profile the journeys of high school dropouts in the San Joaquin Valley. Creating a network of local contacts, he will follow his subjects as they work the oilfields, or become farmhands, or join gangs, or get pregnant, or commit to God. Not all will make it to twenty. Along with his big story, he will also catalogue elementary schools with lead in the drinking water, residents debilitated by air pollution, the victims and perpetrators of auto theft. In the evenings, he will unwind in honky-tonk bars where Merle Haggard is still the greatest country musician who ever lived, where roughnecks, shitkickers, and truckdrivers start fights and laugh until last call. On the weekends, he will hike the Tehachapi Mountains, where, on the few clear smog-free days, he can almost see downtown Los Angeles.

But on this morning, Dale Raven is just a young man leaving his hometown for an adventure. Packing his bags, he will travel by bus. He will need to buy a clunker when he gets to California, but he's already found a reliable seller.

Ethan accompanies his best friend to the transit center, where they sit in the outdoor shelter, waiting. Traffic passes on its way to the coast. Dale Raven studies the rundown façades of downtown Aberdeen, the material conditions of the place that raised him.

One day, he says, we're gonna need to explain this to our children.

Explain what? Ethan asks.

Deforestation and deindustrialization. The people on the street. The people in tents by the railroad tracks. Clear-cuts and abandoned buildings. The rape epidemic. The brutality epidemic. Things that aren't natural but that we've decided are natural. Y'know what else I'm sick of?

What?

Well-to-do culture warriors who only care about the etiquette of power, not power itself. Cliques of self-satisfied hall monitors competing on Twitter, pretending their petty conflicts and personal grievances are leading to a better society. Y'know what it's really leading to?

What?

Neither do I.

Dale Raven will say something similar when he reports on the government's response to Standing Rock, too.

A white and orange coach pulls in, Olympia the destination. They embrace. Dale Raven hopes Ethan gets that job in Seattle, that his romance with Holly is healthy and long, and that our father can stay on track. He wishes him luck dealing with me.

AFTER SEEING OFF his best friend, Ethan comes into the kitchen, where I'm cooking up steak and eggs on a cast iron skillet. Dad is sitting at the table. I've been awake for hours—never went to bed—slipping out for a walk around town in the dark, passing saloons and feedstores and abandoned houses until I was almost in Hoquiam.

Today's breakfast is shoplifted from the Safeway on Heron Street.

I ask Ethan and Dad if they'd like their eggs scrambled or sunnyside. When neither responds, I scramble them. The steaks will be served medium rare, seasoned at their discretion. As I set down three plates, they thank me quietly.

I make conversation.

Did you know they used to call Aberdeen the Port of Missing Men? Because of that serial killer Billy Gohl? Well, alleged serial killer. They say he killed over one-hundred sailors. Supposedly, he would shoot them in the union hall, then use a trapdoor to dispose their bodies. At least one scholar thinks this is all bullshit. He says there was no serial killer, and that Billy was set up because he was a powerful labor leader. But how do you like that nickname? The Port of Missing Men?

They also used to call Aberdeen the Hellhole of the Pacific, Dad says.

I burst out laughing. Ethan salts his beef and eggs. He eats like a scavenger. Dad relaxes, taking his fork and knife, digging in. He has a long shift today. Protein will serve him well.

I ask my brother what he has on the docket.

Nothing, he says.

I ask a favor.

THE PICKUP TRUCK should be fixed by now. Without a cellphone and without his number memorized, I can't contact Edwin to confirm. But I can pay what I owe. This is why my brother is driving me up to Forks.

Probably, I'm not a person-of-interest in the pharmacy burglary anymore.

Probably.

We drive in and out of the rain. Somewhere nearby, the road to Taholah is still washed out from heavy winter storms, the village cut off from the rest of the reservation. We are deep in the Old Growth Kingdom, veering past thousand-year-old trees. Logging trucks articulate the relationship between the Olympic Peninsula and its dependents. Every time one passes, my brother thinks about his old friend, Wilhelm Kunst, and the last sound he ever heard, though I do not know this yet. Sitting behind the wheel, I can see the way my brother's knuckles are clenched.

I want to give Ethan the gift of certainty. I want to convince him I have a plan.

I bet I could get work as a firefighter, I say. That would be an honest living. They can train me and everything. Like those inmates who fight wildfires for less than a dollar an hour.

What about your spine? Ethan asks.

I'll get a new spine.

You're clean, right?

I told you I am.

Well, if you stay clean, I could see about getting you a job at Queets Recovery House. You'd be a peer counselor. I need to stop in for my W-2 anyway.

Thanks, friend.

With Ethan's permission, I set my boots on the dashboard. Out in the forest, I picture trails from the end of the Ice Age, twelve-thousand years of paths losing their form to the rain. Out on the coast, I picture monuments marking where shipwrecked sailors washed up on shore, sailors from Norway, Japan, Russia. So many men.

WE STAND OUTSIDE Edwin Guthrie's apartment. In a courtyard of grass, a rusting jungle gym collects raindrops.

Edwin opens the door. He looks me up and down, then looks at Ethan.

Who's this?

My little brother. Remember when we camped in your van?

Edwin tilts his head. Behind him, I hear the burble of a television. I take out a wad of cash and a plastic bag of quarters. Edwin counts the money. My brother and I are still out in the rain.

Can we speak inside? I ask.

I got the little ones, Edwin says. Things are still a little hot for you around here.

Alright, alright. How's the truck? She fixed?

Edwin nods.

One sec.

He closes the door, sliding the chain. Reopening half a minute later, Edwin drops the keys in the palm of my hand. In the background, the television is louder. He passes me a note with his phone number.

Now get a phone, Edwin says. Get in the saddle and earn. See you around, Jamestone.

See you, I say.

I take Ethan out back, where my truck remains under a blue tarp, license plates obscured by duct tape. I remove the tarp and tape, get in the driver' seat, and turn the key in the ignition. She roars.

I grin at my brother. We'll be returning to Aberdeen separately. I turn off the engine.

Hey, I say.

What?

I got another favor to ask. Do you think I could use your phone later?

For what?

To talk to my daughter.

Don't you want to call Isadora first?

I say nothing. Ethan takes a moment. He decides Isadora needs to be included. If she gives approval, he'll text Belinda. He's got uncle privilege. Preferably, we could all do a video call together. I would have to stay sober.

I agree.

Ethan types out the message and sends it to Izzie. When we meet up at 67 Simmons Street, he'll have a verdict.

Before leaving town, he detours to the bridge over the Sol Duc River, where he parks and stays for half an hour, lost in thought. I arrive in Grays Harbor well ahead of him. Without a key to the house, all I can do is wait. When my brother pulls up, he has answers from my ex-fiancée and our daughter.

Yes.

And, somehow, a second yes.

HOW SHE MUST feel when my pixelated image appears on the screen.

Scared. Angry.

Sad.

I'm calling from the upstairs bedroom where Dad spent his childhood, where Ethan sleeps on a bare mattress beneath a wood-paneled ceiling. He and Billie enjoy that rare rapport where they can tell jokes, tease each other, and share personal news in the first ten minutes of a conversation. He is her lifeline to the Jamestones.

I steal a quick look at my girl's appearance: her half-shaved head, the maturity in her eyes. Like most afternoons, Belinda has the house to herself, a time of instant ramen and Tumblr. She's grown into a confident fifteen-year-old, but right now, little of that confidence is on display.

I hear my daughter is a poet, I say. Is that right?

An embarrassed smile, covered up with her sleeve. Yeah, she admits. But she's not ready to talk about that. I ask what else she's into. Pygmy marmosets, Billie says. She doesn't know how she feels about the term pygmy—maybe it's offensive, maybe it's not—but she's in love with the tiny, wide-eyed primates. They're the size of her hand, maybe tinier. They can be groomed with just a toothbrush. Though she's never seen a pygmy marmoset in person, she scrolls through videos and photos of the critters every day, learning everything she can.

They're gummivores too, Belinda says.

Gummivores? I ask.

They only eat tree sap. Maybe some bugs, but mostly tree sap. They live in riparian forests. Do you know what a riparian forest is?

Can't say I do, darling.

A forest by a river.

I tell her that phrase sounds like the title of a poetry collection. I suggest she incorporate words like gummivores and riparian into her stanzas. She blushes, waving off the possibility. We move on. I ask about music: who she listens to, who's important. Her favorite song is something called So High, but she won't elaborate on what it's about. She also loves St. Vincent, the art-rock guitarist. Tacocat is another favorite. Candy and pop-punk, tattoos and dyed hair. Then, there's Sleater-Kinney, who dropped *No Cities to Love* last month. My daughter's torn between who she idolizes the most: Corin Tucker, Janet Weiss, or Carrie Brownstein. She leans towards Brownstein because she has a memoir coming out in October, *Hunger Makes Me a Modern Girl*. Belinda always wanted to know what makes her a modern girl. Maybe now she'll find out.

I used to be labelmates with Sleater-Kinney, I say. That one album they dropped in 2005, *The Woods*, came out the same year my debut was supposed to come out.

Really?

I tell her how Sleater-Kinney is also the name of a road in Olympia—Exit 108B or Exit 109, depending on if you're traveling I-5 North or South—taken in honor of a gig around there. Billiebat loves Oly. She hasn't been back since that fateful night in 2012, but she is still drawn to its grungy magnetism, the lore of its artesian waters, the creative independence of Sword Fern State. She's accepted Spokane for now, but the moment she can leap back over the Cascades, she will.

Do you know how to drive yet? I ask.

Yes! she says. Well, no. In the State of Washington, one only has to be fifteen to obtain an instruction permit if they're in driver's ed, fifteen and a half if they're not. Since Izzie can't afford private classes, Belinda has to wait. I tell her how Izzie went through our entire relationship never knowing how to drive.

I could teach you, I say. Maybe if you come out here for summer break or something. Your mother would have to be comfortable with it, of course. We won't do anything without her permission.

Billie nods. We talk about it, she and I. We talk about it.

LATER THAT EVENING, my brother takes me to Queets Recovery House. While he collects his tax form, I sit down with Mr. Josiah.

He likes me. He believes I could be an exceptional peer counselor, but I need more formal experience. To be honest, he's also uncertain about the future of the facility, hinting they may not survive the fiscal year.

The visit isn't a loss. Mr. Josiah is gregarious. He tells me about New Orleans, how he and his wife used to be preachers. His new career is a way to continue God's mercy. He tells me about his preteen son battling leukemia. Faith will carry them, just like it carried them out of Louisiana.

He invites me to play guitar for the boys sometime.

My brother is welcome too. The boys love him, which they show by clowning on him. They invite him to play chess, an activity that breeds mutual respect as they strengthen one another's skills. After the games are over, Ethan and I return to the house, where Dad is asleep.

IN THE MORNING, my brother's phone vibrates. It's the before-and-after school program at Maynard Middle School. The site director wants to schedule an interview.

Twenty-Three

Tsunami Evacuation Route

THE HOUSE IS forgiveness. This is what my brother says. This is what the rain says too, tapping on the roof and glass. Rain from the Kuroshio Current, the remnants of a squall whirring over Japan before slipping into the North Pacific, taking the reverse path of the tidal wave from three centuries ago, pouring into the sloughs of Grays Harbor.

Last year, when he rediscovered this house, Ethan had also come here in a storm.

Panic.

Late one night, just before graduation, just before Dad was released from jail, he hopped onto the highway between Oly and Aberdeen, rocketing at 110 miles per hour, moving so fast the doors were rattling. Towns exploded and disintegrated at his side. McCleary, Elma. He remembers the lights on the never-commissioned Satsop Nuclear Power Plant flashing like a warning. Rolling into Aberdeen, the madness evaporated, even as the rain strengthened.

Slowly, my brother turned into the community by the Wishkah River. He passed the yellow house on East 1ˢᵗ Street where Aberdeen's most famous son lived as a teenager. He turned around at the Young Street Bridge, where The Saint Who Slept On Mud used to take shelter, a myth Aberdeen's second-most-famous son disputes whenever asked about it. Then, deep in the neighborhood they used to call Felony Flats, he found the house at 67 Simmons Street. Nobody in the Jamestone family had remembered it until that night. Nobody remembered anything about Aberdeen.

This is my legacy, Ethan tells me. That, and the way I taught him to see. The way I taught him to separate himself from the competitiveness of his peers, and the strife between Mom and Dad. The spite. For the few months I interrupted his youth, I changed everything. As long I have my brother, I have an advocate.

This is how I start over.

We discuss my options. I could finish my education, try vocational training. Or, I could jumpstart this music career again, talk to Sub Pop or their new subsidiary, Hardly Art.

Anchor myself in something plausible while everyone tries to trust me.

What we need is a family reunion, I say. How about I see to that?

Ethan laughs.

I say good night and leave him be. Descending downstairs, I hear Dad snoring in his bedroom, one of the few sounds trailing me from childhood to adulthood.

ETHAN TAKES HIMSELF to the ocean at dawn, leaving a note on the kitchen table. If he gets the job, his opportunities to see the Pacific will be cut short. He wants to visit while he can.

Dad knocks on my door. Frightened.

What's wrong? I ask.

Can you drive me somewhere? Dad says.

The home improvement store has sprung a surprise drug test on him. Before his afternoon shift, he is to report to a testing facility and urinate. If he tests positive, he will be fired. He won't know the results for a week.

I get dressed and throw on my coat.

THE OTHER TESTEES are a sample of Grays Harbor's working and hustling classes. Calloused palms, pierced lips, neck tattoos, hardened knuckles. Wage earners and parolees.

Dad tries to fill out a form on a clipboard, the plastic pen shaking in his fingers. When I volunteer to fill it out for him, he snaps, apologizing immediately. He's not trying to be rude, but he's paranoid he might get in trouble if someone else's handwriting appears on his documents.

Paranoia is another tool they use.

Dad finishes and signs. He passes the form to the receptionist. She gives him a number like we're at the Department of Licensing. She does not meet his eyes. Dad lowers his body back into his seat.

How would you feel if I organized a family reunion? I ask.

Dad coughs.

What?

I'm serious. We could do it in Seattle, probably.

Nobody is in Seattle anymore. Except for Izzie's mom. And I assume you don't want to involve Sunshine Madera.

She's welcome, even if she hates me. Hell, if I'm welcome, anyone's welcome. We could rent out a few rooms at a hotel. Converge for a weekend. Families do that. Money won't be a problem if we pool our resources.

Don't expect your mother to show up, Dad says.

She's invited too, I say.

Dad's number is called. He lifts himself out of his chair and ambles to the clinical hallway. The piss test will take less than a minute. Fewer than twenty-four hours later, his employer will be notified that his results are negative, results his employer will sit on for several days. Though he is clean, until his boss says so, my father will feel anything but.

WE TAKE THE morning. In a diner, we lunch on steaming bowls of geoduck chowder, sourdough bread, and coffee.

We talk jobs. Always jobs.

Dad suggests I get a newspaper route. He's not kidding. He admits it wouldn't be great—I would be classified as an independent contractor so that the newspaper wouldn't be on the hook for benefits; I would be using my pickup truck without any compensation for gas mileage—but I should give it a shot. Maybe, I say.

We talk about Ethan, how proud we are, how hopeful. Twenty-three is the perfect age. By the end of this decade, I'll be forty. That's no kind of age to be bouncing from one underpaying music gig to the next, or from one retail job to another. Of the three of us, Ethan has the most potential, even if he doesn't see it yet.

There was a time I wasn't sure he would live this long, I say.

Dad stirs his coffee.

You mean how he used to cut himself.

Yeah, I say. That.

I tell Dad how, a few years back in Palo Alto, the moneyed, high-achieving center of Silicon Valley, a dozen teenagers killed themselves in rapid succession. Pressure to succeed was the common factor in their deaths. Reading about the Palo Alto suicides, I always thought about Ethan.

Dad looks out the window.

I failed you, he says. Both of you. And your mother.

Pop…

I'm sorry, Terrell.

Dad talks some more. Ever since he was a child, he's always felt alone. He remembers how Grandpa Hugh mocked him for mourning the death of Grandma Lilith, hitting him, calling him weak. He remembers how Grandpa Hugh sneered when he received his acceptance letter to the University of Washington. Jealousy and rage. For the entirety of his law firm years, he felt like a fraud. Every positive performance evaluation felt like a practical joke. He never felt like he deserved to advance, yet he would never be satisfied until achieving the peak of his profession. In his loneliness, he hoped to someday work out of the Governor's Mansion, or the Office of the Attorney General. His dreams always felt conceited. Yet he demanded them.

He could hardly bear to feel alive.

We talk about therapy. Dad's not sure he needs it anymore. Losing his attorney's license was the second most stress-relieving event of his life, second only to the death of his father. So long as he holds onto a job—and Ethan is okay, and I am okay—he will be okay.

We pay our lunch bill, and drift through downtown.

In an alley behind the restored D & R Theatre, local high schoolers have painted dozens of murals: stencils of pop culture figures, Shepherd Fairey-esque stickers, portraits of the graduating class. There are messages to choose pancakes over black tar heroin, to seek grace and courage in God, to never abandon your family in the pursuit of vice. The youth of Grays Harbor, showing the rest of us how to live.

DAD'S ABERDEEN IS unlikely. But he will thrive here.

One day, before it burns down, he will visit the Aberdeen Museum of History, studying the version of Grays Harbor that brought the Jamestones to the Pacific Northwest, absorbing the steam-powered logging machines, the antique camping gear, the saws and axes and lanterns, the photographs of firs the height of small skyscrapers. In the gift shop, Dad will sift through yearbooks from J.M. Weatherwax High School, where he'll find Lilith Hopkins in the Class of 1939. Bright-eyed and sly, graduating at sixteen, precocious in every way.

He'll keep the yearbook in his bedside table. Thankful he found her again.

His professional life will get better, too, getting hired part-time as a copyeditor at *The Daily World*, which he will try to parlay into serving as legal review.

For the foreseeable future, he will continue attending his sobriety meetings at the Alano Club, where he will form a friendship with Mr. Josiah, who begins serving as a moderator. In their friendship, the two men will do volunteer charity work, tending to the town's most vulnerable, carrying boxes of food and hygiene supplies into abandoned buildings. He will listen to the mumblings of the dispossessed, sincere but hard to follow. Some phrases will never leave his mind, phrases like Christlike Systemic Collapse. With Mr. Josiah, Dad will search for the bodies of the overdosed, encountering his first in a room where pigeons roost in the shadows. For every person he and Mr. Josiah recover, a family receives closure. His volunteer work will come from radical love.

OLD MAN EUGENE will never be far from his mind. He will always be looking for him: in doorways, in alleyways, in riverways. Sometimes seeing.

AND MOM?

I don't know.

When Ethan leaves for his job interview, I sit at the kitchen table with a yellow legal pad, writing a letter to Tanner Ranch.

DEAR MOM—

I love you.

This is Terrell.

Your first-born and last-remembered. That's supposed to be a joke.

I'm back in Western Washington, trying to settle. Much is up in the air, but much is already being planted. I want a family reunion. You, me, Dad, Ethan, Holly, Izzie, Billie. Our loved ones, our complications. Our contradictions. Uncle Rod & Aunt Dottie too. I want to see the Jamestones & the Tanners & the Maderas in some swanky hotel, swapping stories, sharing dinners, hugging, praying—whatever praying looks like for each of us.

Two days. That's all I'm asking. Two days.

You can get to know me again, scary as that may be.

You want the hard truth?

I will always remember how I grew up.

Those bad nights—that hairbrush in your fist, smacking my five-year-old face; the flipped-over chairs & TV-trays; the wad of cash you threw at me when I threatened to run away—those bad nights hit me hard.

For decades, I've tried to figure it out. Figure out why. Panic is my best conjecture. Panic looks like anger in you, a kind of self-defense. But I was your child. Your small boy, who you read to in bed, who you sang to in the bathtub, who you put out peanut butter & crackers for in the afternoon. I used to speculate that you weren't mature enough to be my mother. You did better with Ethan, after all. Now I'm curious what you might have to say.

I hope you're recovering in Montana. I never got a handle on what the ranch means for Nora Tanner. Uncle Roderick is so tight-lipped. A loyal brother. But I had clues. Silas Tanner's old-time religion always did hang heavy, though I never heard much about it. Your own mother got hit by a train while you were in kindergarten. You were tiny, marooned in grief until the piano freed you.

Write me back. I don't got a phone yet. Laptop neither. Haven't really got the mind to make such purchases. I also haven't got the money. Not that I'm asking for any.

Your (Resurrected) Son,

Terrell H. Jamestone.

ON DAD'S ADVICE, I visit Mr. Robbin.

The therapist is amused. I am the second Jamestone he's met. He warns me that he will not be able to disclose any of what he discussed with Ethan. Then he asks the classic Carl Rogers question.

Who is the person you are becoming?

Before we get into that, I ask Mr. Robbin to tell me about himself, his twenty years in the Coast Guard. A lot of what he did was participate in rescue missions. The mouth of the Columbia is home to some of the most unpredictable waves along North America. You could be an international barge, a floating city of a vessel with the most experienced crew, and still capsize. Most of who he rescued were private boaters with neither training nor the common sense to be there.

The thing about the Columbia Bar, Mr. Robbin says, is that you have all these ridges hidden beneath the surface. All this sediment collecting the entire length of the river and its tributaries. Some of the soil comes from as far away as the Bitterroot Mountains.

I let out a long whistle. I picture myself as a tugboat operator, navigating farther and farther inland until I'm in Montana. All I say is that I need to get down to the Columbia for myself.

· Twenty-Four ·

The Last of the Cedar Choppers

YOU COME TO believe you've been touched by something important. Maybe once in the Hill Country, maybe now in the Pacific Northwest. Touched by an ember. You believe, in the sinew of your tissue, that your manner of being alive is alright.

Then one of your tires blows out on the way to a job interview. You've got no way of contacting your interviewers about the delay because you never purchased a cellphone. Not even a burner.

I am somewhere on Highway 101.

Pulled over in the rain, I unscrew the wrecked tire with a rusted old wrench. My fingers hurt and slip. The replacement tire is the same one that's been in the truck for twenty years, slightly deflated. I'm out of options. As I work, my knees press into the asphalt, grit and pine needles embedding into my jeans. Rain soaks my jacket and hat. I look feral, forgotten. Logging trucks rumble by.

A few days ago, Dad told me that the big mill in Raymond was holding walk-in applications. Every type of position is open: saw operators, forklift drivers, security. Every level of education, every level of experience. Each job is full-time with benefits. Health insurance, overtime pay, vacation days. With some luck, some real luck, I could qualify. I could be a modern timberman, earning a paycheck off the same wooded bounty Hugh Jamestone exploited, the bounty we somehow have too much of and too little of. If I could reach Raymond on schedule, I could have a chance.

The tire change takes thirty minutes. When I finish, I climb into the truck. I sit and look at the clouded sky.

I feel overrun by tree roots. Swallowed by muck. Within that overgrown sensation, I hold onto my breath: the glacial wind blowing off Mount Rainier, the salted air over Puget Sound, the oxygen of the West Coast. I feel the breath that was in my mother's lungs. Within my respirations, I identify a stillness, the emptiness of what I was before birth.

I am still a man without a job.

Across the highway, I notice a Roosevelt elk peeking out at me. He is the King Herbivore from the Humptulips River, a survivor of the Ice Age, megafauna and confidant. His eyes twinkle in perception.

I wait for another logging truck to pass. Thirty minutes later, I arrive at the mill. I fill out a form, dripping from rain. I'm not even granted an introduction. Nobody wants to see me.

I move along.

WITH MY BLACK guitar case strapped to my back, I stroll through Raymond. Ninety-eight inches of rain falls here every year. The sidewalks are slick under my boots. This is a town of fraternal lodges and antique stores. A few lots are vacant and weeded. The Willapa Hills rise around the river and the bay, oysters everywhere below the surface. A place that feels like a raft about to be cut loose into the ocean.

I approach the Tsuga Alehouse & Inn. A hardwood lodge exterior, neon beer signs blazing in the windows. A gargantuan stump sits in the parking lot with a rusting crosscut saw sunk halfway through. Inside, a woodstove heats the booths and tables. Taxidermy deer heads are mounted on the walls. Flannel-clad locals sit at tables and booths. Retirees and alcoholics.

At the bar, a silver-haired waitress introduces herself as Frida. Frida passes me a menu of craft beers and fancy sandwiches. This place used to be a dive—I can tell— rehabilitated into something more upscale, probably for tourists out of Portland and Seattle. Maybe that's what the chic hostel out back is for. But in February, it's locals only.

I order the cheapest high-point beer they have. Frida is chatty. She wants to know if I'm the entertainment for the evening. Some rockabilly band was supposed to perform, but nobody's heard from them. She points at the stage underneath the flat-screen television.

No ma'am, I say. I'm on nobody's schedule.

In a conspiratorial voice, Frida tells me Krist Novoselic sometimes pops in on random nights, all six foot seven of him. He takes the stage with his accordion, always a solo act, always a big hit. His home is not too far from Raymond, on a farm near the Columbia. Frida tells me she's been instructed not to talk about it.

I laugh.

Beer after beer passes through me. I feel nothing. Every now and then, I consider asking to use the phone so I can call Dad, to tell him not to worry about me. I won't drive home drunk. I'll take the time to sober up.

But I don't.

The night goes on. The crowd grows. Younger now, workers now.

Frida comes back with a real proposition. If I play for the crowd, the Tsuga will cover my tab. Plus, I can take home whatever tips I earn.

Heck, I say.

I set down my glass, take my instrument, and hop on stage. A microphone is already set up. As I unlatch my case, customers cheer. I sit on the stool under the bright light, giving my best smile.

You don't know who I am, I say. But I believe we've met before on countless nights. My name is Terrell Jamestone. Let's try to keep up with each other. Alright, folks?

Their attention is mine.

I pull off three songs—Pickin' Blackberries, The Space Needle is a Jackhammer, Don't Fly Away—picking as well as I ever could, straining my voice to the limits of its range. When I finish, I get a round of applause.

Oh, you like that, I say. That's good. Being a musician ain't paying the bills, and folks, if you ain't pay the bills, the bills will find out sooner or later. I was lucky. For me, they found out later.

Cheers.

I tune my guitar.

I'd like to dedicate the next few songs to my brother, Ethan, I say. Ethan got a job this week. A job! We love ourselves a job in Raymond, Washington, don't we, folks? Let's hear it for Ethan.

Every voice roars.

From then on, it feels like every person in Willapa Bay is streaming into the bar, coming in from the night to hear me sing.

MY BROTHER INTERVIEWED early Wednesday afternoon.

Acing it.

Maynard Middle School was almost identical to how he remembered it: the same two-story brick building, the same divide between bus kids and neighborhood kids. The site director, a woman named Zeinab, met him in the cafeteria, where the Maverick Mentors program is held. Born and raised in Seattle just like him, Zeinab performs her duties in a black hijab, black blazer, jeans, and flat-heeled shoes. She carries herself like she could someday be the principal, if not the superintendent. And, probably, she will be.

My brother, dressed in his most respectable khakis, recounted his qualifications. Everywhere he's been, everything he's done, everything he knows. He described the relationship between behavior and learning, the necessity of structure, how maintaining a consistent mixture of kindness and authority is necessary to allow preteens to be preteens.

That's all we want, Zeinab said.

For preteens to be preteens.

Maverick Mentors provides something between childcare and academic support. As site director, Zeinab prioritizes socialization and emotional intelligence. Though some parents are pushing for the program to be an extension of the classroom, with its own curriculum, she won't budge. Zeinab keeps lists in her office of which parents are still allowed to complain to her and who have had that privilege revoked.

You may have worked with gangmembers and addicts, Zeinab said, but these Queen Anne types are something else. You would not believe how aggressive some get. Screaming, throwing things. Some are banned from campus. If you are able to deescalate them, I have every confidence you will make an excellent therapist someday.

Ethan nodded.

After the interview, he hung around to observe, shadowing snack time, a group game, homework time, cooperative problem-solving. As he asked questions and helped with cleanup, Zeinab called his references, then hired my brother on the spot.

A typical week will be thirty hours, three every morning and three every afternoon, paying fourteen dollars per, eventually fifteen. He will reach full-time status on spring break and summer vacation. From there, he'll figure out grad school.

Until then, five days every week, he will commute from Holly's apartment up and down the Counterbalance. That old impossible force we've always known.

TO CELEBRATE, ETHAN and Holly are hitting up a show in Little Saigon. Three acts are playing, two of which Holly has designed posters for.

In her Lower Queen Anne apartment, she dresses my brother in a tight, dark gray t-shirt and stonewashed jeans. The sexiest thing a man can wear, she says, are clothes that fit. She purchased his outfit at a secondhand store near Bellevue. The best thrift shops are on the East Side, where rich people discard fabulous garments for nothing. For herself, Holly has procured high-waisted leather leggings, a black-and-teal t-shirt, and a faux-leather jacket punctuated by imitation rhinestones. Nothing fancy about her shoes, perfect for the underground.

She and Ethan look at themselves in the mirror.

We're so hot, Holly says.

They leave for the bus.

THE VENUE IS a nondescript office building on South Jackson Street, a satellite of the city's basement scene. As a Hmong girl, Holly says she'll probably be the only attendee who looks like she belongs in Little Saigon at this hour. Mostly, she's right.

Outside, hipsters smoke and drink beer. One woman drops her bottle by mistake, glass shattering, the doorman hissing at her indiscretion. Holly and Ethan step over the broken bottle, pay the three-dollar cover, and get their hands stamped. Inside, they are led into a conference room turned performance hall. The crowd packs the venue wall to wall.

The show begins.

Neuroplastik is up first, a rapper who composes her own melodies and beats, champion of the Central District. Setting up her laptop on a table, she plugs a cord into an amp and hits play. Releasing the first instrumental—booming sci-fi house music—she slinks into the center of everyone's attention, showing off her velvet purple dungarees and imitation luxury shoes. Hipsters sway with loopy grins; some vogue; some are confused. Neuroplastik holds off rapping, encouraging her audience to vibe with her.

Suddenly, a historical photograph appears behind her: an ancient woman in front of a wooden shack, holding a cane with gnarled hands, staring out at a muddy waterfront. Everything is in sepia, except for her bright red scarf. This is Kikisoblu, daughter of Chief Si'ahl, better known to history by her Christian name, Princess Angeline.

Neuroplastik paces, holding the microphone to her lips.

Before we begin, Neuroplastik says, I just wanted to remind you all that we Black and Brown girls have always belonged here. We always will. That's not a diss to the rest of you. It's a celebration. I'm inviting you to celebrate with me tonight. If you're with that, let's get it!

She presses a button on the laptop. A new track comes out: a remixed Spaghetti Western melody, looped over 808 drums. With great technical skill, Neuroplastik unpacks her rhymes, interweaving stories from the South End to Rainier Valley. Everyone is mingling and sweating. Holly holds Ethan's hands, grinding against him. She whispers in his ear.

AN HOUR LATER, a pop-punk quintet takes the spotlight. Five pale women strut out in pink plastic leotards, purple tights, and red platform boots. One is holding a saxophone.

We're the Oh Oh Ohs, the vocalist yells. We play songs about masturbation and sex!

They begin their set.

My brother is alone. Disappearing out of the conference room, Holly has a scheme. When the saxophonist does her thing, Ethan is to reach into her purse, which he is holding for her, unzip the inner pocket, and take out whatever he finds. He does not know why.

Three songs in, the saxophonist leans back into a wide stance. She shuts her eyes and blows a howling solo.

This must be her thing.

Ethan opens the purse. He takes out a key, tagged with a note telling him to use it on a closet in a nearby hallway. Detaching himself from the crowd, he does as told.

Inside the closet, Holly is waiting for him on a king-sized mattress. Candles light up their private space. She laughs. Her friends helped her set this up. They can take as much time as they need. Nobody else has access.

My brother kneels, kissing her on the lips.

IN RAYMOND, THE rockabilly band shows up at last. I cede the stage. The singer sounds like Roy Orbison. The audience is a tidepool of rowdiness, passing me plastic cups of liquor. The rockabillies last forty minutes. Not bad. As they take a break, I pull them into a huddle. I ask if they could play backup.

Don't worry about getting the rhythm right, I say. We can jam it out. Sound good?

They're into it.

A few shots of whiskey later, the rockabillies and I are ready to serve the people. Applause rolls out as everyone in the Tsuga realizes the show is not over.

I take the microphone.

If you all don't mind, I say, I'd like to dedicate these next songs to my wife and my daughter. I wish they could be here tonight. I love them so.

I nod at the rockabillies. We play into midnight, and beyond.

JAY KRISTENSEN JR.

AS ALWAYS, I play for her.

ISADORA TOSSES CLEAN sheets onto her bed in Spokane, worrying about our daughter like she has since 2012, always breathing in relief when Billie shows up in the morning for breakfast. For a long time, Isadora would open her door in the middle of the night, checking to see if she was still there, causing fights at two a.m.

Despite Isadora's misgivings, she wants her daughter to have a relationship with me. Hers is a pain she's held onto for ten years. She believes we could make it work, the three of us. I do too. I see us meeting up for coffee by the Davenport Hotel, taking hours-long walks along Riverfront Park. Talking, just talking. Communication and acceptance, a process of months. Attending couple's therapy in Spokane, Isadora taking advantage of her professional connections. Sometimes, Belinda would sit in on our sessions, interjecting with her opinions.

We'd be alright, getting to know each other again.

We'd be alright.

Maybe, just maybe, Isadora would invite me to the brown ranch-style house she owns—yes, owns—by the mall. Belinda and I would help prepare dinner, something with brown rice and steamed vegetables. No teriyaki sauce allowed. That's a story I'll hear about. Over our meal, the three of us would have a serious discussion about our future. We'd take things week by week. I see Sunday hikes in the Channeled Scablands, the desert riverbeds carved out by biblical floods, and trips to Lake Chelan and Coeur d'Alene. We'd visit the rolling hills of the Palouse, the three of us standing side by side, peering out for miles. Sharing the same view.

I see myself teaching Belinda how to drive in my pickup truck, too, our daughter escorting me in uneventful, tree-lined suburbia. Billie would be elated, calm, in control. When she passes the test with a near-perfect score, I could earn a permanent place in their household. As a guest anyway.

I see so many permanent places. In Eastern Washington, in Western Washington, in the hyphen between Madera and Jamestone. But maybe impermanence is the only truth.

OLY IS WHERE our girl will come into herself.

Early at Sword Fern State, she'll pair off with a lover named Lorelai, freckled and red-haired, a nonbinary femme our girl loves immediately. Lorrie and Billie will be a sight on campus, always teasing each other, always play-fighting by the clocktower. Celebrating their love with photo collages, taking pictures of themselves in front of Oly's infamous Black Houses. In Lewis County, they'll kiss beneath the fussy Uncle Sam billboard, who's rhetorically asking whether Sword Fern State is home to eco-terrorists and homosexuals. In Capitol Forest, they will stumble onto an illegal shooting range, yahoos firing into a gravel pit. Rather than condemn them, Billie and Lorrie join in, and in a coup, Lorrie will prove themself to be the best shot in the bunch. My grandparents taught me, she/they will say. Returning to the hiking trail, Lorelai will have to hold Belinda back after a trio of ATV riders nearly crashes into them, my girl screaming and cussing, ready to fight. One of their greatest adventures will be exploring a sprawling rural property rumored to be owned by Courtney Love, a rundown mansion with rundown horse stables. Coming down to McClane Creek, they will pay respects to Ms. Love's late husband.

Our daughter will host poetry readings in coffee shops around town, carrying a copy of *Night Sky With Exit Wounds* by Ocean Vuong wherever she goes, a collection she tries to memorize in full, every verse of war and family and body hunger. Through an independent learning contract, she will spend two quarters in Port Townsend interning at Copper Canyon Press, honing her passion in a dreamscape of Victorian houses.

Victorian architecture will punctuate many of my girl's fondest memories. A spring road trip will take her and her lover into California, to the tiny town of Ferndale, ornate with Butterfat Palaces, a name that will cause Billie to laugh and laugh. She will be fascinated by the Golden State's mingling of pine trees and palms. On the Lost Coast, she will envision a future with Lorelai, working in a bakery by day, smoking the best cannabis at night.

Traveling into San Francisco, Billie will visit the same places Uncle Ethan did, including the Poetry Room at City Lights, yearning for the same city slipping beyond the grasp of the unmoneyed.

In the summer, Belinda and Lorelai will take seasonal jobs at a cannery in Alaska. Hiking the mosquito-rich woods, they will cause a brief stir when they climb a tree and hang out for a few hours, spurring rumors of an environmentalist stunt. The story will make the papers, a copy of which Billie will frame and hang in their bedroom. Renting a room on Oly's East Side, their housemates will be two retired Jesuits, a nice couple who keep a vegetable garden out back. This is the house where Isadora will visit them after graduation, spending a few nights on an air mattress on the floor gazing at the dark ceiling, heart pounding because she's seen her daughter from birth to womanhood. Her pinnacle achievement.

Hers. Not mine.

WE NEAR LAST call at the Tsuga. I'm alone on stage.

How many people in here have heard of the Hill Country? I ask. The Hill Country, down Texas way?

Some cheering.

Alright, I say. Let me tell you something about the rolling woods and caves west of Austin. Used to be, they were inhabited by people known as the Cedar Choppers. They were called that because chopping cedar was how they made their living. Every one of them, men and women, sons and daughters, everybody was raised with axes in their hands. Soon as you could walk, you could chop. Their hills were filled with ashe juniper, and ashe juniper was what built Texas. Every ranching fence, every telephone poll, every-everything. All of it was made possible by the Cedar Choppers. They lived off their labor for over one-hundred years, until Austin's gentry decided the land was theirs for the taking. Most of the Choppers didn't have any heat or electricity or running water. Most of them couldn't read. But they were rich in their way. Kept their sense of awe about them. And ain't that something we've all been missing lately? A sense of awe?

The bartender yells.

Ten minutes til closing.

Last thing I want to tell you about the Cedar Choppers, I say, is that there ain't none left. All that new money choked them out. We all know what that's like, don't we? And me? I'm just a kid from Queen Anne. Just like my brother. Difference is, my brother is doing alright. Me, well…I'm still me.

I down my whiskey. Counting off in my head, I play one last song, a number called Bee Cave Blues. At two a.m., the bar closes.

OUT OF GRATITUDE, the manager gives me a room free of charge. Helping me onto a bottom bunk, she places my guitar by the door. She doesn't steal anything.

I fall asleep.

HOLLY AND ETHAN are the last ones out of Little Saigon. They stand on South Jackson Street, catching the Night Owl, riding through downtown. Alone on the bus, Holly rests her head on Ethan's shoulder. He kisses her.

How would you feel if I drove us to Aberdeen? Ethan asks.

She raises an eyebrow.

You mean like now?

The highways are empty, Ethan says.

She laughs. Sure.

Twenty minutes later, Holly and Ethan are in the Jetta, cruising down I-5 towards Olympia, where they will turn towards Aberdeen. They will find Dad sitting on the doorstep, red-eyed with worry.

THE MANAGER AT the hostel checks on me in the early morning.

My bed is empty.

Down by the Columbia, under the bluff at Point Ellice, someone calls in my pickup truck, reporting it as abandoned. Like a bad joke, my black guitar case is sitting in the driver's seat. Someone else calls in a report of a lanky young man on the four-mile bridge to Oregon, holding onto his prairie-yellow hat, dancing across the river. State troopers shut down the bridge in both directions, trying to get a handle on who I am and what I'm doing. Eventually, I arrive in Astoria, a town of barking sea lions and old docks, and gladly accept my arrest.

Maybe I'll spend a couple nights in jail. Maybe my truck'll get impounded. But after smoothing everything over—paying a fine, writing a few new songs—maybe I'll settle down like I was always supposed to.

Acknowledgements

Thank you for reading.

Queen Anne Cowboy, as a concept, first emerged from my therapy sessions with W. John Gass in September 2018. For sixteen months, we met in his office on the third floor of the Security Building in downtown Olympia. Mr. Gass was always compassionate and insightful, and generous with his servings of licorice tea. Wherever he hangs his hat these days, I wish him peace and balance.

To develop the outline, I drove once a week from Oly to Queen Anne, sketching my thoughts inside El Diablo Coffee Co., a funky and beloved spot in one of the city's most buttoned-up neighborhoods. After surviving a sudden lease termination and emergency relocation, the COVID-19 pandemic closed El Diablo permanently in April 2020.

Work on the first draft began in Spider House Café in Austin, Texas, another funky and beloved spot the pandemic would claim. For two weeks—a quarter-life crisis peaking in September and October 2019—I lived out of a motel off the interstate, driving to Spider House every afternoon and settling into a red-vinyl booth with my laptop. Fueled by Frito pie burgers from Arlo's and house-made dirty horchatas, I began with Chapter Nine. The city, roiled by triple-digit heat, seeped into the story.

I rewrote the novel multiple times from February 2020 to February 2021 in my apartment in Tucson, Arizona. Those twelve months proved to be the driest and the second hottest in the recorded history of the Southwest. In that same period, the COVID-19 pandemic resulted in the deaths of 1 in 500 residents of Pima County. I will always be grateful to my neighbors who participated in measures protecting everyone's safety. Special shoutouts to the Food Conspiracy Co-op, Antigone Books, Café Passe, and the regulars at Catalina Park.

From the early 2010s, I'd like to give special shoutouts to: the Crisis Clinic of Thurston and Mason Counties, Gateways for Incarcerated Youth, Naomi and Miguel, Candace, the Sem II Café, the Flaming Eggplant, Last Word Books (in the White Building), Orca Books (on 4th Avenue), Burial Grounds (on Washington St.), the Reef, SIZIZIS, Nammy's, Caffé Vita (at 4th and Washington), California Tacos (on Harrison), Basil Leaf, the Suburban Dream Home, the Texaco (on Cooper Point), Dick's (on Broadway), Oasis Tea Zone (in the ID), Post Alley, Aladdin's (on the Ave), Caffé Ladro (in Fremont), Café Allegro (in the alley), Bauhaus (at Melrose and Pine), Black Coffee Co-op, I-5 (at night), the Bay Bridge (at dawn), North Beach, the Poetry Room, Taqueria Zorro, Caffé Trieste, Fourth Wave Coffee (at Polk and Pine), the Mission District, Taqueria Cancun, Taqueria Vallarta, Philz (the original on 24th St.), Clarion Alley, Balmy Alley, the Tenderloin, and the corner of Geary and Larkin.

The West Coast, from the Sound to the Bay.

To everyone who put up with my misadventures in that era, thank you. To the people who proved to be those misadventures, thank you too.

Rick, who built Yesler with two bricks, is a lot like Rick, who built Garfield with two bricks, and passed away in February 2021. He was a Central District legend.

Mr. Lavender is a lot like Mr. Fielder, who passed away in December 2011. He was a Queen Anne legend.

Shoutouts also to: Evan Sanders, for participating in many of the real-life scenarios and institutions that inspired this book; Callie Jones, for the same reasons, and for supplying the anecdote about the pig; and Stacy and Ryan Juhre for the enthusiasm they've shown for my work since our shifts in Cottage C.

I would like to thank my early readers and fellow Unsolicited authors, Tara Stillions Whitehead and Taylor Garcia. As always, I would like to thank my editor, S.R. Stewart, and the entire team at Unsolicited Press. As always, I would like to thank my family too.

About the Author

Jay Kristensen Jr. was born and raised in Seattle. He has also lived in Southern Appalachia, Philadelphia, and the Sonoran Desert. He took this selfie after narrowly avoiding a car wreck in Yuma, Arizona.

His first novel, *Light in Rosadero*, was published on Tuesday, September 21st, 2021, and was nominated for the 2022 Maya Angelou Book Award and the 2022 Washington State Book Award. *Queen Anne Cowboy* is his second book.

About the Press

Unsolicited Press based out of Portland, Oregon and focuses on the works of the unsung and underrepresented. As a womxn-owned, all-volunteer small publisher that doesn't worry about profits as much as championing exceptional literature, we have the privilege of partnering with authors skirting the fringes of the lit world. We've worked with emerging and award-winning authors such as Shann Ray, Amy Shimshon-Santo, Brook Bhagat, Kris Amos, and John W. Bateman.

Learn more at unsolicitedpress.com. Find us on Twitter and Instagram.